"I am Alaric of the Wolves." He kept his voice gentle as though he were speaking to a child. She held her ground, and he took another step toward her. "What are you doing in these woods, Lark?"

Her eyes darted around, looking for an answer or a way out, he wasn't sure which. The hem of her dress was covered in dirt, and her cloak was worn and faded. She had come from the direction of the castle; perhaps she was a maid.

"I was out for a walk," she lifted her chin and met his eyes as she spoke, "and I am hardly in the woods."

He nearly laughed. She was right; she had barely crossed the tree line into the shade. "Hasn't anyone told you there are dangers in these woods, men that would harm you?"

She swallowed hard. He could see her pulse racing in her neck. Her dark eyes were wide, but they hadn't left his face. His muscles tensed under her appraising gaze. What did she see when she looked at him?

"Harmful men are not confined to these woods."

Her words stilled his approach and sent a jolt of regret through his body. Why had he used such menacing words? His fists curled at his sides. And who were these other men? Perhaps the goddess put her in his path because she needed help as well.

Marked for Each Other
Other
The Princess and The Barbarian

by

Melissa McTernan

Here's to large barbarian men! Hope you like this one! ♡ Melis

Marked for Each Other - The Princess and The Barbarian

Cover Art by *Jennifer Greeff*

The Wild Rose Press, Inc.
PO Box 708
Adams Basin, NY 14410-0708
Visit us at www.thewildrosepress.com

Publishing History
First Edition, 2023
Trade Paperback ISBN 978-1-5092-4718-9
Digital ISBN 978-1-5092-4719-6

Published in the United States of America

Dedication

To my dad, for being the first one to realize I was writing Romance. Thanks for clearing that up and for encouraging me to keep going.

Chapter 1: Lock and Key

The man in her bed didn't love her. At least not in the way she needed him to. Odessa came to this realization as she looked out over her father's lands from behind the thick glass of her bedroom window. The pane was cold and fogged over with her breath in the chill of the morning.

"Come back to sleep." Nolan's voice was distant and muffled from under the covers. Odessa didn't move from her perch at the window. There was a time, not long ago in fact, when she would have rushed to his side, curled up beside him, and soaked in his attention. But not today. Today she wanted more. And wanting was dangerous.

The sun rose higher in the sky and the fields turned from gray to gold in the morning light. Her kingdom, Kalon, extended from the castle to the edge of Asherah's Wood where her father's authority could not touch. It was there her eyes wandered to the wild tangle of trees standing beyond her father's reach, and her heart followed.

The woods had captured her imagination ever since she was a little girl, locked in her chambers so her grieving father wouldn't have to look at her. The burgundy birthmark covering half her face, like a clumsy party guest spilled wine across her pale skin, served as a constant reminder of her tragic birth. Her father, the king, couldn't seem to forgive her for killing her mother. He kept her locked away, allowing the rumors to grow and twist until tales of his cursed and disfigured daughter traveled far across the kingdom.

Odessa brought a hand reflexively to her cheek. She was no more cursed than anyone else born to a selfish father. And she certainly wasn't evil or demon possessed as some claimed. At least not as far as she could tell.

A new restlessness twitched inside her like it was a living beast attempting to scratch its way out. For years she had stared out this damn window. For years she had tamped down her desire for freedom, for a life beyond these walls. But it wasn't working anymore. The desire had grown too strong to contain. It wanted out. She wanted out.

Nolan groaned and stretched in her bed, drawing her attention away from the window. He wore nothing from the waist up and his blond hair flopped over one eye. Odessa tipped her head, considering him. She had known him nearly a year now and familiarity sometimes blinded her to his charms. He was pretty. That much was true. And brave. His exploits as her father's loyal knight were well known. There were plenty of women at the castle who would appreciate having him in their bed. For all she knew plenty of them already had. Her stomach turned. Why had she let him in? Again.

"Good morning, princess." He nodded at her and stood to pull his shirt over his head. Odessa cringed at the name. She didn't need a reminder of what she was. "You're up early today."

"I couldn't sleep." She didn't sleep much these

days, the growing restlessness keeping her awake until the early hours of the morning. She pulled her robe around her shoulders. The chill of autumn had already started to seep into the stone walls of the castle. Frost glittered on the grass below her window.

As she watched Nolan dress for his day, she was reminded of exactly why she had let him in again. She had hoped he was the answer to her prayers. He had been sneaking into her room for months now. One of his first duties after becoming a member of her father's inner circle was as a night guard outside her chambers. For her protection, she was told and didn't believe in the slightest. The guards were there to keep her in as much as to keep intruders out. It was a job her father only trusted to his most loyal knights.

Nolan had been the only guard to speak to her, to treat her as a person. She had been so starved for any sort of human interaction she gobbled up his attention like it was a feast. For a year now she waited for him to do more than slip into her bed in secret. She wanted more than clandestine meetings, needed more. Any woman would. Odessa took a breath and steeled herself for what she was about to do.

"Nolan." She stood from her window seat and joined him in front of the fire. He ran a hand through his hair, smoothing it away from his face. He still hadn't met her eye.

"I have quite a busy day. I'm not sure I'll have time to visit you again later." He sat to pull on his boots. "Perhaps in a day or two."

"Nolan, I…"

He kept talking, tugging his second boot into place. "Your father has me training new men every day. It is a lot, but who am I to argue with my king?"

"Yes, well about that…"

"I am one of his most trusted men." Nolan stood and grabbed his jacket from the back of the chair.

"Trusted, of course. But Nolan…"

"I really must be off. Be well." He leaned in to place a chaste kiss on her cheek, but she dodged and grabbed his arm instead, forcing him to stay put.

"Nolan, please." The urgency in her voice finally caught his attention.

"What is it, Essa?"

The nickname he gave her made her heart flip. Perhaps this was the right thing to do after all. She rolled her shoulders back and stood straighter. "I want you to ask my father for my hand."

The astonished, slightly sick look on his face told her everything. But she was a desperate woman with few options. The restless beast urged her on.

"As you said, my father trusts you. You are his most faithful knight. If anyone could convince him, it would be you."

Nolan shook his head and backed away from her as though her head had spun around, and bile spilled from her mouth. She reached for him, but he evaded her grasp.

"It's impossible." His voice was stern when he found it, unyielding. Her hopes slipped. "Your father has forbidden it."

"But you could convince him otherwise." She was nearly begging now, and she hated herself for it. A princess on her knees. "If you love me—"

"Don't."

"Is what we do here in my bed, not about love?"

She rounded on him, closing the gap between them. He twitched like a spooked horse. "If it isn't, perhaps you shouldn't come anymore." There. Let him deny it. Let him revoke the words he whispered to her in the night.

His eyes raised to hers and for the first time that morning, he met her gaze. "Essa, you know I can't give you any more than this." He swallowed hard, looking away. Too much of a coward to face her as he denied her. "Your father fears for your well-being. He wants to keep you safe."

Odessa nearly scoffed out loud. Her father did nothing for anyone's interests but his own. He loathed her and wanted her out of his sight. She had been told on multiple occasions she was lucky he had let her live past her birth. She owed both her life and her imprisonment to him.

Nolan's voice was softer when he spoke, "I will be back in a few days. Do not worry yourself." He took her hands and kissed them, keeping his eyes lowered as he did. Odessa watched him stride toward the door. He stopped with his hand on the knob. "At least you are not locked in anymore, princess."

With the reminder of how much worse her life had once been, he was gone, and Odessa was alone again. The air left her lungs in a long sigh. She was no longer locked in with a key but the rumors about her ensured she had nowhere to go. How dare Nolan imply she should be grateful for such small mercies? She may be free to walk the castle grounds, but not without stares and curses, prayers and scowls. She was still the marked princess. And the title afforded her no real freedom.

The sun was up in earnest now and her

whitewashed walls glowed in the morning light. She had insisted on covering the gray stone and now the room's bright cheerfulness mocked her. The mural she started on the far wall still waited to be completed and stacks of books littered the floors. More could be sent to her whenever she wanted. She could have more rugs and draperies, more paints and ink, more gowns and tea sets. But she was not allowed anyone to wear them for or anyone to drink with. Her father denied no request as long as it kept her in her chambers. As long as the people did not have to look upon his cursed daughter, he was happy to oblige.

Another sigh escaped her lips. How foolish she had been to beg Nolan to help her. How foolish to think he actually would. She ran her fingers angrily through her dark hair, working out the tangles from the night before. Tangles he had put there as he crushed her into the mattress. Of course, he wouldn't risk angering his king to marry her. Why would he? She was here whenever he wanted her, to take when he pleased. A captive and docile woman. What man wouldn't want that?

Odessa twisted her hair into a messy plait and wandered around the room, setting things straight. There were plates from the night before to be taken back to the kitchen. She stacked them neatly on their tray. The bedsheets were twisted and tangled, so Odessa straightened them, smoothing her favorite blue quilt over the top. It was not a secret to the staff what went on between her and Nolan, but seeing it so boldly displayed made her cheeks heat.

The mess on her desk had nothing to do with Nolan's visit, but she went to straighten it also. Papers and drawings covered in ink splotches were spread across the wood surface. Further evidence of her ever-growing boredom.

Perhaps it was the change in season that had her so unsettled, so eager to change her situation. Or maybe it was the fact she turned twenty-four this year, the age her mother was when she died. Her mother was a married queen with two small children at the time. But at twenty-four, Odessa was frozen in time, trapped in a suspended state of dependency on her father. Or it could have been the simple fact she was tired of being at the mercy of a powerful man's whims. Whatever it was, she was at her wit's end, and she wanted out of this room and out of this life.

She brought her gaze to the window, staring out as far as she could see to steady herself. Her eyes again landed on the woods beyond her father's land. There were people who lived in that forest. Four clans made their home there, independent of the surrounding kingdoms. A small seed of an idea planted itself in her heart. She wasn't locked in anymore…

A soft knock at the door disrupted her thoughts.

"Come in, Sylvie."

Her lady's maid bustled in, a tray filled with breakfast balanced precariously in one hand and a bundle of clean laundry in the other.

"Let me help you!" Odessa hurried to her side and took the tray from her hand.

"Oh, thank you, my lady! It seems I tried to carry a bit more than I can handle!" Her cheeks were pink with exertion. Little brown curls escaped her otherwise tidy bun. She hustled farther into the room and laid the laundry out on the bed, quickly getting to the task of hanging everything in the wardrobe.

"Won't you take a break for a moment and have a cup of tea?" The tray she had carried in held only one cup, but Odessa asked anyway.

Sylvie shook her head so hard more curls escaped their pins. "Oh no, dear. I will take my break later. Too much to do." The woman wouldn't meet her eye. Odessa wouldn't push her. She swallowed another rejection. It seemed this morning would be full of them.

She sat sipping her tea and nibbling a scone trying to ease her twisting stomach while Sylvie worked. When she was done with the wardrobe, she insisted on taking a brush to Odessa's hair. Her dresses were simple enough for her to dress herself but wrangling the thick layers of her hair was never something she was good at. Sylvie's fingers worked quickly through the long strands.

"Sylvie."

"Yes, princess?"

"Tell me everything you know about the clans of the wood."

Chapter 2: The Clans of the Wood

Alaric pulled the furs over his sisters' small frames, not wanting them to catch a chill. Their heads peeked out from under the blankets, one dark, and one copper. The girls stirred a little, burrowing deeper under the fur, but didn't wake. He moved to the center of the A-framed house and added more kindling to the fire. Fall had begun in earnest now and the small home was cold first thing in the morning.

He didn't bother to wake his brothers, who slept along the opposite wall from the little girls. Often, they would join him for the hunt, but today he craved the quiet of the woods. By the time he got back, the cramped house would be filled with bickering voices and too many demands. His brothers were thirteen and fifteen now, nearly men themselves, and his sisters were getting bigger and more boisterous by the day.

He paused, warming himself by the fire for a moment and the grief hit him as sharp and fresh as the day his mother died. It should be her, here by the fire, tucking in her children. He was ill-equipped for this job and had never wanted it. The role was thrust upon him when the sickness took her two years ago. He was barely eighteen at the time.

There were rumors the sickness was back like it had blown in with the autumn wind. Two of the clan's women had already passed. Alaric's chest tightened in familiar panic at the thought of keeping his siblings safe.

His fists clenched at his sides as he inhaled slowly through his nose. He was a warrior built for battle, but how could he fight an enemy he couldn't see? His weapons and his strength were useless against this enemy and yet four small souls relied on him for safety. It was nearly too much to bear. He waited, eyes closed, breathing deeply until his chest was loose enough to move again.

Hunger was a problem he could solve now, today. So, he pulled on his boots and a thick fur-lined vest, grabbed his bow, and strode out the door.

The air outside was crisp and clear. Alaric sucked the cool air into his lungs and already felt better than he had inside the crowded house. He didn't linger, having no desire to spend time in the shadow of the other house on his family's modest property. The one that was supposed to be his.

The second house stood unfinished and abandoned next to the first. After his mother died, he saw no reason to finish it. His siblings needed him close. He left the yard without a glance at the skeleton of the incomplete structure and picked up his pace through the village.

The village was quiet. The sun had not yet risen over the horizon, but wisps of smoke streamed from some of the chimneys. A cinnamon-colored goat ambled into Alaric's path, bleating mournfully at him.

"Oh, things aren't so bad now Magnus, are they?" He gave the goat a pat on his wiry head and moved around him before Magnus could begin to chew on the leather of his vest.

The smell of woodsmoke and dry leaves drifted through the air. The village was silvery in the early morning light. Alaric's steps were lighter as he made his way to the hunting trail on the outskirts of town, but a stern voice stopped him in his tracks.

Connell was the last person he wished to speak to this morning, but he couldn't ignore his chief no matter how much he wished to. He turned slowly and came face to face with the man.

"Where are you going so early this morning?"

"Hunting." He lifted his bow. Where else would he be going? The words rose in his throat, but he held his tongue.

"I expect all is well with your family?"

"It is." Alaric shifted, wanting to be gone. "Is there something you need?" His voice had an edge to it just short of insolent. Connell's eyes narrowed. Shame heated Alaric's face as he waited for the reprimand that never came.

Connell ran a hand down his beard. Gray streaks had begun to show through the deep black of his hair. Lately, he looked even more like the Great Wolf he was named for.

"The clan is in trouble."

Alaric was shocked by his abrupt admission.

"The sickness has returned," Connell went on, his voice a low rumble, "We will need a miracle if our people are to survive the winter."

Alaric's stomach twisted at the older man's words. He had the sudden urge to run home and barricade the door. The houses of the clan stood sleepy and quiet around him. Which homes would be affected? Which families would lose members?

He cleared his throat, but his words were stilted when he spoke. "And what do you ask of me?" *What can I possibly do?* The real question lay right below the one he asked.

"Only for you to be a better man than your father was." Connell's words were like a physical blow, and Alaric could find no response.

Be a better man than your father was. The words might as well have been tattooed next to the howling wolf on his chest. It was all he had ever tried to do. His father was an angry coward. But a dead one. Alaric had no intention of being anything like him.

The chief waited, his stare cold and unyielding. For a heart-stopping second, Alaric thought he might go on, that he might speak further about his father and the circumstances surrounding his death. His hands were numb at his sides, and his jaw was clenched so tight his teeth ached. He would confess nothing to this man. If the clan wanted him punished, they would have done it years ago. And yet, he still felt the weight of their judgment every day. Were Connell's words a warning? A warning to stay in line, to serve his clan, to not fail his family.

Alaric made a gruff sound of acquiescence, enough to appease his leader for the moment. Connell nodded and stalked away—message received. Alaric struggled to regain his composure. He tightened his grip on his bow and strode off into the woods.

Frost-covered leaves crunched under his feet as the quiet of the forest embraced him. The farther he walked from the village, the more his heart slowed, and his breathing calmed. Up ahead the trees thinned and opened into a field littered with fallen leaves.

He crouched low behind a rotted log and waited, silent as the trees around him. Somewhere above him, a raven cawed. A message from a neighboring clan? No, this raven had no ring around its leg. It didn't belong to anyone. It was free. It cawed again and flew into the lightening sky.

A doe stepped into the clearing, her head raised, ears twitching, listening. He raised his bow and aimed. Liquid black eyes stared back at him. The deer could feed his family for weeks. His arm shook, his desire wavered. The deer flicked her tail, her back legs poised and ready to run. Alaric lowered his bow. He didn't have it in his heart to kill something so beautiful. Not today. He shifted in his hiding place and the deer ran off into the trees.

He continued his hunt, catching a few small animals on his way, enough to feed his siblings for a day or two. Alaric tried to focus on the task at hand and on the peace of the forest, but his conversation with Connell played over and over in his head.

The clan had barely recovered from the last time the sickness swept through the village. Not to mention the harassment they received at the hands of the kingdoms beyond the woods. The kingdoms' soldiers who traipsed through the clans' sacred trees on their way to murder each other always managed to find a reason to attack a clansman or two. Or to steal their livestock. Or to taunt their women. His clan faced dangers from inside and outside their walls. Their numbers were low. How could they withstand another onslaught of the disease?

An image of his mother, thin and frail in her bed, her face pale and covered in sweat, came to mind. Even with her dying breaths, she instructed him on how to run a household, on what foods his sisters liked best, and how to treat a fever. Then she was gone. How could he survive it again? Who would be taken this time?

Connell said they needed a miracle. Alaric raised his eyes to the treetops, a prayer forming on his lips.

Asherah, goddess of the wood, Narah, goddess of the wolf. I beg you, be with us. Keep my people safe.

As he walked, the words became a chant accompanied by the steady drumbeat of his heart. If he said it enough, maybe they would hear. Maybe this time would be different. Maybe this time he wouldn't be alone.

Chapter 3: Life in the Shadows

Sylvie hadn't told Odessa anything she hadn't already heard about the clans. There were four, named after the animals who guided them: wolf, bear, fox, and raven. They lived in the wood stretching from Kalon to the kingdom of Melantha in the south. She had heard all of this before.

Of course, what she really wanted to know was something she couldn't simply ask. Were the clans as bloodthirsty as they say? Would they welcome a stranger? Would they keep her hidden? The questions were foolish and she a fool for considering them. A desperate fool. So desperate for an escape, she had briefly considered running into clan territory. Being cooped up in the confines of her room had clearly started to addle her brain.

She tugged her favorite green dress, faded from use and frayed around the hem, over her head. She needed to get out of the castle; she needed air. Smoothing her hair away from her face, she searched for her cloak. The clothes Sylvie had so neatly organized were soon in a tangled mess once again, but Odessa would fix it later. Her need to get out of the room grew stronger by the minute. Surely, she would suffocate if she didn't get some fresh air into her lungs.

Odessa let out a small cry of triumph as she yanked her amber cloak from its hook in her wardrobe. She draped it around her shoulders and hurried toward the door. There were no mirrors in her room; she had no need to check her reflection. Odessa had no desire to have a daily reminder of her marking. It didn't matter anyway. She saw evidence of her curse on the face of anyone who looked at her. The pity or the fear in their eyes.

So, she walked out the door to her chambers without checking her appearance. She tugged the generous hood over her head, keeping her marked cheek in the shadows. The fresh air would have her thinking straight again. There must be another way out, another option left for her.

Odessa scurried quickly through the dim halls, light on her feet. When her father stopped locking her in her room, when the rumors about her became worse than the truth, she had been both elated and terrified to walk these halls. They were wide and cavernous in spots, but tight and dark in others. She got lost a lot in those first days of exploration, but she had gradually learned the way.

Two maids carrying bundles of linens hurried past, chatting to each other. Their gaze drifted toward her, but they quickly looked away. Odessa tugged her hood out further, hiding deeper in its folds.

Several ladies of the court strolled toward her like swans drifting on a lake. She turned quickly toward the narrow window in the alcove beside her and feigned interest in the goings-on outside. While the ladies didn't often spit in her direction to ward off the evil spirits as some of the villagers did, they did treat her as though her condition were contagious. As though they could catch her birthmark and her curse. Odessa's fingers tightened on the windowsill as they passed, willing them to keep going, making herself invisible.

Her body relaxed once they moved on, leaving her alone in the empty hallway, but movement through the window caught her eye. Nolan was below, training the new men. He stood tall and proud in front of his new recruits, and despite the distance, it was obvious he was barking orders at them. A burning embarrassment pooled in her stomach when she thought about what she had said to him this morning and his thorough rejection of her idea.

She brought a hand to her cheek, trying to cool her heated skin with her chilled palm as she watched Nolan and his men. The soldiers were an attractive bunch, young and strong. Their faces shone with sweat from their exercises and their skin ranged from dark to light. Every color of the kingdom was represented in the men below. But her coloring had come with a curse, had come with death and fear and anger. So, she was locked away.

Air. She needed air now. Her strides were long and determined as she made her way through the last hallway before the servants' entrance. She turned the corner and nearly knocked over the queen, her stepmother. Would luck never be on her side?

"Mother." She made a hasty bow in front of the woman she would never think of as a mother. The queen was only ten years her senior after all.

"Odessa." Her stepmother, Louise, took a step back and ran a hand along her skirts, smoothing them. A small face peered out from beside her. "Where are you off to?"

"For a walk. Good morning, Faye." Odessa turned

toward her half-sister and waggled her fingers in hello. Faye's face broke into a smile, but Louise held out an arm as though restraining the girl. "How are your studies going?" Odessa asked.

Faye opened her mouth to speak, but her mother cut in before she could utter a word. "Her studies are going well. Thank you."

Faye's brow creased in frustration, and the faint purplish spot marking her temple came into view. It was small and Louise had styled her hair to cover most of it. Faye's skin resembled the warm dark hues of her mother's instead of the pale skin of their father. Perhaps it was for this reason the little princess was not considered marked. Or perhaps it was because her mother still lived and stood beside her, and Odessa's had died on the day of her birth. Either way, she was glad the girl's life did not resemble her own.

"I'll be on my way, then." Odessa gave another perfunctory bow, with a quick wink to Faye, and she was out into the sunshine at last.

"Oh finally!" She filled her lungs with the crisp fall air as she left the castle behind her. She slipped out through the kitchen garden. Pumpkins and squash ripe for picking lolled in the dirt. Odessa hopped over the late-season lettuces, planted in neat rows. Past the garden, a gate in the wall was open for the servants coming and going. A single guard on duty did not pay her a second glance. Most people had never laid eyes on the cursed princess, and as long as her face was covered, she moved through the world anonymously. It was thanks to her relative invisibility that her daily walks on the castle grounds became longer walks through the surrounding fields.

Her thoughts and plans were a tangle in her mind. She would walk until they unwound. Nolan should have been her best chance and his answer stung each time she thought of it. He wasn't even willing to try. He was perfectly happy to continue on the way they were forever. But Odessa was a grown woman living a half-life, a life confined to the shadows, a life lived on other people's terms to appease other people's fears. For twenty-four years she had lived like this. She couldn't do it anymore.

Her two older sisters were just as useless. Odessa had written to them many times seeking a way out, but her sisters had married men from faraway kingdoms and seldom looked back. If she was determined to leave, she would have to do it on her own.

Odessa pulled her cloak tighter around her, a sudden chill from the shade of the trees seeping through the thick wool. So focused on her plans, she had wandered to the edge of the forest without meaning to. She glanced back toward the castle sitting high on the hill; its white stone gleamed in the bright fall sun, scarlet flags flapping on the walls surrounding it. The mist of the morning was lifting all around the castle, and the golden and amber trees of autumn surrounded it on its perch. It was objectively beautiful. It should have been a beacon calling her home, but she didn't have a reason to go back. Not a single person would miss her. The light of the castle didn't call to her but the quiet darkness of the forest in front of her whispered to her soul.

Leaves crunched underfoot and her head whipped back to the trees. A man stood watching her. She gathered her skirts in one hand and took a step back.

19

"Wait." His low growl of a voice sent shivers up her spine.

Run! The word tore through her body, but his gaze kept her rooted to the spot.

Chapter 4: A Sign from the Goddess

Alaric had expected her to run. Her skirts were gathered in her fist, her chest rising and falling rapidly. He had seen hares stare at him in much the same manner as she was now. The wind blew through the branches of the trees and her hood fell from her head. A stain the color of over-ripe cherries ran from her temple to her chin, caressing the side of her nose. The other cheek was pale and unblemished.

Her face was light and dark, like the moon, like the goddess Narah of the wolves. Finding a woman such as this was no coincidence. Not after all he had prayed for, begged for. This woman must be part of the answer. The goddess would not have put her in his path otherwise. His heart thrummed in his chest, and he took a step toward her.

"Who are you?" he asked. The woman's muscles twitched, ready to run. He would chase her if need be.

Her gaze shifted to the side and then back to his face. "Lark," she said. Clearly a lie, but he did not challenge her.

"I am Alaric of the Wolves." He kept his voice gentle as though he were speaking to a child. She held her ground, and he took another step toward her. "What are you doing in these woods, Lark?"

Her eyes darted around, looking for an answer or a way out, he wasn't sure which. The hem of her dress was covered in dirt, and her cloak was worn and faded. She had come from the direction of the castle; perhaps she was a maid.

"I was out for a walk," she lifted her chin and met his eyes as she spoke, "and I am hardly in the woods."

He nearly laughed. She was right; she had barely crossed the tree line into the shade. "Hasn't anyone told you there are dangers in these woods, men that would harm you?"

She swallowed hard. He could see her pulse racing in her neck. Her dark eyes were wide, but they hadn't left his face. His muscles tensed under her appraising gaze. What did she see when she looked at him?

"Harmful men are not confined to these woods."

Her words stilled his approach and sent a jolt of regret through his body. Why had he used such menacing words? His fists curled at his sides. And who were these other men? Perhaps the goddess put her in his path because she needed help as well.

"Are you in danger now? Are you running from someone?" He looked her over again. Other than her worn clothing she appeared to be in good health. Her long dark hair was plaited neatly and hung over her shoulder like a silken rope. Her pale cheek was flushed pink with the cool fall air and her eyes were bright and alert. Those bright eyes stared back at him as his gaze roamed all over her body. He cleared his throat, his own cheeks heating.

Her lips curled into a small smile. "I am fine. No dangers have followed me." She stepped forward this time, close enough for him to reach out and grab her. His body's reaction to the idea unnerved him. He kept his arms rigid at his sides, but he could all too easily imagine them wrapped around her waist.

"Do you intend to cause me harm, Alaric of the Wolves?"

He liked the sound of his name spoken in the accent of the Kalon. "Never."

Her smile widened at his earnest reply. Surely even his ears were red now. Damn it. He was acting like a boy. This woman must be the key to helping his people. He needed to find a way to get her back to his village, but he was suddenly less inclined to throw her over his shoulder. He opened his mouth to speak but the woman was faster.

"Perhaps you can help me. I need to get away from here."

If Alaric had needed more evidence to prove the woman was goddess-sent, this one request would have sufficed. His mouth hung open for a moment before he pulled himself together enough to speak.

"You can come with me. The Clan of the Wolf will welcome you as an honored guest."

It was the woman's turn to be shocked. He watched as indecision crossed her face. She glanced back at the castle and hesitated a moment before turning to Alaric.

"An honored guest?" She arched a single black eyebrow as though she doubted his words.

"Yes. I'm sure of it." As sure as he could be. He could see she was sent by the goddess; his clansmen would see the same.

She ran her foot in a slow arc through the dirt in front of her, considering his offer, stalling for time. Alaric took a breath and waited. Finally, she lifted her face, pinning him with her stare.

"If you promise no harm will come to me, I will

come with you to your village."

His swift nod brought another smile to her lips. He ignored the warmth the smile brought to his chilled body.

"It is a few hours' walk from here." As the words left his mouth, he realized how far he had wandered from home. It was almost as if something had pulled him here. "I hope you are up for the journey." He glanced at her feet and was pleased to see she wore sturdy boots. Her cloak should keep her warm enough and he had food to share in his pack.

"I don't mind walking."

With another silent prayer he was doing the right thing, Alaric turned to lead the woman with the goddess's face back to his village.

Chapter 5: Wolf Territory

Alaric strode ahead of her on his long legs and Odessa did her best to keep up. The vigorous pace was useful in keeping her mind quiet. If she had the energy for thought, her brain would be screaming in panic to turn around and go back. But as it was, she needed all her strength to not get left behind.

Following a strange man into the woods, a clansman no less was obviously the most foolish thing she had ever done. But it wasn't only her own desperation pushing her to follow him. It was the way he looked at her. Not even the way he looked at her but the sheer fact he did look at her. Without flinching, or spitting, or cursing. He looked at her like she was something good. He looked at her like no one else had before.

So perhaps she was a desperate fool, but at least she had her reasons. And was there nothing to be said for fate? What was this man doing at the edge of the woods, so close to the castle grounds at the exact moment she was there? She had lived long enough with the fate she had been dealt at birth, maybe a new destiny was being written for her, maybe she could have a hand in writing it.

Alaric stopped suddenly, and she ran face-first into the solid wall of his back. So much for not thinking.

"Oof." She stumbled backward but Alaric caught

her arm before she could fall. He yanked her toward him to correct her momentum, his strong fingers digging into her flesh and the heat of his hand searing through her wool dress. Her other hand shot out to steady herself and landed on his chest. He was firm and warm against her palm. Her face was nearly buried in his furs, and his scent of woodsmoke and pine wrapped around her.

Her gaze rose to meet his and she found him staring at her. Up close he was different from what she had first imagined. His short beard was neatly trimmed, and his long hair was pulled back away from his face. His skin was tan and smooth. He was younger than her, perhaps. But it was his eyes that held her frozen in place, her hand still resting on his broad chest. One eye was as blue as the sea and the other as brown as the earth beneath her feet. Odessa had the sudden and absurd thought that she would never tire of looking at them.

She took a step back, breaking the connection between them. Alaric dropped his hand as though he had been bitten.

"Sorry. I didn't notice you had stopped." Her voice was small in the vastness of the forest.

He gave a curt nod. "I thought you might need a break. There's a stream nearby."

"A break would be nice. Thank you." She sat on a fallen log, gathering her skirts underneath her while Alaric filled a canteen with water.

She ignored the racing of her heart and instead took in the ancient forest around her. Asherah's Wood. Even the name sounded like a whispered prayer. Gnarled branches covered in thick green moss twisted toward the sky above her. She ran her fingers over the nearest trunk. The bark was layered and ridged beneath her fingers. The golden leaves rustled in the wind and a shiver ran from her fingers to her core. Her father's kingdom worshipped more gods and goddesses than she could count, but none felt as close to her as the goddess of the wood did right now.

She dropped her hand in her lap and turned to find Alaric returning. She curled her fingers into a fist, attempting to hold onto the feeling she got from the tree and Alaric's body.

He handed her the canteen, and she took a long swallow of the cold water.

"Thank you."

He answered with the nod she was already growing accustomed to. Were all clansmen so quiet? She would find out soon enough. He sat next to her on the log and pulled bread and a hunk of cheese from his pack. Wordlessly he broke off a piece of bread and handed it to her along with some cheese.

She had forgotten her hunger until she started eating. The bread was soft on the inside and perfectly crunchy on the outside. Odessa sighed as she ate it. As she popped the last piece in her mouth, she turned to find Alaric studying her from the corner of his eye. He cleared his throat and began repacking his bag as soon as she caught him.

"How do you know?"

Alaric looked at her, his eyebrows raised in question.

"How do you know your clan will welcome me?"

He let the pack drop from his hands and rested his elbows on his knees. He looked out over the trees as he spoke, his voice a low rumble.

"Narah is the goddess of my clan, of the Wolves."

The people of Kalon did not worship the gods of the forest, but Odessa had heard of the wolf goddess before. What did she have to do with anything?

"She is also the goddess of the moon," he went on, "those blessed enough to have seen her say her face has a light and dark side like the moon."

Odessa's hand went instinctively to her own face. "I am not your goddess."

Alaric huffed a small laugh. "I know."

Her cheeks heated. Of course, he didn't think she was a goddess.

"But your face," he turned to her, studying her. "It must be a sign."

"I…you must be mistaken. I bring no messages or signs for your people. Perhaps I should go back." Odessa stood, fresh panic coursing through her blood. If his people were looking for a messenger, she was not it. How would they react to her presence? She had no desire to anger the clans.

Alaric stood in one graceful motion and grabbed her hand, pulling her close again. Her breath caught in her throat. She hadn't been paying attention to their route. She could never get back on her own.

"My clan is in trouble." His voice was thick when he spoke, and his eyes flashed with pain. "Please. Come with me."

Odessa swallowed hard. "I am not a strong or a wise woman. I cannot help your people."

He shook his head, gripping tighter to her hand. Her heart fluttered rapidly in her chest; every cell in her body urged her to run.

"Please. Come speak to the elders. They will know what to do."

His grip loosened, but he still held her fingers in his hand. He ran a thumb lightly across her wrist and warmth spread through her. "I will keep you safe from whatever it is you are running from. And my people will do you no harm." He repeated his promise from earlier. But could she trust him?

Her gaze skittered across the overgrown trail before landing back on his face. His eyes pleaded with her. She couldn't imagine what she might do for his people, but the idea of having a purpose, of being needed, was too tempting to ignore. Alaric wasn't the only one who benefited from her coming with him. He had offered her the escape she wanted.

She nodded in agreement, and he dropped her hand. She ignored the part of her that missed the steady touch of his fingers, and they walked further into wolf territory.

Chapter 6: The Elders

An awed sound of surprise escaped the woman's lips as the forest opened into a clearing ahead of them. Rays of sunlight streaked through the trees, casting the small village in a welcoming glow.

"It's lovely."

Alaric grunted in agreement. He had to admit his home looked warm and inviting after a day in the chill of the forest. He was pleased with how well the woman had coped with the journey. She was slow and a bit clumsy, but she made no complaints.

As much as he longed to return to his house and check on his siblings, he needed to speak with the elders first. He reminded himself his brothers were perfectly capable of taking care of things for a day. They'd done it plenty of times before, and his aunts were never far if help was needed.

Alaric stopped at the edge of town and turned to face his guest. Her hood remained at her back, and her marked face was turned toward the sun as though she were soaking in its rays.

"Lark."

She blinked her eyes open and looked around before realizing he was speaking to her. Soon he would have to learn her real name.

"Will they come looking for you? Whatever it is you are running from, will it follow you here?"

She paused for only a moment before assuring him, "No one will come for me." He heard the sadness accompanying her statement, but the woman's emotions were not his concern. The safety of his family was all he cared about. He would have to trust her. The goddess would not have put her in his way for nothing.

"Come with me." Before walking through the village, he lifted the hood back over her head. Pain flashed through her eyes, quick and sharp, but he saw it and immediately regretted his actions. Who else had forced her to cover herself? He shook the question away; he didn't have time for the woman's feelings.

Alaric didn't want to cause a scene before he was sure what the elders would say. He left the hood in place and turned quickly, striding toward the meeting hall. The sound of the woman's footsteps followed close behind.

A thin line of gray smoke streamed out of the chimney of the longest house in the village. It stood in the center of town, in the middle of the concentric circles of houses making up the rest of the village. The elders were sure to be inside.

He didn't bother to knock but instead wrenched the heavy wooden door open and entered under the howling wolf carvings above him. Lark stumbled in after him.

At the opposite end of the long dim room, the elders shouted at one another. Their argument was so intense no one had noticed Alaric enter. He stood for a moment allowing his eyes to adjust to the low light and took in the scene in front of him. The heads of the five families of the Wolf Clan were seated in high-backed wooden chairs. Well four of them were. Connell paced the floor like a caged animal.

"It's the only answer!" he shouted at the others.

Merrick, Alaric's uncle, rose from his seat and faced the chief. "It can't be. We must never return to the old ways." His voice was steady and firm, the voice of reason among a group of hotheads.

Ayana with her fiery hair was next to speak, "The healers—"

Connell cut her off before she could continue. "I don't want to hear another word about the healers! What could the healers do when my wife lay dying! Nothing." He spat the last word, and Alaric felt his desperation in his own bones.

Caspian ran a hand through his gray beard. Too old and stooped to easily rise from his seat, he spoke from where he sat. "The clan has lost its way. We are being punished."

Nix scoffed. "Old superstitions! Going back is never the answer." Her voice rose above the rest. Caspian glared at her from under his bushy eyebrows. Nix's mother was a Wolf, but her father hailed from a Kalonian village. She didn't grow up among the Wolves, and many didn't trust her.

"We need to pray. We need a sign." The words died on Caspian's lips as the men finally caught sight of Alaric and Lark standing in the doorway. She had moved closer to him, her body shivering against his arm. He put a firm hand on her back and led her to the front of the room before he could lose his nerve. Goddess, help him.

"Connell, Uncle, elders," he greeted them. "You speak of a sign, and I believe I found one." Lark attempted to scoot behind him, but he held her steady. He turned to her and whispered, "All is well, remove your hood."

She stood paralyzed while the elders waited. He nudged her gently. "You are safe with me." She glanced at him and the fear in her eyes made his own heart clench, but she lifted a shaking hand and tugged her hood away from her face.

"Alaric, what have you—" His uncle was the first to speak, stepping toward him, but Connell quickly cut him off.

"Who is this?" he asked.

"This is Lark. I met her near Kalon. She agreed to come with me. Her face…it must be…"

"Her face. Yes." Connell prowled forward, reaching out a hand to touch her but she pulled back and he dropped it.

"A sign from the goddess, surely it is! She looks like Narah herself!" Caspian sputtered from his seat. Ayana and Nix hadn't taken their eyes off the woman since they came forward. Nix's mouth hung open in disbelief.

Lark shrank farther into his side; her body trembled against him.

"I assured her she would be treated well here. As an honored guest." He took a step forward, shielding her from their stares.

Connell's gray eyes swung to his and a predatory grin spread across his lips. Cold dread pooled in Alaric's stomach. "Of course. She is clearly goddess-blessed. The clan's luck is sure to change now."

The tension in his gut only loosened slightly at Connell's words. He met his uncle's eye, and the man nodded his approval. Ayana shifted from foot to foot. No one spoke and Connell's words hung heavy in the air. This woman would change their luck. But how?

"She will play a vital role at the solstice. She will bless us all." Connell went on, answering Alaric's unasked question. Ayana choked and coughed, but Connell's cold glance silenced her. "Until then she will stay with you and your family. You have done well bringing her here." Connell was close to him now, his voice a low growl. "Keep this gift from the goddess safe and you may well prove you are better than your father after all."

Alaric swallowed hard. With this one task, he could save his siblings from the sickness and restore his family's name. He could save his clan. And what a simple task it was, keeping one small woman safe. The solstice was just over a month away. Perhaps the goddess had changed his luck already. Relief flooded through him.

He nodded in agreement, and Connell dismissed them with a wave of his hand. Alaric led Lark back outside, feeling lighter than he had in months.

As soon as the door closed behind them, she collapsed in his arms and the yelling from inside the building resumed.

Somewhere, the goddess laughed.

Chapter 7: An Honored Guest

Strong arms held her as her legs gave out beneath her. She squeezed her eyes shut, trying in vain to rid herself of the face of the Wolf chief. He had looked at her like she was his next meal.

"Lark?" Alaric's voice was in her ear. She had lied when he asked her name, on the off chance he'd heard of the princess, Odessa. It was a good thing there had been a bird chirping nearby or she would have called herself Branch. But every time he spoke it, she had to remind herself he was talking to her.

"Are you alright?"

She was crushed against his chest, his arms wrapped around her. She opened her eyes to find him staring down at her with his mismatched eyes. His forehead was creased in worry. His concern eased her terror. For the moment. Slightly.

"I'm fine." She managed to choke out. Alaric loosened his grip but kept a strong hand on her arm. "Truly. I am." A flush of embarrassment covered her fear for the moment. She hadn't fainted. Her legs— exhausted from so much exercise and her panic at facing the elders—had conspired against her, leaving her a shaking mess in this man's arms. Odessa had been a lot of things in her life, but a swooning maiden had never been one. She straightened and smoothed her hands over her skirts. Alaric dropped his arm and cleared his throat.

The voices of the elders boomed behind the thick wooden door. Their words were muffled but their anger was clear. Her gaze returned to the building, lingering on the howling wolves carved above the door. A shiver ran down Odessa's spine. Were they arguing about her? She pulled the hood back over her head.

Alaric winced as the voices grew louder. "Come." He led her away from the meeting house, a firm hand on her back.

The village they walked through was tidy and quaint. The thatched roofs of the houses were so steep they nearly touched the ground on either side, making the dwellings look like perfect triangles. Each home had a small garden beside it. Goats ambled along the road and chickens scattered as they passed.

Her fear loosened its grip on her racing heart as they walked. Nothing, not even the icy stare of the Wolf chief, could make her want to be back in her chambers. She breathed deep, the smell of wood smoke and dry leaves filling her lungs. She would not let the elders intimidate her. After all, she was here to help them, even if she didn't understand how. They needed her.

The sun had begun to sink lower in the sky, coloring the clouds a rosy lavender. There weren't many people outside, but the chimney of each house poured streams of smoke into the evening sky. The smells from their fragrant suppers drifted by her on the wind. Her stomach growled in response.

Alaric glanced at her, and her cheeks heated in embarrassment for the second time since they arrived.

"You're hungry." A statement, not a question.

"A bit."

His nod this time told her they were nearly home. She hoped the food would be waiting for them.

"Are they always like that?" she asked as they turned down a path leading to the outer circle of houses. "The elders, I mean."

His hand pressed more firmly into her back as he steered her around the bend in the path. The houses were more spaced out here and closer to the trees surrounding the town. It took a moment for him to answer, and the silence hung between them. When he did speak, Odessa could hear the tension in his voice, as though he was still trying to work it out himself.

"They are not always so...intense."

Odessa huffed a small laugh. Intense was a bit of an understatement. Alaric glanced down at her again, mouth stern, unamused.

"They have a lot to worry about. As I told you, the clan faces many trials at the moment."

"You did not mention what sorts of trials. I still don't understand how I am going to help you at all." Odessa could hear the frustration in her own voice. She was tired and scared and hungry. She did not have the patience for cryptic messages delivered from stoic clansmen right now. Regardless of how comforting his enormous hand felt on her back.

Alaric stopped in front of a large house, wooden like the others with a steep thatched roof. Another smaller house stood next to it, although that one was missing a roof, and instead, its frame was covered by several large canvases to keep out the elements. A few chickens scurried to greet them, pecking around their feet. Alaric tossed a handful of breadcrumbs he pulled from his pack and the hens scattered in a puff of feathers and dust.

He peered into the shadow of her hood. The intensity of his gaze was so strong, she wished she could draw herself even deeper into its protection. To go from having people actively avoid looking at her, to the directness of his stare was unnerving, to say the least.

"I have not been fair to you," he said, at last, breaking the silence but doing nothing to ease the tension. "I have not given all the details, but neither have you." He raised a dark eyebrow. She thought for a moment he would press her for information, force her to reveal who she was and why she had run, but instead, he went on.

"There is a sickness here among the clan. It is not the first we've seen of it and the last time it killed many of our people." A shadow crossed his face when he spoke, a sadness returning to his eyes. "Our healers can't seem to control it, so we have appealed to Narah for her help. She sent us you."

Odessa swallowed the thick knot of panic forming in her throat. She had run to a town infected with a deadly sickness. And now she was expected to help them.

The horror must have shown clearly on her face because Alaric clapped a firm hand onto her shoulder. She was sure the skin would be branded with his touch when he pulled it away. Her face flushed hot, and she was glad for the protection of the hood.

"My house has not been affected. You will be safe with us." He nodded again, as though there was nothing more to say, but Odessa's face must have told him otherwise. He sighed as though all this talking was taxing for him. "Connell says you will take part in the winter solstice ceremony. That is all we expect of you. The goddess will do the rest."

Odessa relaxed slightly at his words. Maybe it would be enough; her presence alone would comfort these people. She could do that. She could simply be here as a sign from their goddess. A sign they were not forgotten. The clan's ceremonies were a mystery to her, but already she trusted this man not to lead her into danger.

"Alright. I will stay." She said it as though she had a choice. And maybe she did. Maybe if she told Alaric right now that she changed her mind, he would have taken her back. Her eyes ran over his muscled arms and his hulking frame, his set, stern face, his bow slung over his back, and his dagger sheathed and hanging from his belt. Or maybe, he would have forced her to stay, slung her over his shoulder and carried her into his house. It wouldn't have been hard for him to do.

Odessa rolled her shoulders back and met his ethereal eyes. "I will stay," she said again, asserting it, choosing it for herself. She had wanted out of her old life, away from her father and Nolan, and everyone else who made her decisions for her. She wanted to leave her curse behind. So, if these people saw her as a blessing, she was not going to argue. And besides, this man was the first to ever offer her help. Only a fool wouldn't accept it.

Alaric nodded his approval and turned toward the house. "Let's eat." Odessa followed close behind.

Before Alaric could lift a hand to open the door, it flew open, and a streak of copper and brown tore out into the yard.

"You're home!" The little girl who was now wrapped in his embrace, her feet dangling off the ground, squealed into his chest.

Odessa was less surprised by the girl's sudden attack than she was by the blinding grin spreading across Alaric's face when he saw her. He was smiling. She hadn't known if he was physically able to do so. His face had been so stern, his mouth so unyielding; it seemed it would never lift into a smile. But now, his face rivaled the glow of the sun setting behind him.

"You've been gone all day!" the girl admonished, and Alaric laughed. Laughed! The sound was rough and deep like it came from some hidden place far inside his chest. It was as Odessa pondered this secret sound that the girl noticed her, and her blue eyes went wide in her freckled face. She didn't look much younger than Odessa's own sister Faye's ten years, but there was a wild joy about her Odessa rarely saw anywhere in the castle. Her rust-colored hair was braided away from her face, and she wore the same style of leggings and tunic as the women elders.

She wriggled free from Alaric's arms and stood staring at Odessa.

"Who is she?" she whispered.

Alaric cleared his throat, the smile fading from his lips. "This is our guest. Lark."

"Hello there." Odessa dropped into a small curtsey, and the girl's eyes widened even more.

"This is my sister, Arowyn."

"Nice to meet you, Arowyn."

The girl peered into her hood, trying to get a better look at her, and the familiar panic at being seen clutched at Odessa's heart. How would the girl react?

Alaric took his sister's hand and led her toward the house ahead of Odessa. "Let's go in."

Arowyn followed his lead, but not without several backward glances at Odessa, who forced her feet to move from the yard and into the house.

Inside, she was greeted with three more curious faces, and the urge to crawl away crept up her spine. Revealing herself to new eyes was never easy, and she had done it enough for one day.

"This is a guest of the clan. Lark. She is to stay with us until the solstice." Alaric hung his bow on the wall as he spoke. Odessa stood awkwardly in the doorway.

"This is my other sister, Rieka." He gestured to a girl, stirring something in a pot over the fire. She was taller than her sister and her hair was jet black instead of copper. Her gaze shifted back and forth between Odessa and Alaric, her brow crinkling in concern.

"My brothers, Weylyn and Faolan." The boys he pointed to were exact replicas of their older brother, but with smoother faces and smaller frames.

"Hello," Odessa managed to choke out.

"She's to stay here?" The larger boy, Weylyn, spoke to Alaric, ignoring her greeting. "There's barely room for us."

Odessa used the uncomfortable pause in the conversation to quickly take stock of the home she had barely entered. The ceiling was tall, crisscrossed with wood beams. A small platform in the center of the house held the fire pit; pots and pans hung over the top of it, waiting to be used. A long wooden table next to the cooking platform ran through the rest of the home. On either side, beds piled high with furs and blankets

41

lined the walls. And that was it. The family's entire life was lived in this one room. Odessa began to sweat under her heavy cloak, her skin itching and her lungs tight. She had escaped one confined space to be thrown into another. She took a step back, colliding with the door behind her.

Alaric glanced in her direction with his brow furrowed. When he spoke, he addressed his brother, "She will sleep here tonight. Tomorrow we will finish the roof on the other house, and she will stay there."

Arowyn's eyes grew wider, and Faolan's dark brows rose in surprise at Alaric's announcement about the other house, but Odessa's body sagged with relief. At least she wouldn't have to stay crammed in this house for more than one night.

"We?" Weylyn crossed his arms on his chest. "So, you have us all roofing tomorrow?"

"Were you not complaining about close quarters?" Alaric's voice was an impatient growl. "This is the solution."

"Who is she anyway? Why is she here?"

Odessa watched Alaric's jaw clench and unclench as he breathed deeply through his nose. "A guest of the clan."

Weylyn looked as though he would argue further. How much longer would this discussion go on before they could eat? Without thinking she pulled the hood from her head and tugged the cloak from her shoulders.

The silence filling the room was so sudden and so complete for a moment Odessa worried the whole thing had been a dream and soon the house and the people and the whole day would disappear as she woke up.

Alaric recovered first, clearing his throat and

hanging her cloak on a hook by the door, he announced it was time to eat. The stunned faces of his siblings, however, said differently.

"Rieka, what did you make us?" he asked gently. The girl shook off her shock and blinked up at him.

"Rabbit stew."

"I made the bread!" Arowyn piped up, her surprise already fading.

Alaric gave her his smile again. "And you make the best bread, little wolf."

The little girl beamed at his compliment and Odessa couldn't blame her. She found herself longing to be on the receiving end of that smile. Instead, he cleared his throat and with a gruff nod, directed her to a seat at the table.

Weylyn still eyed her suspiciously, but the youngest brother, Faolan, gave her a shy smile from across the table. And without further explanations about her face or her identity, Odessa spent her first night with the Clan of the Wolves.

Chapter 8: Moonlit Confessions

He heard the door open and close. Whoever had left was trying to be quiet, but Alaric never slept soundly anymore. Not since taking responsibility for his family. He sat in bed and silently counted the bodies asleep around him. Weylyn and Faolan were still in their bunks, stacked one on top of the other. Arowyn's copper hair peeked out from her covers on the other side of the room, and one of Rieka's feet dangled over the edge of her place next to her sister. They each had their own sleeping bunk but often insisted on snuggling together in one bed instead.

Alaric's gaze scanned the far wall of the house, where he had made up an extra bed for their guest, but it was now empty. He cursed under his breath and yanked on his nearby boots and a coat before following her out into the night.

It didn't take long to find her, and Alaric said a quick prayer of thanks that he hadn't failed at his task on the very first night. She sat with her back to him on an old bench his mother had added to the garden years ago. He watched as she ran a hand over the worn wood.

Something told him she had no plans to run, and he could go back into the house without worrying. But he found himself padding softly toward the bench, not wanting to leave her out here alone. He told himself he was being cautious. He told himself he was protecting the key to the clan's safety.

He cleared his throat to announce his presence, and Lark turned with wide, startled eyes.

A soft "Oh!" escaped her lips and her hand pressed against her chest. "You scared me!" She kept her voice low as if worried she might wake someone.

"That was not my intention." He stood halfway between the house and bench, unsure if he should approach or return to his bed. He was a fool.

Her mouth lifted into a small smile. "I couldn't sleep. I didn't mean to worry you."

He opened his mouth to respond and then closed it again. He was struck dumb with indecision. The heat rose in his face as he struggled with what to do next and he was glad for the darkness.

"Are you having trouble sleeping too?"

She was throwing a rope to a drowning man. He grabbed it.

"Yes. I haven't slept well since…" His voice faded into the night air. He didn't want to talk about his mother right now, with her.

She patted the bench beside her, and he forced his heavy feet to move toward it and sit.

"We can keep each other company. I haven't been sleeping well lately either." She tilted her head to face him, her unbound hair tumbling over her shoulders. She shivered a little, wrapped in a light blanket she must have pulled from the bed.

He slipped off his coat and wrapped it around her shoulders. Her fingers brushed against his as she took it and held it tight around her. He ignored the shiver running through him, the one that had nothing to do with the chill.

"But now you will be cold," she whispered, her eyes never leaving his face.

He had to tear his gaze away before he could speak. "I am used to the cold."

Lark murmured a word of thanks beside him, her warmth seeping through the sleeve of his shirt. Even in the night air, sitting next to her, he would not be cold.

For several minutes, neither spoke, but instead, let the sounds of the night fill in the silence. The sky was clear, and each star shone brightly above them. Alaric glanced to the side, peeking at the woman next to him. She looked small inside his coat. Her head was tipped back, her gaze at the heavens.

Alaric leaned forward on the bench, and his fingers curled tightly around the edge of its weathered surface. He returned his stare to his old, scuffed boots and cursed himself for the warmth spreading through his chest at her nearness, for the words cutting through his thoughts.

Perhaps she was not meant for the clan. Perhaps she was meant for me.

He inhaled sharply at the absurdity of it. He felt Lark shift her gaze from the stars to the side of his face. He continued to study his boots, not ready to meet her eye. Again, he was glad for the darkness so she couldn't see her effect on him.

"How did you come to be responsible for your siblings?" she asked, breaking the quiet between them.

He paused before he spoke, taking a minute to clear his head. "My mother died two years ago. She was ill." His voice was gruff, harsh, even to his own ears.

"My mother is gone also. Since the day of my birth."

He straightened and turned toward her as he spoke, gentling his voice. "Do you have siblings of your own?"

Her mouth tilted into a small smile, the one that made it look like she was keeping secrets from him. "I have three sisters."

He raised his eyebrows, and a laugh escaped her lips. "My father felt the same way about having four daughters. He wished for a son, of course." The amusement had faded from her face and her features set into the determined sadness he had seen when he first encountered her in the woods. As though she were used to a life of disappointment but went looking for something hopeful anyway.

"We are not close," she went on, "My sisters and I." She glanced back toward the house behind them. "It must be nice to have your siblings close to you."

"A bit too close sometimes." The words escaped his lips before he had a chance to think them over.

A short laugh burst from Lark's mouth, and she clamped a hand over it to muffle the sound. A smile crept onto Alaric's face as well. Lark's eyes twinkled above the slender fingers she still had clasped over her mouth.

"There are a lot of them, aren't there?" she asked with a grin, dropping her hand to her lap.

His smile deepened. "Sometimes it seems as though more appear in the middle of the night. It's possible half the children in there aren't even related to me."

Lark's shoulders shook with the laugh she was trying and failing to hold in. Her giggles squeaked out and made him laugh in return. She looked at him so shocked to hear his laughter, her eyes comically wide, that they both started laughing anew.

"Thank you, for that," she said, catching her breath. She placed a hand on his shoulder. "This day has been…" her words faded away, but her fingers stayed on his arm.

He cleared his throat. "This day has been different for us both."

She nodded, still watching him, her fingers still searing him through his shirt. His own fingers twitched in his lap, suddenly longing to cup her stained face and push the hair from her temple. His gaze skated across her mouth. He would run a thumb across those lips and feel their softness. He would…

"Will you show me the house?"

He blinked, breaking the fantasy he was so recklessly engaging in. What had she asked?

"The house?"

She gestured toward the other house on the property. His house.

Alaric hadn't set foot in it since his mother died, since the day his life had veered permanently off course. He looked at it now, a dark hulking shape on the other side of the garden. He would have his work cut out for him tomorrow to make it livable for her to sleep in. But Weylyn was right, the big house was too crowded for another person. Especially a person who roused such inconvenient feelings in him.

"It will be hard to see much in the dark," he told her, but she was already up and moving toward it, the nearly full moon lighting her path. He had no choice but to follow.

"What is it doing here? Does it belong to your

family? Has anyone lived in it before?" She asked the questions faster than he could respond.

"It's mine." The answer was curt and too loud for the stillness around them. Lark stopped at the door and looked up at him.

"It's yours?" She placed a palm on the door and ran her hand over the smooth wood, wood he had planed himself until it was as smooth as glass.

He nodded, but she continued to stare, his nonverbal answers were never enough for her.

"It was meant to be mine. I built it for me and my wife…"

"Your wife?" Her eyebrows rose nearly to her hairline, and Alaric had to clamp his lips together not to smile at her shock.

"My future wife. Or so I thought at the time."

She waited only a beat before asking, "What happened to her?"

He sighed and ran a hand down his beard. This tiny sprig of a woman had him talking more in one night than he had in the past several months combined. He supposed he could turn around and go back to bed, leave her and her questions behind. But instead, he found himself opening his mouth to answer.

"Nothing happened to her. She's alive and well, the mother to a feisty little boy, in fact." And now he was adding in details like a regular storyteller! What had gotten into him? Lark leaned forward in interest, her eyes on his. He had no choice but to go on.

"It happened to me, not her. After my mother was gone, nothing was the same, including my feelings for the girl. I never moved into the house, never finished it." He ran a hand over the door now too, brushing his fingers past Lark's. "My aunts took in the little ones, but they kept turning up at my doorstep. What could I do? I couldn't turn them away, my own siblings. So, we stayed together, in the end."

He breathed out slowly when he was done. Lark watched him with dark eyes and then, as though she had decided something about him, something critical, she placed her hand on his chest. She left it there for only a second, right over the place where his heart thudded inexplicably hard, before pulling it back and tucking it inside the coat still hanging over her shoulders.

"Can we go in?" she whispered it and he nodded, having no words left. He pushed open the door, and it protested loudly on rusted hinges. It hadn't been open in over two years. Lark stepped inside, pausing to let her eyes adjust to the darkness. The window he had carved out above the door let in the moonlight, but most of the space was nothing but shadows.

If it were light, they would see a typical cooking platform in the middle of the space, one that had never been used, wooden bunks on either side for sitting or sleeping, and a sturdy wooden table next to the fire pit. And that was all. Well, that and two years' worth of dust and dirt. Even now he heard the scurry of feet as whatever had moved in over the years was disrupted by the human visitors.

The sudden heat of failure and embarrassment started in his belly and worked its way to his cheeks. A feeling so familiar to him over the years he wasn't surprised by it. How could he have offered this dirty, half-completed house to this woman? She must think him a savage, a barbarian. She came from Kalon, after all, and that is what they all thought of the clans.

Lark turned to him, and he opened his mouth to explain, to apologize, but the sight of her face stopped him. It was lit by the moonlight shining through the window and by something else, something inside her. The heat in his belly cooled. She was smiling.

"It's perfect." Her voice was quiet, reverent, and another thought came unbidden to his mind.

You make it perfect. I built this house for you. He swallowed the words and led her silently back to the big house.

Chapter 9: A Loyal Knight

Arowyn was teaching her how to pull squashes from the vine when they heard the pounding of a horse's footsteps. Not many of the clanspeople used horses and Arowyn's eyes were round with surprise. Odessa stood from her crouch in the dirt with a vague sense of foreboding gathering in her stomach. It couldn't be.

She glanced back at the little house she had already, in just a few days' time, begun to think of as hers. With its new roof and the thorough cleaning Alaric and his siblings had given it, it was a handsome little building.

The sound of the horse was getting closer and was now accompanied by a voice. A voice shouting her name.

Damn it. Odessa cursed softly, wiping her hands on her borrowed apron. Arowyn was right by her side as she strode toward the path that wove its way through the village. The girl had become her shadow over the past few days, helping Odessa with the day-to-day tasks Odessa had insisted on being a part of.

From where she stood, she could see other neighbors coming out of their homes, craning their necks to see what the commotion was all about. Whatever was about to happen, she would have an audience for it. She tucked a wayward strand of hair behind her ear and steadied herself.

A sleek black horse rounded the corner, and for a fraction of a moment, her heart leapt at the sight of him. The habit hadn't yet had time to die. A relic of her past feelings for him, resurfacing one last time. But her eyes met his, and she remembered. She remembered how long she had waited for him, how long she had suffered while he lived his own life. She would not go back to it. He pulled the horse to a stop and jumped down in front of her.

"Odessa!" Her name on his lips was both a sigh of relief and a reprimand. Nolan's eyes ran over her, checking for damage she assumed, but diligently avoiding her face. Had he bothered to look up he would have seen the truth: she had no desire to be rescued.

"Odessa?" Alaric's bewildered voice behind her startled her into action. She turned to explain, but before she could open her mouth, Nolan was already speaking.

"Princess Odessa of Kalon. Do you not know who you stole?" Nolan scoffed, drawing his sword in the same breath. He stepped between Odessa and Alaric.

"Careful knight, you are on clan lands. And you are alone." Alaric's voice was a menacing growl. It made the small hairs on Odessa's arms stand on end. Nolan was not a fool; he lowered the sword. But he didn't step back. The men stood nearly nose to nose.

"I am here to return the princess to her family." He spoke loud enough she was sure the entire village knew by now who she really was.

"The princess," the word was harsh and mocking from Alaric's mouth and Odessa cringed internally, "came willingly and can do as she wishes." He looked over Nolan's shoulder as he spoke, his eyes on her face. Whatever softness she had found in those eyes in the last few days was gone. Now she could see nothing but his anger.

"She will return with me." Nolan's answer was so swift and so confident Odessa nearly agreed out of habit.

But before Alaric could hand her over like an errant sheep that had wandered too far from the farmer's field, she found her voice.

"You do not speak for me." Both men turned to look at her, and she instinctively raised a hand to her uncovered face. But she wore no hood to hide in, so she had no choice but to speak out in the open. "I did come here willingly. And I do not wish to leave."

Nolan's eyebrows rose so high it would have been comical had she not felt like she was fighting for her life. Alaric's face was impassive, his massive arms crossed over his chest, impossible to read. Would he send her back with Nolan? Perhaps he was tired of defending her place here, first to his people and now to hers.

She glanced toward the big house where both Rieka and Arowyn stood in the doorway with watchful eyes. Weylyn and Faolan had crept into the yard and stood menacingly silent behind their brother.

Odessa swallowed hard. Surely, she had caused these people enough trouble, but the idea of returning to her room squeezed her lungs tight in her chest. Returning with Nolan meant returning to the shadowed life of the cursed princess, and she wouldn't go back. She couldn't.

"Princess," Nolan's voice was full of sweet

indulgence like she was a simple child or a spooked horse. She could kick him. "I'm sure you have had quite the ordeal, but we must return you to your father."

Mention of her father only increased her desire to stay. "I have not had an ordeal. I have been treated very well, and I have no desire to return home."

Nolan's smile was growing tight. He was losing his patience. "Odessa," he hissed. And even while he spoke to her directly, his eyes flitted from place to place, never landing on her face for more than a moment. "What is this about? Surely you don't think you can stay here!" He said the last part like it was a joke, but not surprisingly no one was laughing.

She dared a glance at Alaric and were it not for the rise and fall of his chest, she would have thought he was made of stone. Only his eyes moved. They followed her as she stepped closer to him, choosing sides.

Alaric's brothers moved toward him also, as though sensing things could get out of hand at any moment. Odessa felt as though the eyes of the entire clan were on her. Certainly, she couldn't explain how Nolan had many chances to rescue her from her prison and never had. She couldn't explain that she had no real plan, only to escape the life she had been living. How could she tell these men all she wanted was to make a choice for herself, that her only real motivation in coming here was to decide on her own path?

Heat rose to her cheeks, and she was sure the pale one was pinkening to match the marked one. How foolish she had been to think she could live here amongst these people who were not hers, that she could be of use to them, that she could build a life here. Her eyes flicked back to Alaric, where he stood stoic and unflinching. Foolish.

But she had come this far. She rolled her shoulders back and faced Nolan even as his eyes darted away from hers. "I'm sorry. You will have to return without me."

His eyes did meet hers then, and for a moment something like sadness or regret flickered through them before they returned to anger.

"Essa." The name on his lips no longer held any power. He reached out to grab her hand. Alaric stepped between them in one graceful move.

"Your princess wishes to stay."

Nolan's hand went to the sword at his side. The entire village held its breath; even the birds in the trees were silent. A muscle twitched in Nolan's tightly clenched jaw. The wind blew a strand of hair across Alaric's face. Neither man blinked. Their chests rose and fell in the same steady rhythm. Odessa bit hard on her bottom lip to keep from speaking. There was nothing left to say. Nolan broke the stare first, his eyes sliding to hers for one last moment. With a terse nod, he turned and remounted. He rode away without looking back.

****

She found him later—after Nolan had gone, and the children had wandered away, and the neighbors had stopped staring from their own gardens and doorways—behind the house splitting wood. She stood for a moment and listened to the repetitive whack of the ax into the logs, adding to the already substantial woodpile.

His back was to her. His bare arms rose over his

head with each swing, tan and muscled, distracting her from her reason for seeking him out. She had intended to apologize for the lies, but he was hacking apart those logs with a simmering anger that burned her from where she stood. He tossed the pieces of wood he had cut into the pile and glanced over his shoulder, catching her watching him. He hesitated, the ax hanging at his side. He wiped the sweat off his brow, and she worried he would go back to chopping without speaking to her, but he propped the ax against the pile and turned to face her.

"You're a princess." He surprised her by speaking first.

"I…uh…yes, but…"

"You lied."

"I did. And for that I am sorry, but…"

He stepped toward her, closing the space between them. The sweat glistened on his chest. She swallowed hard.

"Do you know much about the clans, princess?"

The title from his mouth grated on her, rubbing raw her already battered heart.

"No. Not much."

"Let me fill you in. The clans living in this forest have an uneasy truce with the kingdoms to the north and south."

She nodded. "That I knew."

He took another step toward her, so she had to tip her head to look at him. "And how do you think the peace is going to last if the king of Kalon believes we have stolen his daughter?" His voice was menacingly quiet.

"I…"

"You have made things very dangerous for me and my people. You told me no one would come for you. Who was that man?"

The long-held tension inside her snapped at his accusations. She poked a single finger into the solid chest of the man accusing her of endangering him. His mismatched eyes widened in surprise.

"You begged me to come with you. You told me your goddess sent me! So now you doubt your goddess? Now I am no longer useful to you?"

It was Alaric's turn to open a shocked mouth, but no words came out.

"My father locked me in my chambers for the first half of my life. For years I saw no one except the maids who fed and clothed me." Alaric's eyes widened, something in his face softened, but she went on.

"They say I killed my mother, that my face is evidence of my curse. My father both hates and fears me. He only let me out of my rooms when the rumors about me became worse than the truth." The tears slid down her cheeks. Alaric's hands gripped her arms as though willing her to stop, but she couldn't, not after finally starting.

"For years, I have been alone, spit on, pitied, and feared. And all I wanted was to get away. And you…" Now the tears would not stop, and she sniffled, her words thick with emotion, "you told me you would help me, and I could help you in return."

He squeezed her arms tighter, pulling her closer to him, so when she spoke next her cheek was against the rough fabric of his sleeveless tunic and the smell of woodsmoke and pine was in her nose.

"Is it no longer true?"

He dropped his hands from her arms and slid them around her back. He rubbed circles between her shoulder blades until her tears stopped, holding her close until her breathing slowed.

When she finally pulled away to look at him, his eyes reflected her own sorrow.

"It is still true," he promised, his voice low and rough. "We will help each other, just as I said."

Chapter 10: Prophecy

Nolan raced back to the castle; his fury fueling his ride. How dare she? How dare she turn him away? After he had worried about her safety, after he had risked his own life to come find her. He had gone to the king immediately after realizing she was missing and volunteered to go after her. He was the one person in all of Kalon who cared for her, and she turned him away, choosing that hairy beast of a man over him. His hands gripped so tightly to the reins his knuckles were white. He dug his heels into the sides of his horse, urging her on.

He took the Warriors' Pass back through the woods toward Kalon. The way was cleared years ago; the trees burned, and the path widened for the soldiers, horses, and artillery passing through this forest, fighting the never-ending war between Kalon and Melantha to the south. In the beginning, the two kingdoms were ruled by brothers, and their people lived in peace with each other until the wife of one was caught with the other.

A duplicitous woman, Nolan thought to himself as he rode, isn't that always the way? And from that act of betrayal, countless lives were lost, seemingly endless blood was spilled.

Nolan's horse shied away from the edge of the trail, and the flesh rose on the back of his neck. He could feel the eyes on him. If any of the clansmen of these woods took offense to him being there, he wouldn't stand a chance against them. The woods were sacred to the clans who lived in them, protected by their goddess, Asherah. They had not been pleased to see a swath of it burned to the ground, and their precious woods split in two.

The forest had grown between the two kingdoms as the animosity between the warring brothers also grew. Nolan didn't know where the clans had come from. It seemed they belonged to the forest itself, sprung from the animals who still protected them: the wolf, the fox, the bear, and the raven. It was absurd, of course, for the clans to worship the animals and the trees the way they did. Further evidence of their primitive and barbaric nature.

Nolan had faced men from each clan at one time or another. The clans often raided the war caravans for food and weapons, and the men from the warring kingdoms didn't hesitate to take what they needed from the clans as well, a wife or two, some unguarded horses. The peace between the clans and the kingdoms to the north and south was relative, not perfect.

He had never been into a clan village until his visit to the Wolves today. Stealing from savages wasn't his way, although he said nothing to deter his men from doing so. It was a risk, coming here alone, a rash decision made out of fear and his own foolish pride. As soon as he discovered Odessa was missing, he started imagining their reunion. The bile rose in his throat at the image that greeted him instead, his princess standing next to the barbarian, choosing him over Nolan.

The day he first laid eyes on Odessa sprang to

mind as he raced through the forest. It was the morning after his first shift as the night guard outside of her room. He had been about to return to his chambers to catch a few hours of sleep before he needed to be on the training field when Odessa had opened the door and peered out into the hallway.

"Oh, I thought you left." Her voice surprised him, and without thinking he looked at her face. It was half-hidden by the large hood of her cloak, but bright eyes shined out at him. His gaze lingered a moment too long, and the princess stood frozen in the doorway.

"I was just leaving." He tore his gaze away and stepped aside.

"Thank you."

She left the scent of rosemary and lavender in her wake as she moved past him. She glanced over her shoulder at him, and he met her stare again. This time her face broke into a beaming smile.

It was the smile that did him in. He couldn't seem to stop thinking about it for the rest of the day. He needed to see it again. He craved it.

And so, the next time he was on watch, he found himself lingering into the morning hours, waiting for the princess to leave for her daily walk. Soon the smiles became words, and the words became touches, and Nolan couldn't help himself. He found himself in Odessa's bed, convinced she had cast a spell on him.

Despite what the people said about her, despite the rumors of curses and a princess marked by evil, Nolan couldn't stay away. Odessa showered him with attention and admiration. That was the spell she cast, one that made him believe he could do anything. He liked being adored.

Had she ever meant any of it? He cursed aloud as a low-hanging tree branch whipped across his arm, wrenching him from his memories. Damn this forest, and damn Odessa and her lies.

He remembered their last conversation; she had been upset, unreasonable. She wanted too much. The king had forbidden marriage for his marked daughter, and who was Nolan to argue? But did he not visit her? Did he not spend time in her chambers and between her sheets? She should be thankful he didn't run like every other man in the kingdom. And still, she had the audacity to turn him away. He nearly choked on his own rage.

As he rode through the clans' desecrated forest, the path worn beneath his horse's hooves, he wished he could burn the rest of it to ash. Surely, the king would feel the same. Marked or not, Odessa was his daughter, and the king could not possibly stand by and allow his family to be kidnapped by savages.

The blood boiled in his veins the more he pictured Odessa standing beside that man. He would single-handedly fight the four clans himself. The Ravens and their faces painted black like the night, like death. The Bears, wearing the skin of their sacred animal. The Foxes, so cunning he never saw them coming. And the Wolves, starting with the man who dared to steal Odessa from him. Nolan would strike them all down to take back what was rightfully his.

He took a long shuddering breath. Rashness would get him nowhere right now. He had managed not to kill the barbarian in his own front garden. He would need to keep a level head if he was to get Odessa back. First, he must speak to the king.

****

Nolan strode into the great hall, not bothering to bathe or change his clothes before meeting with the king. He stunk of horse and sweat from days on the road, dust, and grime stuck to him, but he had no time to spare. The king wanted him to be discreet in his search for his daughter, but discretion takes extra time. It would have taken him even longer had he not heard the gossip in the market about a stranger among the Wolves. Bitterness rolled through him. Odessa had ruined his triumphant return. She should be by his side.

His footsteps echoed in the cavernous space as he approached the dais. Villagers who had come for an audience with the king and queen scurried out of Nolan's way. His face must have looked as black as his mood.

"Your majesties." He gave a curt bow in front of the king and queen, noticing the little princess was present as well. She looked so much like her older sister he nearly choked. Her birthmark wasn't nearly as visible as Odessa's, but he could make out the faint outline of it on her temple. How could the king lock up one of his daughters and sit beside the other? For a moment, a familiar sadness washed over him, the same pity that had compelled him into the cursed princess's quarters in the first place. He had liked being her only companion, and that fact alone made her betrayal cut him even deeper.

"I have news of your daughter."

The king's face remained impassive at this announcement, his response a mere nod of the head. At first glance, it would appear the royal family hadn't heard his words at all. But Nolan did not miss the flush of red starting at the king's neck, slowly working its way up, or the queen's white knuckles as she gripped the arms of her chair, or the shift in the princess's posture as she leaned toward him. Perhaps he was not the only one concerned for Odessa's welfare.

With a wave of his hand, King Orion had the room cleared of everyone but Nolan and a guard near the door.

"Speak." He turned his bulk toward Nolan, the eagerness for information burning behind his eyes.

"I found Princess Odessa among the Wolves."

A small sound of shocked worry escaped the lips of the little princess, and her mother's hand shot out to cover hers. Nolan's gaze lingered on their clasped hands where the mother protected her daughter from worry. Was that the thing keeping Faye safe, the mother sitting beside her? He shook his head. These thoughts would get him nowhere.

"She is unharmed but…" The words stuck in his throat. How could he explain what happened next? It was still so unfathomable even to Nolan himself and he had witnessed it firsthand.

"Out with it," the king barked.

"She does not wish to return, your majesty."

The redness that had started on the king's neck had now spread to his entire face.

"She what?" he sputtered.

"The princess does not wish—"

"The princess has no right to wish for anything!" The king's voice bounced off the stone walls of the great hall and echoed through Nolan's bones.

"I would have brought her back by force, your majesty, but I was greatly outnumbered. It would be my honor to lead a group of men…"

The king was no longer looking at him or listening to any of his words. He ran a hand down his weary face and turned toward his wife. She sat rigid in her chair, her face the picture of stoic grace, but Nolan saw the fear behind her eyes. If one princess could be taken by barbarians, what would stop them from taking another?

"We never should have unlocked her door," the king hissed at her.

She turned to her husband, her face a practiced calm. "And would it have been better to have the kingdom believe a mutilated monster had sprung from your loins? That is what they said about you before I came, before I married you and released your cursed daughter. They needed to see for themselves what she was. Nothing more than a marked girl."

The king stood, glaring at his wife, his breath coming so hard, he looked to Nolan like a bull about to charge.

"Leave us!"

Queen Louise rose, in a slow graceful movement, her daughter doing the same. She tucked the small girl's hand into her side and led her from the dais. Impatience radiated off the king. The queen made no effort to hurry.

She turned back toward her husband. "Do not let the clans get away with this. Or you risk us all."

The king glowered at her retreating back, and Nolan shifted on his feet.

"Your majesty," he said, in an attempt to steer this meeting back in the direction of Odessa, "with enough men, I'm sure we could bring the princess back safely."

Orion's gaze swung back to Nolan's face, his eyes

narrowed, assessing. Nolan straightened to his full height, rolling his shoulders back. With a sigh, the old king sat back in his chair, running a hand down his ruddy face.

"This is about more than the princess."

"Of course, we must consider the safety of the whole royal family—"

The king raised a hand to stop his rambling. Nolan bit back his frustration and waited for Orion to go on.

"I speak to you in confidence, so you'll be aware of the severity of our situation. But what I tell you must not leave this room." Icy blue eyes stared into him. Nolan nodded.

The king cleared his throat and closed his eyes, preparing for a speech. Nolan groaned internally. Every minute spent here listening to his king's tales was a minute he could be spending preparing for his next attack.

"The day my third daughter was born was a terrible day for the kingdom. Not only was she born marked, but my queen died bringing her into this world." The king shook his head, his graying hair rustling against the back of his chair. "I knew this child would cause me nothing but pain."

Again, pity pricked at Nolan's heart. Had the king spoken to Odessa in years? Laid his eyes upon her and truly believed she was cursed? That she was to blame for her mother's death? The image of Odessa standing outside the clan house, her face uncovered, her voice unwavering, came to his mind. A flicker of pride ran through him. She had escaped the man who sought to keep her hidden.

Pity and pride were quickly overshadowed by the

memory of the man who stood beside her and her refusal to return with Nolan. She had betrayed him in the worst way, and he could not easily forget it. He hardened his heart as the king continued his story.

"After my wife died, I was sick with sorrow and rage. As I gazed upon my wretched child for the first time, the midwife whispered a message in my ear, a prophecy."

Nolan looked up, his focus returning to the task at hand. He never heard mention of a prophecy, which was rare in a castle so ripe with rumor and gossip.

"The old woman told me one day my child would unite the clans against a mighty kingdom."

Unite the clans? The idea alone chilled Nolan's blood. As a leader of the king's forces, he knew more than most that the kingdom's success relied on the clans remaining divided. If they were to unite against Kalon, he could not be confident in the outcome. It had never been done.

The king's eyes were open now, studying Nolan from where he sat above him.

"Now you see why I kept my daughter locked away. Now you know the danger we face. It is for the good of the kingdom I give you this task. Do what you must to return my daughter to me."

"As you wish, your majesty." With another bow, Nolan stalked out of the great hall. He would happily kill anyone who stood in his way of rescuing the princess, starting with the beast who stole her from him. And now he had the king's blessing to do so.

Chapter 11: Until the Solstice

"You wished to speak with me?" It was rare for
Alaric to face the chief alone, and he was not foolish
enough to believe Connell had summoned him to relay
good news. The older man sat at the end of a long
wooden table, the same as the one sitting in Alaric's
home. Most of the chief's home was similar to his own.
The main difference was the size and emptiness of the
space. Connell had only one daughter and his wife was
dead. The man sat alone with his cup and gestured for
Alaric to join him.

Connell waited before speaking, taking another sip
of his drink, while Alaric squirmed inside. On the
outside he remained stoic, refusing to let the other man
intimidate him. Or at least refusing to let him see that
he did.

"You brought me a princess," he said at last.

Alaric nodded, waiting to hear what else the man
had to say. Connell obviously knew about the scene that
had played out in front of his house the day before.
There was no need to add any details before he asked
for them.

Connell leaned back in his chair, cold gray eyes
never leaving Alaric's face.

"The Northern king will not be pleased to learn
we've kidnapped his daughter."

"I didn't kidnap her." Alaric's response was quick,

escaping his lips without hesitation. He would not be branded a brute who stole women from their homes.

Connell smirked a wolfish smirk. "So, I hear. However, I don't think the king will see it that way."

Alaric opened his mouth to protest further but Connell went on, "You have put me in a tough situation. Our people are sick and dying, and I have promised them answers."

"She doesn't want to return. She wishes to stay."

Again, the smirk. Goosebumps rose on Alaric's arms.

"And I do not wish to return her."

Alaric relaxed slightly. He worried he would have to tell Odessa she had to go back against her will. After hearing her story, he was even more determined to keep his promise to her.

Connell clasped his hands over his flat stomach. The man was a warrior and still built like one, even as his beard grew in grayer and grayer. "The trouble is the king will not simply let her go."

"Should she not get a say in the matter?"

Connell barked a cruel laugh. "You are young, my boy."

Alaric bristled at his tone. Connell spoke to him as though he had not lived twenty winters, as though he had not fought beside Connell in battle.

"As for the princess, of course, we will honor her wish to stay. We as a clan are nothing if not hospitable."

Nothing about this little speech rang true, but Alaric held his tongue, curious to see where Connell was going.

"If we wish to protect the princess, we must be

prepared to fight. I am sure Kalon will attack within the week. And we will be ready."

Alaric gave a terse nod. He had figured as much himself, but he still didn't understand why he had been summoned. He rose to leave when Connell's voice stopped him.

"But remember, in the end, your loyalty must be to the clan, not your little guest."

Connell's eyes were boring into him now.

"You question my loyalty?"

"I simply remind you of your duties. I am relying on you to keep our guest safe until the solstice."

"I know my role."

"Good."

Alaric rose and turned toward the door, eager for this meeting to be over, but again Connell's low growl stopped him in his tracks.

"Because I would hate for the clan to find out the truth about what happened to your father."

Alaric froze. He always wondered if the man knew what he had done, but never had Connell threatened him so directly with the truth.

"The princess is safe with me," he ground out, his jaw so tight his teeth ached. He pulled open the door into the sunlight, nearly running to get out of this house, away from the man who threatened to upend his life.

"Until the solstice…"

Alaric could hear the laughter in the chief's voice as he fled the house, his parting phrase ringing in Alaric's ears. He would keep Odessa safe, he would do his duty, and he would never give Connell a reason to tell the clan what he did to his father.

****

71

The sound of his sisters' giggles pulled him from his thoughts of Connell and his father as he neared home. The simple joy of it was a balm to his worried heart. Odessa's bright laughter joined his sisters, and his stomach flipped in anticipation of seeing her.

He crept silently toward the house and peered around the side of the building where Arowyn and Rieka were doubled over in laughter. He took in the scene, a smile creeping across his own mouth as he watched.

"You can't milk a goat?" Arowyn squealed in delight as Odessa clumsily squeezed the goat's teat. "I have been milking the goat since I was five!"

Alaric grinned. Being the baby of the family meant Arowyn rarely got to be an expert at anything. There was always someone around who knew better than her. Her cheeks were flushed with pleasure at getting to be the instructor.

"And how old are you now?" Odessa asked, still squeezing and getting very little milk for her efforts. The goat shifted in agitation.

"I am eight and Rieka is ten."

Odessa looked up at the girl with a smile. "Ah, see! You have been doing this for three years, and it is only my first day!"

Arowyn laughed again, delighted at this announcement. Rieka squatted next to the milking stool, attempting to readjust Odessa's fingers. The hiss of milk hitting the sides of the pail followed, and Odessa's face lit up almost as brightly as his sisters'.

"There! I did it!"

Arowyn did a little victory dance in celebration, and Rieka smiled at her student proudly. Alaric's chest tightened at the sight of Odessa beaming at his sisters from her seat on the stool. He rubbed the unfamiliar ache above his heart. He had forgotten what happiness felt like.

Odessa was dressed in the style of the clan, in a tunic and buckskin leggings he had borrowed for her from his cousins. Her hair was braided away from her face and the rest hung in a riot of waves down her back. Both sides of her face were beautiful in the late afternoon sunshine.

The truth settled over him quietly, like a whisper in his ear. He wasn't keeping her safe because his chief demanded it, but because she had asked him to. And because he wanted to.

A shriek disrupted his thoughts as the goat bleated, kicked over the bucket, and tore past him, Arowyn and Rieka on her heels.

"Oh no! The milk!" Odessa stood, goat's milk dripping from the front of her tunic, staring despondently at the puddle of fresh milk soaking into the dirt. "Damn it." The curse was soft, spoken under her breath.

"Such language from a princess," he chuckled, stepping out from behind his hiding place. Odessa startled and clapped a hand over her mouth, but when she pulled her hand away, she was grinning.

"My first lesson did not go so well," she said with a shrug. "Even though I had very eager teachers."

"It was kind of you to humor them."

"Humor them? No, I truly wanted to learn! Sadly, your goat had other plans." She laughed, the sound of it filling him up. Her eyes were on his, and her face turned serious. He shifted under her gaze.

"What did your chief say? Am I to be returned to Kalon?" Sadness eclipsed the humor on her face.

"Connell says we will honor your request to stay."

She let out a relieved sigh, and stepping closer to him, she placed a hand on his thudding heart. She must feel how rapidly it beat against her palm.

"Thank you."

He cleared his throat searching for something more to say. "Who was the man that came for you yesterday?" The question was not one he had intended on asking but it flew from his mouth before he could stop it.

Odessa dropped her hand and took a step back. He should not have mentioned the man.

"He is one of my father's knights."

"He seemed to be more than that." What was he doing? He had no right to ask any of these questions, but the imprint of Odessa's fingers was still warm on his chest, and he needed to know if this man was more to her than one of her father's men.

Her eyes flicked to his and then looked away. He grabbed her chin gently and lifted her face. Her skin was soft under his fingers.

"He was more than that once," she answered honestly, holding his gaze, "but no longer."

Alaric held her face a moment more; her dark eyes held his, unflinching in their inspection of him. What did she see when she looked at him?

"He did not look at me like you do," she confessed, her voice husky. The heat crept into his face, but he did not look away.

"He could never seem to bring himself to look upon my face for too long, but you do not flinch."

Alaric brushed her cheek with the back of his hand, first the pale one and then the marked one, caressing the reason for her imprisonment as though he could take the curse away from her. She leaned into his touch. A small sigh escaped her lips, echoing in his heart. He took a step closer until their bodies were nearly touching.

His gaze roved the contours of her face and landed on her full lips, parted slightly, inviting him. He leaned toward her, all rational thought leaving his brain completely, when the goat meandered back into the yard, bleating loudly around their feet. He jerked away from Odessa, dropping his hand and leaving her blinking at his sudden movement. His sisters would not be far behind the old goat.

"I should go." He cleared his throat and turned toward the house, his sisters nearly running him over in their pursuit. He left the girls with Odessa in the yard and hurried inside, shaking the imprint of her skin from his fingertips.

Chapter 12: Burnt Offerings

Alone in her room, Odessa had plenty of time to imagine a future for herself. Not a single one of those daydreams involved her living with a clan of the woods. Most had starred her father having a change of heart, and plenty included Nolan. Never once had she considered leaving Kalon on her own until the day she finally did it.

It had been over a week since she left, and she had no clear vision of what the future held for her. For the first time, it was wide open. The door of her confinement had been flung open and her life stretched out before her, unplanned and unrestricted. She felt hollowed out by it.

This life expanded before her. Like a soap bubble on the wind, she worried she would float away. She focused on the current moment to keep herself firmly on the ground, and the current moment contained a horribly scorched pot of stew and two disappointed teachers.

"It seems I may have burned it," she grimaced. The smell of charred vegetables wafted up from the heavy pot.

Rieka put her hands on her hips, her small mouth pinched, and her eyebrows furrowed. It was clear the girl was trying to find a kind way to tell her she was a horrible cook. Arowyn took a more direct approach.

"Not 'may have.' Definitely. It's worse than when Weylyn cooks." Her whole face puckered in disgust as she lifted some of the burnt contents onto a long wooden spoon. "I doubt the goat will eat it, and she eats old shoes," she added, wafting the smell away from her crinkled nose.

Odessa suppressed a sigh. She had failed at nearly every domestic task the girls had taught her this week. Afraid she would become a burden to the family who had so kindly taken her in, she had insisted on helping out, but so far, every attempt had been unsuccessful. She didn't have a single practical skill. And yet she had imagined she could start a new life for herself. Were it not for these two little girls in front of her, she would have starved by now.

Rieka took pity on her and patted her reassuringly on the arm. "Perhaps you should stick to bread for now." She gestured toward the table where a lump of dough sat, waiting to be kneaded. Odessa approached it slowly as though it may bite her like the goat had. Rieka let out a small laugh.

"It's easy, push and fold, push and fold." She demonstrated a few rounds before stepping aside to let Odessa try.

She sunk her hands into the warm dough, the yeasty scent filling the air. She pushed the heels of her hands in like Rieka had done and folded the dough over itself and repeated the process.

Rieka gave her an approving nod before returning to the disaster in the pot. The girls muttered quietly to themselves, plotting a way to save the supper. Odessa watched them for a moment, heads bent over the pot. She liked being near them. They reminded her of Faye and made her wish she had been allowed to be closer to her younger sister.

Her older sisters had found ways to sneak into her chambers when they were children, following busy maids carrying loads of laundry, flirting with the guards outside her room once they got older. But their visits were brief and rare; the girls feared what their father would do if they were caught.

Her interactions with Faye had been limited to brief meetings in the halls, with her stepmother never far away. It was as though the queen worried her beloved daughter would catch the curse that hung over her, but it wasn't possible. Faye's birthmark was as plain as day on the girl's face, but their father had never acknowledged it. He blamed Odessa for the death of his wife. Her face was merely a convenient excuse to make her pay for her sin.

"You don't need to be so rough with it." Rieka's comment broke through Odessa's memories. The mutilated dough squished out from her clenched hands. She had kneaded a hole right through it.

"Right. Sorry." She patted the dough back together, smiling sheepishly at the girls. There was no need to think of her father anymore. She was safe here. If she could just learn how to feed herself, she might be alright on her own.

The door swung open, and Weylyn and Faolan tumbled in, their older brother not far behind.

"I would have hit it, if you hadn't distracted me," Faolan was saying.

Weylyn rolled his eyes and gave his younger brother a teasing shove. "You wouldn't have hit that rabbit no matter what I was doing! It was too far."

"Too far for you maybe," Faolan huffed, "but I would have hit it."

Weylyn opened his mouth to argue the point further, but he cringed as he caught a whiff of the smoky air. "Please tell me that's not the smell of our supper. We leave you girls to cook for one night and see what happens!"

"Oh, shut it, Weylyn. You nearly burned the whole house down the last time you cooked." Arowyn stood on a chair to meet her brother face to face, her hands on her tiny hips. "Besides, it wasn't us…" Her gaze slid to Odessa, but she clamped her lips together, suddenly deciding not to blame their guest.

"I'm so sorry—" Odessa began, but Rieka piped in from beside her.

"She tried her best. And she did a fine job kneading the bread for the morning."

"And what good does that do us now?" Weylyn snapped back.

Odessa looked across the room to Alaric for help with the situation, but he stood pinching the bridge of his nose between his fingers as though his head might explode at any moment.

"We could have had rabbit, had you not distracted me," Faolan muttered, sitting at the table.

"Get over it." Weylyn pushed him hard on the shoulder and Faolan nearly upended the entire table before spilling out of the chair and onto the floor.

All hell broke loose in the small house. Faolan jumped up and tackled his brother, both landing on the sleeping platform behind them. Rieka shrieked dramatically as though her life was in danger, and Arowyn joined the fray, pummeling both of her brothers with a rolled-up blanket.

Alaric looked at her then, and she couldn't help the grin that crept onto her face. Despite the complete chaos surrounding her, there was nowhere she would rather be. For the first time in her life, she was part of a family. Even if it was only temporary, even if she didn't understand her role, she liked the feeling.

Alaric tipped his head toward the door and gestured for her to follow him. She left the pile of yelling, scrabbling children behind, and snuck out after him.

He let out a sigh, closing the door quietly. "Sometimes it's best to let them tire themselves out."

Odessa nodded. "I'm sorry to cause so much trouble, I mean with the supper and all."

"It's nothing," he said with a shrug. "There's always something to bicker about." He walked toward the small bench in the garden, and she followed, remembering the night they had sat here together.

He stretched his legs out in front of him and scrubbed a hand along his face. A house full of children was a novelty for her, but for him, it was an exhausting reality. She sat beside him and stretched her legs out as well.

The dark came earlier and earlier as they neared the solstice, and the sun was already low in the sky. Odessa shuddered; the solstice ceremony was a black spot on her time here. She still didn't know what would become of her after she fulfilled her role.

Alaric cleared his throat, and she glanced at him from the corner of her eye. He was large and imposing next to her, his body solid and warm. His steadfast presence pushed the worries from her mind.

She found herself drifting toward him as though he were pulling her closer by an invisible thread. Her thoughts wandered to the day he held her tight against him, promising to help her. His chest had been so firm beneath her cheek, his hands rubbing comforting patterns around her back. What else could those hands do…

"We can return to the house soon." His gruff voice broke through her daydream, and she straightened a bit. She needed to stop thinking of him like that. Look at where it got her with Nolan. Nowhere. Alaric was being kind to her out of an obligation to his clan. He needed her as much as she needed him, and there was no need to muddle things between them.

But when he looked at her with those mismatched eyes, she couldn't help the way her pulse quickened, or the way her skin prickled like she was hot and cold at the same time. Try as she might to ignore it, he stirred things in her she didn't know existed. Things she was determined to keep hidden from the man beside her.

The door to the house opened, and Arowyn skipped out into the garden.

"Can we go see what Auntie is making for supper?" she asked, vaulting herself into Alaric's lap.

"Oof," he huffed as she made her landing. She giggled and placed a kiss on his cheek. He smiled at her and poked her nose with his finger. It was clear she had him in the palm of her small, dirty hand.

"Not tonight, I'm afraid."

"Why not? She loves to feed me. She said so herself." Arowyn's mouth turned down into a well-practiced pout. Odessa stifled the laugh bubbling up in her throat.

"Your cousins aren't feeling well. So, we'll stay here." He kept his voice light for the child, but Odessa could see the worry in his eyes. "Why don't you go see if you can round up some eggs from the hens, and I will cook them the way you like."

She broke into a grin and hopped off his lap, scurrying to the back of the house where the hens were kept. Alaric stood to go in, but Odessa grabbed his hand, stopping him in his tracks.

"Your cousins, will they be alright?" she asked, afraid of the answer.

Lines of worry appeared between his eyebrows. He gave a slight shake of his head and met her gaze. It still unnerved her how he looked at her. "I pray they will be, but nothing is certain. My aunt had the sickness before and survived. It is not likely she will get it again. Hopefully, my cousins will be as lucky."

"Have any of you had it? I mean other than your mother…"

"I did, and Rieka as well. But none of the others. We will keep to ourselves, for now, to be safe." He gave her a reassuring smile, but the sadness did not leave his eyes. "You need not be worried."

It wasn't herself she was worried about, well not entirely herself. She had grown to care for the little family in the short time she had been here. He squeezed her hand, and she realized she was still holding it.

"Let's go eat." He strode toward the house, Odessa following close behind. She didn't have much of a choice; he still held tight to her fingers. She couldn't find it in herself to pull away.

Chapter 13: Rumors

"Everyone knows she's cursed, and any man who looks upon her face is cursed as well."

"She's wicked. It's the mark of the devil on her."

A cold drizzle rained on Nolan as he listened to his men. Not a single one had begun the morning exercises despite the late hour, and instead, they sat around gossiping like old maids. The sparring field had been reduced to a muddy pit and the morning was cold and damp.

Roderick tossed an apple core into the mud. His bright orange hair had turned rust-colored in the rain, but he still stood out like a sore thumb from the other dark-haired men. Blaine, an oafish, hairy beast of a man, lazily picked the dirt from under his fingernails with a small dagger. They were a wet and miserable bunch, none too keen on their current assignment.

Jayce, one of Nolan's oldest friends, one he had trained with since they were boys, spat onto the ground beside him and told his version of the tale.

"Oh no, I heard she's not even the king's daughter at all. Her mother bedded another, and the baby was cursed because of it." He waggled his thick eyebrows and cackled. Nolan's fists curled at his sides with the need to throttle the man he once considered a brother.

"You have it all wrong. She's evil. It was her wickedness that killed her mother. The queen was innocent. She died at the sight of her hideous baby," a man named Oliver chimed in. He was young, new to Nolan's company and he already spoke ill of the princess.

Nolan's jaw ached from grinding his teeth together, listening to these well-worn tales. Anger and embarrassment washed over him in equal measure, the emotions churning together in his gut. Odessa was none of the things people claimed about her, but self-preservation stopped his protests before he spoke them. Defending her would confirm other rumors swirling around about the princess, rumors involving him.

But he had to do something.

"This is how you speak of the king's daughter? The king you swore to serve and protect?" The men startled at the sound of his tense voice and swiveled around to greet him. They spoke over each other, apologizing and explaining their true intentions, several jumping up, grabbing swords and shields, and heading out onto the soaked field.

There was one man who refused to grovel at Nolan's feet. Lawson still believed he should have been named head of the king's guard.

"We don't see why we should risk our lives for the devil's princess," Lawson said, squaring his shoulders to face Nolan.

He knew perfectly well how his men felt about the matter, and he did not need this sneering idiot to explain it to him. Blaming Odessa was a convenient way to hide the truth; his men were afraid. They were not eager to go head-to-head with the Clan of the Wolf, even the heartiest among them. The southern kingdom of Melantha was an enemy they knew, and they welcomed the chance to do battle with their sworn enemies. But when it came to facing the clans' people, they had no desire to charge headfirst into clan territory and its hidden dangers.

His men were accustomed to facing their opponents in an open field. It was all they had trained for. A battle in the sacred wood was something that struck fear into even the most battle-worthy knight, so Lawson spoke for them all when he asked, "Is it the king who wishes it or you?"

"The king," Nolan spoke through clenched teeth, waiting for what came next.

"We know she has you under her spell. You've seen her face, and she's enchanted you," Lawson went on, "What else have you seen? Has she taken you to her bed? Is she purple anywhere else?" He sneered, glancing at the men around them. A few chuckled nervously.

Nolan's face flushed hot with shame. He was not proud of what he did in Odessa's chambers. He'd tried to stop their affair many times, but he couldn't bring himself to do it. There was something about the woman he couldn't seem to stay away from. From the start, she had been so open to him, so eager to please. The way she clung to him, needing him to save her from her lonely days, made him feel invincible. He had been her everything. Or so he believed, until she tossed it all away, wanting more from him, wanting things he couldn't give her.

He would rescue Odessa to save the kingdom—and if that towering beast of man she found wandering the woods happened to be killed in the process, all the better. He would figure out what to do about the princess once she was back where she belonged. He shook himself free of his tangled thoughts and faced Lawson toe to toe.

"The king has commanded us to bring back his daughter. You can join us or be hanged for treason. It's your choice."

"Of course, I am with you," Lawson said with a mocking bow. He turned to join the other men, but Nolan did not miss what he said next, whispered loud enough for him to hear. "I still think if the princess wants to fuck barbarians, we should let her go."

Nolan's anger rose in him so quickly, it nearly choked him. He was on top of Lawson in an instant, every rational thought gone from his head. Blind with rage, he cracked his knuckles into Lawson's face. Blood poured from the other man's nose. Lawson squirmed beneath him, attempting to throw him off, but Nolan kept him pinned to the ground.

"Take it back. Take those disgusting words back." His breathing was rapid, and spit flew from his mouth and landed on Lawson's face. "The princess was kidnapped. Say it you bastard," he growled the words, pressing the man's shoulders deeper into the mud.

Nolan's knees dug into the mud around them, his hands slipped, and his grip on Lawson's arms weakened.

"Say it!" he bellowed.

Lawson narrowed his eyes and he smirked; he had found Nolan's weakness.

"The princess was kidnapped," he repeated, slowly. "But you, Nolan, are cursed, and we are cursed to follow you."

Nolan released Lawson's shoulder and slammed

his fist into the man's face again. The impact reverberated through Nolan's arm. Later his knuckles would be bruised and swollen. Lawson attempted to curl in on himself, blocking his face with his now free arm. Blood poured into the dirt. Nolan's lungs burned with ragged gasps. He wanted nothing more than to beat the man senseless, but he was lifted off Lawson and dragged away by Jayce and Roderick. He struggled against their grip, but there were two of them and only one of him.

"Release me," he rasped, his throat hoarse from shouting.

"We can't let you kill him," Jayce said as they finally dropped his arms and deposited him in the mud. Nolan narrowed his eyes at them, his men, men who swore to follow his command. And now they looked at him like he had gone mad, like he was the one who deserved their pity.

"Leave me be," he growled at them. Jayce paused and Nolan was ready to bark more orders in his direction, but Jayce just shook his head and followed Roderick out onto the field.

Wetness seeped through Nolan's clothes leaving him cold and miserable. He rose and shook his hand, the damage from Lawson's face already stinging his knuckles. The man deserved what he got and more.

The image Lawson's words provoked would not leave his mind, even as rainwater rolled down his nose and dripped from his hair—even as he barked orders to his men to begin sparring and even as Lawson limped from the field to mend his injuries. As Nolan took his place in front of his men, the image of Odessa in the arms of the barbarian would not leave him.

The king had ordered him to bring his daughter back, and he would. But it would not be the king's victory, it would be his. Odessa would see she had made a grave error in doubting him. He would leave the Wolf village with her on the back of his horse, or he would not leave it at all.

Chapter 14: Preparing for Battle

Rough hands dragged her from sleep, a gruff voice spoke her name. The room was still dark, and her brain worked slowly piecing together where she was.

"We have to go." Alaric's voice reached her through the fog of sleep. His hand squeezed her shoulder until she sat up, rubbing her eyes.

"What's going on?" Fear blossomed in her gut. Alaric hadn't entered the little house since she had moved into it. His face in the semi-darkness was placid, as though he were carved from stone, but Odessa knew him better now. She saw the worry swimming behind his eyes.

"You will be safer in the big house."

"Safer than what? Tell me what's happening." She tossed off the fur blankets, and the cold immediately seeped through her thin shift. Alaric held out her cloak, averting his eyes from her state of relative undress. If it weren't so dark in here, she was sure she would see the blush rushing up his neck to his face. It would have struck her as charming if she wasn't terrified.

She snatched the cloak and wrapped it around herself, then yanked on her boots. "Do I not even have time to dress?"

"No."

She stood to face him, waiting for an explanation, but he turned to leave. She grabbed his arm to stop him.

"Tell me what's going on."

Alaric let out a long sigh. "Our scouts tell us, Kalon attacks today."

All the air left Odessa's lungs. Kalon attacks? How could this be? Why wasn't her father happy to get rid of the curse that had plagued him for so many years? Why would he not let her go?

"I…" she looked up at Alaric with no words to express the rush of emotions tumbling through her. "I'm sorry. I truly didn't think…"

"Your father's actions are not your fault. But we need to go. You will stay with my siblings for now."

His siblings. This man who was the sole caretaker for his family was about to go into battle because of her. What would happen to them if he didn't survive? Her lungs squeezed tighter, her breaths coming in short bursts.

"I will go with the soldiers. Please. Let me turn myself over to them and stop all this." She clutched his arm, digging her fingers in, desperate for him to listen. She needed to end this before it began. She refused to be the reason blood was shed, even if it meant returning to her life in the shadows.

"It's not that simple, princess." His voice was soft, comforting, even when he was the one in danger. "If Connell says we fight, we fight."

"But surely, he would not keep me here against my will. If you explain to him that I want to return home…"

Alaric looked away, and his brow creased. The realization hit her hard in the gut. She was no longer here by her own free will. She had traded one prison for another. Her throat constricted in panic and sweat trickled down her back despite the chill in the house. She was an animal in a trap and no matter which way she turned she only ended up more tangled, her struggle tightening the ropes around her.

Alaric stepped toward her, and she fell into his embrace. A small sob escaped her as his arms wrapped around her. She rested her cheek against his chest, soaking in his strength while her tears soaked his tunic.

"It is my fault. Not yours." He spoke into the top of her head, his breath warming her scalp. "I should not have brought you here, but I will keep my promise. You will not be harmed." He ran a hand down her hair, smoothing it, his fingers raking through it. The touch was an echo of an intimacy they had not yet shared, and Odessa found herself missing something she never had.

"I chose to come. You cannot blame yourself." It was a reckless and desperate decision, but there was no way to change the past. She pulled back to look at him. His stoic demeanor had cracks in it now, his brow furrowed, and his mouth turned down in the corners.

They stood staring at each other in the small space, the gray morning dawning outside the window. Once again, Odessa was trapped, overruled, and helpless. There was nothing she could do to stop the coming onslaught.

She huffed in frustration, and she saw the emotion reflected in Alaric's eyes. He had no more say in the matter than she did. She wouldn't make it harder for him than it already was. Odessa wiped the tears from her face, and Alaric dropped his hands from where they lingered on her back.

"Let's go then," she said, and with a nod, he strode toward the door.

****

Everyone was already awake by the time he returned to the big house with Odessa. The tortured expression on her face had been replaced by an eerie calm like she had resigned herself to her fate.

He cursed the goddess Narah for ever putting Odessa in his path. He had only wanted to help his people, not lead them into further bloodshed.

Arowyn launched herself at Odessa as soon as she entered, and the princess hugged her tight, whispering comforting words to the child. Even as he wished he had never laid eyes on her; his heart told a different story.

"I will go with you." Weylyn's foolish assertion broke through his regrets. He could not undo what was already done. All he could do was focus on keeping his family safe, Odessa included. He would not be the reason she was harmed.

Pushing his thoughts aside, he turned to his brother. "You will not."

"I am prepared to fight," Weylyn insisted, already reaching for his bow.

Alaric shook his head. He did not have time to argue. "You have not reached your sixteenth winter. In the eyes of the clan, you are still a child, and you will not fight."

Weylyn's face turned bright red at being called a child. He puffed out his thin chest, facing his brother. "What difference do a few months make? I am man enough."

His brother should not be in such a hurry to die. Alaric bit back the words. They wouldn't help. It was not so long ago that Alaric was fifteen, and he remembered the restless energy that propelled him, the need to prove himself always on the surface. In many ways, it was still there.

Weylyn practically vibrated in front of him, staring daggers at Alaric for calling him a child. He clapped a hand on the boy's shoulder and lowered his voice.

"I need you here to protect the family."

Weylyn's dark eyes searched his face. The pain in them cut deeper than his anger. Alaric could handle the boy's anger, knew how to calm it, but the sorrow lingering in his brother's heart he could not erase. It was easy to forget his siblings, especially Weylyn, had also borne the weight of their father's cruelty and the soul-deep sadness of their mother's death. He did everything he could to protect them, but he could not undo the pain they had all endured.

His brother's body relaxed under his hand. Alaric would not make the mistake of calling him a child again.

Weylyn gave a quick nod. "I will do it." He grabbed his dagger, the one he had been practicing with lately, and dragged a chair closer to the door. "I will be ready."

Alaric watched the boy, his limbs long and spindly still waiting for him to grow into them, his face still smooth, and he prayed it would not come to that. If soldiers made it this far into the village, Weylyn and his dagger would not stand a chance. Which meant his family was as good as lost. He glanced toward Odessa where she sat, Arowyn and Rieka flanking her on the bench. She had an arm around each and spoke softly to them, but her eyes followed him as he prepared for battle.

She blamed herself, but they were nothing more than pawns in their rulers' games. They would always find a reason to fight; an insult to avenge, a treasure to hunt. He had only lived twenty winters but he was already weary of fighting his chief's battles.

Alaric donned his leather breastplate and yanked his shield from the wall. These would be his only protection. He was lucky to have the leather plate to protect his chest. Many of his fellow clansmen would fight in nothing but thick wool tunics.

When he looked up again, his family's wide eyes were on him and the weight of the lives he defended settled heavily upon his shoulders. He had fought many times against the small raiding parties of the north and south, but it had been many years since the clan was attacked by the Northern king's army.

Again, he wondered why the goddess had placed Odessa in his path. Why did she bring war upon them when they already suffered so much? He breathed out a long sigh and attempted a reassuring smile for his family.

Fear creased their small faces, but it was Faolan who broke the silence. "May the goddess protect you."

Alaric nodded, words sticking in his throat. He would not say goodbye to them. He would return. There was no other choice. He turned and left them, praying to a goddess he no longer understood, but he had no others.

Footsteps behind him stopped him before he reached the road. He assumed Arowyn had followed him for the hug he couldn't bring himself to give her, for the goodbye he refused to say. But it was not his sister behind him.

Odessa closed the gap between them and brought her hands to his face. Without a word she stood on her toes, stretching until her mouth grazed his. He didn't move, didn't cup her face in return, didn't run his hands through the silken strands of her hair like he longed to do. His racing heart was the only part of him that dared to respond to her touch.

When she pulled away, returning to her normal height, tears glistened in her eyes. She placed a palm over his heart, calming it with her touch. She didn't speak a word but held his gaze a moment longer before turning and hurrying back to the house.

Alaric strode off to battle with the taste of a princess on his lips and the blessing of a goddess to keep him safe.

Chapter 15: A Thankless Rescue

The howls of his people rang out around him. He threw back his head and added his own, his throat burning with the effort. The other warriors were nowhere to be seen, but they were out there, in position and ready for the attack. The enemy would never see them strike.

Only the Wolves would fight today. The clans rarely came to each other's aid and more often than not they were openly hostile to each other. His people would face the Northern army alone.

The morning was gray and cold, and the smell of rotting leaves filled his nose. The birds were quiet as though they too waited for the attack. Or maybe they were still warm in their nests. He envied them if they were.

Alaric waited in the shadows of the sacred trees, his muscles aching from the tension. The dampness seeped into him. It was the waiting he hated most. He took a deep breath in through his nose and out through his mouth, the way his uncle had taught him, but it didn't do him much good.

He was trained as a warrior from the time of his sixteenth winter, but he did not relish fighting, especially when he couldn't justify the reason. If Odessa wanted to stay, she should stay. Unsurprisingly, no one had asked his opinion on the matter, but he had made a promise to her, and now he would keep it.

His hand rested lightly on the hilt of his sword; his bow was a comforting weight on his back. Connell had positioned him and several others close to the village, the last line of defense against the Kalonians. His chief's only instruction to him was to protect the princess at all costs.

Alaric glanced back toward the village and pictured her comforting his sisters the way she was when he left. The girls already loved her. It was barely three weeks ago he found her, but she had managed to become a fixture in his life. The insane urge to smile came over him at the memory of Odessa's attempt at milking the goat. He clamped his lips together.

She was determined to help with the household chores, never once acting as though she were above them. He admired her for that and for her tenacity, her bravery in the face of an uncertain future, her sweetness towards his family, her beauty, and the way her lips felt against his own...

Dear Narah, save him! What was he doing? Preparing for battle or blushing over a woman like a smooth-faced boy! He swallowed hard and shook Odessa from his mind. Of course, he would protect the princess, but he protected his family too, his people.

A question still remained, whispering to him, refusing to be ignored. When had Odessa become so important to Connell? And why?

He shifted and leaned his back against the tree, the questions echoing through his mind. Connell said she was needed for the solstice ceremony but was that really worth losing lives over? Did it not defeat the purpose? He let out a frustrated sigh. This was not the time for doubting his chief. If this was the way to save his people, he would do it.

The ground began to vibrate beneath his feet. Horses. Many of them. He smirked to himself. The Kalonians were riding horses into the sacred wood. They would not get far. The Northerners were ill-equipped for a battle in the trees, and the Wolves were at home here. They may be outnumbered, but they held the advantage.

A howl rose up, followed by another. The enemy was close. Soon the Wolf archers would pick them off one by one without ever being spotted. With any luck, no soldiers would make it this far at all.

Alaric pushed away from the tree, readying himself beside the old hunting trail leading to the heart of the village. He ran a hand down his face in a futile attempt to clear his mind of the swirling questions and the taste of Odessa's lips on his, but memories of another battle sprung up in their place.

Four years ago, the clan of the Raven sent a raiding party into their borders. It was the first time Alaric was old enough to defend the clan. He stood with his father, waiting for the Raven warriors. His father stank like ale, despite the early hour. He could barely stand, let alone shoot his bow. And yet he spoke to Alaric as though he were a great warrior, and his son was nothing more than a useless child sent to carry his arrows.

On and on the man went, singing his own virtues, and all Alaric could see was the blood trickling down Weylyn's face, the boy crumpled on the floor after their father had struck him with the back of his broad hand. The old man had hit Alaric many times, but he was a warrior now, he could defend himself. His brother was a child. How could he stand by and watch this poor excuse of a man hit his siblings?

What if he went after the little girls? He struck their mother often enough, broken bones even. What would stop him from going after his daughters? It was that thought, the image of little Arowyn not yet four, falling prey to their father that set his hand to action. It was the idea that someday Rieka would be smacked for burning the supper, or Faolan would be backhanded for speaking his mind that sent the arrow soaring into his father's back.

Alaric's only regret was he hadn't faced his father like a man and instead shot him from behind. He would have liked to see the look on his father's face when his son finally stood up to him.

The sounds of battle drifted on the wind to where he stood. Cries of pain mingled with the Wolves' howls, twisting together into a song of war. Looking through the trees, he saw nothing, but the sounds were closing in. He readied his bow, crouching low in the underbrush.

Somehow Connell knew what he did to his father. He didn't plan to add any other crimes to his name. If any Kalonians made it this far, they wouldn't live long enough to reach the princess.

****

The woods were alive with the screams of his men. A wolf's howl sent his blood racing faster, the beat of his heart thudding louder in his ears. Nolan glanced to his sides, but he saw no one. His men had been engulfed by the ancient trees and by the thick fog that settled on the forest as soon as they entered it.

Gods be damned! He had never believed the forest

99

held magic, but as he urged his spooked horse forward through the unending mist, he wasn't sure what he believed anymore. The sounds of metal on metal and shouts of pain reached him through the fog. Somewhere his men still fought, but he had no idea of how many lived or died.

Another howl. Closer to him. He turned in his saddle and narrowly dodged an arrow. He pushed his horse harder. The howling made it impossible to gather his thoughts, to make a plan, to locate his men! But he raced forward, following the faint trail through the trees, praying to whichever gods would listen that it led to the Wolf village. To Odessa.

Her name rang through him, clearing out the sounds of terror around him. His heart beat in rhythm with it, her voice calling to him, the memory of her next to him driving him forward. She was confused last time. She didn't know what she wanted, but he did. He wanted her.

Through a break in the trees ahead of him, he caught a glimpse of the village before the fog swirled in, blocking his view. He kept himself low in the saddle. His horse's mane flew into his face as they neared the edge of the forest. He was practically there!

Until the world tipped upside down, and the air left his lungs as he hit the ground. Pain seared through him as sparks of light flashed behind his eyes. He opened his mouth to breathe, but all that escaped were shallow gasps. He rolled to his side, struggling for air. The faint realization that his horse had fled filtered through him.

Slowly, air returned to his lungs. Pain still radiated through his side, but he was fairly sure it was from the fall and not an arrow. No blood pooled beneath him.

His cheek was against the ground and each shallow breath moved the leaves beside his face. He squeezed his eyes shut and opened them again. If he didn't get up, he was as good as dead. He pushed up to sit and wait for the world to stop spinning.

There was a faint rustle of leaves behind him. He turned. An enormous barbarian stood over him, his sword pointed at Nolan's face.

"Stand." His voice was a low growl.

"Will you not kill me where I sit?" Nolan pushed the words past the painful squeezing in his chest.

The man narrowed his eyes. "Rise and fight."

Nolan stood and drew his sword. Face to face with the savage he would recognize anywhere. It was him.

"You have honor in battle, but you see nothing wrong with stealing women from their homes?"

"I didn't steal her." The barbarian stuck to his story.

"She belongs with her people. Take me to her, and I will let you live." The lie rolled easily off his tongue. The bastard wouldn't live to see another day.

"So you can lock her away again?"

Nolan straightened. How much had Odessa told the man? What else had she said? Jealousy wrapped its claws around his heart and squeezed. It wasn't long ago that he was the only one she confided in.

The man shifted from foot to foot in front of him. Impatient for the fight. Nolan could see now the man was younger than he assumed. The skin above his beard was smooth and even.

"The king did everything in his power to keep his daughter safe. Does your clan not wish the same for its people?"

The barbarian's eyes never left Nolan's face. "My people wish to be left alone to do as they wish without the interference of the Northern king. And so does his daughter."

Nolan's fingers wrapped tighter around the hilt of his sword. Each word the barbarian spoke stoked the fire of his rage. How dare the man speak to him like this? How dare he question the word of a king, this savage who wore animal skins and hid in the forest like a coward?

His sword met the barbarian's with a violent crash. Nolan was fast, but the clansman was pure brute strength, and he easily pushed Nolan back. Sword met sword over and over until both men panted, sweat covering their faces. The mist churned around them, swirling between them as they fought. The village was so close, the strange triangular houses visible through the fog.

Nolan met the barbarian's eyes over their crossed swords. One was light and the other dark. Odessa had looked into those same eyes and seen something in them she didn't find in his. He roared and shoved the man back, coming at him faster than before. One of them would die here and it sure as hell wasn't going to be him.

****

She was suffocating. Surely, she would die here in this house, with these children, waiting. Alaric left hours ago and still hadn't returned. She had nearly chewed her fingernails off listening to the howling warriors. The wind carried the cries of the wounded back to the village, stuffing them down the chimney into her ears. How was she supposed to sit here and listen and wait, while men died because of her?

The children weren't nearly as affected as she was. After a solemn breakfast, the girls had burrowed under the blankets together with a few pieces of charcoal and some parchment and had been drawing quietly ever since. Weylyn and Faolan kept a steady watch on the door, each armed alarmingly—although she supposed in the current situation—comfortingly with a large dagger. But after the first hour or so the boys took to restringing their bows, sharpening their tools, and discussing which girls in the village were the most likely to sneak you a kiss under the sacred trees.

And Odessa was left with nothing to do but wring her hands and allow her guilt to tear apart her insides. Why had she come here? She was perfectly safe at home, well-fed and protected, if not exactly free. But she was selfish. She had put this entire family, this entire village in harm's way. She had to do something to fix it.

"I need to leave." She stood and spoke so abruptly all four children turned and stared with wide eyes at her proclamation.

Weylyn scoffed. "You can't leave. It is not safe." He spoke to her as though she were a fool, which of course she was.

She approached where he sat guarding the door, the dagger laying menacingly in his lap. He narrowed his eyes at her. Could she make it past him if he tried to stop her? Not likely.

"I understand, but I can stop this. I can make the soldiers leave if I turn myself over to them."

Weylyn stood and put his body between her and the door. He was thinner than his brother but nearly as tall. He looked at Odessa and shook his head. "Alaric said none of us are to leave." He crossed his arms. There was no way she could get past him unless she convinced him to let her go.

"Weylyn, please." She stepped in closer, lowering her voice so as to not scare the little ones. Both girls peered at her from under their fort of blankets. "What if Alaric does not return? What will happen to you and your sisters?"

The boy's eyes flashed in anger, a deep red creeping into his cheeks. "My brother always returns."

Odessa let out a sigh and started over. "Of course, I didn't mean to offend your brother. I only wish to help."

Faolan stood beside her listening, but his gaze was on his brother. Weylyn stood straighter.

"What do you plan to do?" His resolve to keep her was cracking.

"I will turn myself over to the Kalonians. Once I am in their possession, they will have no more reason to fight, and they will return home."

"There is always a reason to fight." Faolan's voice was weary and older than his thirteen years. Odessa wished he was still talking about the girls he wanted to kiss. She couldn't stop the fighting forever, but maybe she could stop this one.

She turned back to Weylyn, clasping her hands in prayer. "Please. I cannot have so much blood spilled in my name. Let me go and put an end to this."

Weylyn's brows knit together. Faolan shuffled next to her.

Finally, he nodded. "Find the first Kalonian soldier you can and have him call off the attack." He stepped to the side, clearing the doorway. The girls emerged from their bed. Arowyn clamped onto her side.

"Where are you going?"

Odessa knelt down to look the girl in the eye. "I have to go home. But I thank you for welcoming me. And for teaching me so much." She turned to Rieka and gave the girl's hand a squeeze before she stood.

"Will you come back?" Arowyn's chin quivered, but she bit back her tears.

The answer Odessa wanted to give stuck in her throat. If she went back now, her father would have yet another reason to lock her away. The walls of the small house pushed in toward her, squeezing the air from her lungs, as memories of being trapped in another room wrapped around her.

She looked at each child's face to steady herself. If Alaric didn't return, what would become of them? She needed to end this before it was too late. Even if it meant she never saw him or the outside of her chambers again. She had no other choice.

"I will do my best to visit you." She forced a smile onto her face even as the lie burned her throat.

Arowyn nodded and with one more glance around the room, Odessa turned and left.

Whatever she had been expecting, the unnatural emptiness of the village wasn't it. The sounds of battle still drifted in from the forest, but she was the only one outside. Wisps of mist seeped out of the forest, beckoning her into the shadows of the woods. She took the hunting trail behind Alaric's home and followed the sounds of metal clanging against metal.

Her heart matched her footsteps' frantic pace as she ran into the forest. Gods, help her. What had she been thinking? The woods were alive with screams and howls, the fog erasing her path as soon as she left it. She was lost in a matter of seconds, and her chest tightened in panic.

Odessa had seen many battles fought in the fields beyond the castle walls, the men lined up like chess pieces. Whatever hell she had stumbled into was nothing like that. How would she ever manage to find the Kalonian army? Did any of them still live or had they been sucked into the fog and lost forever?

Her breaths came in shallow bursts. If she didn't calm down, she would die here of asphyxiation and solve nothing. She steadied herself on a nearby tree; her palm rested on the cool ridges of the bark. Again, she heard the clanging of metal against metal and the sound of men's voices. They were close. She could follow the sound and surrender herself.

She crept along the path, keeping a row of smaller pines to her left as landmarks in the fog. Two men battled in a small clearing. Her father's crest shone brightly on one man's heaving chest and the other was dressed in leather and fur like the clan. The men were drenched in sweat, their movements slow and labored.

The fog cleared around them and Odessa's heart stalled in her chest as recognition settled over her. It was Nolan who lunged forward, just as Alaric noticed her as she stepped out from behind the tree. The clansman faltered and Nolan knocked the sword from his hand.

Odessa's throat closed as though it were her neck Nolan held his sword to. A trickle of crimson ran down Alaric's neck as Nolan shoved him hard into a tree. Her scream tore through the trees.

"Nolan, No!"

He whipped his head around to face her, his sword still at Alaric's throat. Their eyes locked for a moment before Nolan collapsed to the ground, a Wolf's arrow in his back.

Chapter 16: Wounded Hearts

Alaric's arms were around her before she could fully register what had happened. She shrieked and struggled against his grip, but his arms were like a vice around her waist as he dragged her away from where Nolan had fallen.

"Let me go!" She kicked and swung her legs wildly, landing several blows on Alaric's shins. He grunted but didn't loosen his grip. "Nolan!" She screamed his name, but he didn't stir, and Alaric pulled her farther and farther from him. Did he still live? He needed help; he needed a healer!

She squirmed against Alaric's chest, thrashing and shrieking until he stopped moving. He lowered his head and growled into her ear.

"Silence, princess. Or you will get us both killed."

She blinked, remembering where she was, remembering the battle still raging around her. The fog thickened, and Nolan's body disappeared from view. Holy gods! He was dead and it was her fault!

The sob rose thick and hot in her throat, her tears blurring her vision. Alaric's arms were still around her. His body was strong and steady against her back. If she hadn't come when she did, he would be the one lying dead in the grass. Would that have been better?

What had she done? Each breath tore in and out of her lungs, burning her. Punishing her.

Alaric whispered softly in her ear. "We must get you back inside. His men will find him."

His arms loosened. She turned to face him on trembling legs. He was covered in dirt and sweat. A thin red line ran across his throat where Nolan's sword had been. What if he had fallen? What would become of her? Another sob rose in her throat and broke through her lips. He ran a strong hand down her arm.

Her gaze raked over him, taking stock, reassuring herself he was still whole. How could someone so large and sturdy ever fall? But she had seen firsthand how close he had come. His right hand still clamped tightly to her arm, but his left hung loosely at his side. Red bloomed through the fabric of his sleeve.

"You're hurt."

His eyes flicked quickly to his arm as though he had only just noticed he was injured.

"Yes. We must get back."

He grabbed her hand and led her through the forest as though the fog wasn't still thick around them, as though the trees didn't all look the same. The ease with which he found his way was only a further reminder that she never would have made it far on her own. Another reckless decision. Another false step.

And this time she may have cost a man his life. Perhaps she was cursed after all.

They were soon back in the village. Men had begun to trickle back, making their way home through the lifting fog. Alaric was not the only one with injuries.

He tugged her along, not letting her eyes linger on the injured clansmen, hurrying her home. Her guilt threatened to choke her, but if she didn't follow along quickly, she would only add to Alaric's troubles.

At the house, an older woman nearly dragged them inside.

"Thank the goddess," she proclaimed, raking an appraising eye over Alaric before moving her gaze to Odessa. "You're alive and you've brought the princess."

Alaric nodded while the woman poked and prodded, assessing the damage. He winced when she got to his arm and her frown deepened.

She had copper hair, nearly the same color as Arowyn but faded from age. Silver streaks mingled with the rust-colored strands in the twin braids running down her back.

"Get all this off." She gestured toward Alaric's torso with a wave of her hand. "It'll need stitching."

Having given the command, she turned back to Odessa and gave a polite bob of her head. "I'm Layla. Alaric's aunt. I came to check on you all and found you missing."

She opened her mouth to explain, but Alaric cut in.

"Yes, about that. Weylyn, what in the name of the gods were you thinking?" He turned on the boy sitting quietly by the fire as though he could disappear into the furniture and escape his brother's fury.

"She told me she wanted to go home! She insisted, in fact." He folded his arms across his chest and lifted his chin. Alaric's face turned an even deeper shade of crimson.

"I did. It's true!"

Alaric didn't bother to take his eyes from his brother's face. The other three children's heads swiveled back and forth between the men as though watching a prizefight.

"I don't care what you insisted on doing. My brother had explicit instructions to keep you here." He ground out the words through clenched teeth.

Weylyn rose to face his brother, but before either of them could knock the head off the other, Aunt Layla stepped between them.

"That's quite enough." She put her hands on her stout hips and spoke with the authority of a woman who had raised many children and had run out of patience. "You..." she pointed at Alaric, "Sit before you hurt yourself."

"And you," she turned to Weylyn, "go make yourself useful and tend to the returning men. In fact, take Faolan with you."

Both brothers looked like they might protest further but with a narrowed look from Layla they did what she said.

"And as for you," she said, taking Odessa's trembling hand in hers. "You have a seat here, and the girls will make you a calming tea. Up, up girls. Let's go! Chamomile should do the trick." She shooed the girls from their hiding place and set to work gathering supplies to stitch Alaric's arm.

Odessa sat and watched the proceedings with detached exhaustion. She took the warm cup when it was offered to her and sipped gratefully. The pained hiss from Alaric's mouth when his aunt began her ministrations pulled her from her stupor. She met his gaze over Layla's head. She must have looked as ill as she felt because Alaric gave her a weak smile.

"Layla is my mother's sister." He let out a long breath and continued. "My mother had the same copper hair, as does Arowyn, of course." Another breath. Sweat began to bead on his forehead. "Layla has two daughters and three sons, same as my mother did."

He winced again but quickly erased the look of pain from his face. He was trying to comfort her, distract her, even when he was the one in pain. A surge of affection for the man shot through her, so strong she had to bite her bottom lip to keep herself from telling him in front of everyone.

"Her husband is Merrick, my uncle, who you met."

She nodded slightly, acknowledging his kindness in speaking to her. She rarely heard him say so many words strung together. It was a gift.

"My cousins have recently fallen ill, and my aunt has been caring for them. How do Asena and Sairsha fair?" he asked his aunt, and she looked up from her work for a moment.

"Asena is quite well; she will recover soon enough." She paused, swallowing the emotion Odessa saw in her suddenly damp eyes. "Sairsha is strong. I have faith." It was all she said on the matter before returning to her work.

Odessa looked back to Alaric, but he was out of words to share with her. His face was a mask of stoic calm, but she saw the needle weaving in and out of his skin, she saw the way his fists were balled up in his lap. He was in pain. She did not look away until Layla pulled the needle through the last stitch.

****

He stepped out of the house into the crisp night air. His arm was stiff and sore from the stitches, and his muscles ached. What he needed was sleep, but he found himself crossing the garden to the smaller house, the one he still thought of as his.

He raised a hand, hesitating before knocking. What if she was asleep? It didn't matter. He needed to speak with her and there had been no time and no space earlier. Not between his siblings' questions, his harsh words to his brothers for letting Odessa out of their sight, his aunt's stitches and worries. He had barely had a chance to breathe, to thank the goddess for his survival, let alone to talk to Odessa.

She had sat quietly all afternoon, speaking only to defend Weylyn against Alaric's admonishment. She barely ate. He had watched, her hand shaking as she brought the cup of calming tea his aunt made to her lips. Only when the fighting was over, and he was assured the Kalonians had been cleared from the forest had he suggested she go home and rest.

Now, he had things he needed to say. He knocked softly and her voice answered immediately.

"It's me."

She opened the door for him and stood aside, letting him in.

"Did they return?" Her eyes were round and trusting, and he cursed himself for worrying her.

"No. Your father's men are gone."

She nodded, drawing in a shuddering breath. Her arms were wrapped around her middle for warmth or comfort, he wasn't sure. He studied her in the soft glow of the fire. Her hair was loose around her shoulders, a black waterfall down her back. An old quilt his mother had made was draped around her, nothing but her shift underneath.

His face warmed and he lifted his gaze back to her eyes. He hated the fear he found there.

"I came to tell you, your knight survived."

Odessa gasped and brought her hands to her mouth. "Nolan lives?"

"Yes. One of our men saw him on the back of another's horse. Alive and returning north."

She breathed out a long sigh and wiped the tears in her eyes. "Thank you for telling me. He was your enemy, but at one time he was my friend." She hesitated on the word friend and Alaric swallowed the bitter taste of jealousy rising in his throat. He had no desire to picture the princess with that man, but the image came fast to his mind.

He shifted, flexing the fingers on his injured arm, the skin pulling and itching beneath his shirt. He winced. She noticed.

"Sit. Please. I forgot about your injuries. You must be exhausted." She ushered him to the sleeping bench along the wall and he sat heavily. The clan often used the sleeping benches for sitting as well, but the awareness that this was her bed sent heat to his cheeks once again. Why did proximity to this woman make him act like an inexperienced fool?

"Does it hurt?" she asked, pulling him from his thoughts. She sat beside him, her fingers fiddling with the quilt in her lap.

"Not much. I've had worse done to me."

"But you almost…" Her voice caught. "I would have never forgiven myself."

"Don't." His voice was too loud, too harsh. She flinched, but he grabbed her hands, engulfing them with his. "This was not your doing. You did not send those men here, nor ask for them to come. You did not hold the sword to my throat."

Tears streamed down her cheeks. He cupped her face with his hand, keeping his other holding hers. He wiped the tears with this thumb, and she leaned into his touch.

"You saved me." He leaned forward and whispered the words along her cheek, his lips grazing her skin. Her eyelashes fluttered against his face. Was it the loss of blood or the proximity to this woman making the room spin around them?

"And you saved me." She spoke the words onto his lips, her breath teasing him.

The number of reasons for not kissing her rivaled the number of stars in the sky, but right now he could not remember a single one. He captured her mouth with his, bringing his other hand up to hold her face close to his. She parted her lips for him and moaned when he slid his tongue inside.

She shifted closer. Her kisses deepened, meeting him with the same urgency rising in his chest. She ran her hand down his bicep and pain radiated through his body. He hissed and she jerked away.

"I'm so sorry! I forgot about your arm!" Her face was flushed a delicious pink and her eyes were wide with embarrassment.

He focused on the pain in his arm, instead of the throbbing in his lap. She was a princess, and he was a clansman. Of all the reasons to stop what they were doing, that one was first to his mind. He was not foolish enough to think the victory in battle today was the end of their troubles.

"It's nothing," he assured her. "But I should return."

Her hand on his stopped him from rising.

"Wait."

Every bit of sense he had screamed at him to leave. But instead, he waited.

"Will you stay? Here with me tonight, I mean."

"Princess…I…"

"Don't call me that. I do not wish to be one." Her rebuke was swift and fierce, and a smile tugged at his lips. In a different life, she would have made a powerful warrior.

"I do not expect…" she sighed and started again, no longer meeting his gaze. "I meant only for comfort. I do not wish to be alone."

He opened his mouth to tell her it was not possible. Instead, he said, "For tonight, only. For comfort."

Her shy smile when she met his gaze again sent his heart racing.

"Thank you." She scooted closer to the wall, making space for him in the bed.

Tonight only. Comfort only. He repeated the words to himself, a silent prayer, a reminder of why he was here.

She rolled over to face him, but he kept his eyes on the wood beams above them. Narah, help him. In one heartbeat, he longed to wrap her in his arms and protect her, and in the next, he wanted to tear that damn shift off and dive between her legs. Both were impossible.

"I don't love him."

He grunted but didn't respond. She didn't owe him an explanation.

"I wanted you to know. I don't love him anymore and I don't think he ever loved me. Not really. I can see it more clearly now, the way I clung to him at first. He was all I had, and he liked it that way."

She sighed and he imagined what her life had been like, locked away, feared, or pitied. He felt trapped at times, burdened by the responsibilities of taking care of his family, but he could not imagine the depths of her loneliness, her isolation from the world. It was no wonder she took the little affection this knight gave her and grabbed onto it with both hands.

"But now I fear he will not let me go. I've wounded his pride, his ego. I saw something in his face today, something ugly, I have not seen it before. And it scared me."

He rolled onto his side to face her. He traced the shadowed side of her face with his finger. "I cannot say what will happen next, but as long as you are here, I offer my protection."

"And I accept your offer." She wriggled closer to him, her warmth radiating through their thin layers of clothes. If he reached out now and dragged her even closer, pressed his body against hers, she would let him, welcome it even. But her confession told him more than her current feelings for her knight. She had little experience in the world. Nolan was the first to treat her with any kindness and she readily gave him her heart. Was it not the same with him now?

He sighed heavily and rolled over onto his back again. She may think she wanted him, but now he knew better. She had not yet learned how to protect her heart, so he would have to do it for her.

"Goodnight, princess."

This time she did not correct him.

Chapter 17: The Old Ways

Alaric left Odessa's bed around dawn and snuck out the door without waking her. It had been a long night of little sleep. He was aware of her every move, her every breath next to him. It was torture, but one he found himself wishing to repeat tonight.

His uncle's appearance in his yard startled him out of his dreams.

"Come." Uncle Merrick grabbed him by his good arm without greeting or preamble and pulled him behind the houses. If his uncle noticed him coming out of the princess's temporary home, he didn't comment on it, but Alaric couldn't help the heat rising to his face. What would his family think of him if they knew he shared the princess's bed?

"I needed to speak with you right away." His uncle spoke in a hushed and urgent voice. The hairs on Alaric's arms stood upright. His uncle was levelheaded and calm in all situations. But now the man was wild-eyed in the early morning light. His hair was disheveled and dark circles smudged the skin under his eyes as though he had been awake all night.

"What is it, uncle? Is Layla alright? My cousins?"

"Yes, yes. They are as fine as they were yesterday." He pulled Alaric closer, glancing over his shoulder before speaking again. "I came to tell you about the princess. And the solstice."

118

A vision of how Connell had looked at Odessa the day he brought her here, like a wolf who had cornered its prey, crossed Alaric's mind. What did the chief intend to do with her? Dread lay heavy in his gut, and he braced himself for what his uncle had to say.

Merrick ran a tired hand through his thick beard. "Connell has a sacrifice in mind."

Alaric's blood ran cold. Surely, his uncle was not saying what he thought he was. "So, the princess will slice her wrist on the altar." His voice wavered as he spoke, but his uncle shook his head, grabbing his arm tighter.

"No. He intends to kill her on the solstice. To appease the goddess and save the clan."

Alaric was vaguely aware his uncle still spoke, but the only sound he heard was the rushing of his blood in his ears. The clan had not made a sacrifice like this in decades. It was barbaric and cruel, and they had done away with the practice years ago. His uncle must be wrong, there was no way...

"Listen to me!" Uncle Merrick shook him until their gazes locked. Sadness and exhaustion lingered behind the older man's eyes. "We have fought long into the night. I opposed him, as did Nix, but the others are for it."

"For it? For murdering an innocent woman?"

"Keep your voice down!" Merrick hissed and Alaric swallowed the bile rising into his throat.

"The people are scared. Entire families are sick. More die every day. Connell has convinced the other elders this is the only answer. I fear he will be able to convince enough of our people as well."

Alaric gripped his head in his hands to keep

himself from screaming. This was madness! The clan was in trouble, and they had lost many lives, but how would more death solve the problem! Narah did not put Odessa in his path for this. If he knew only one thing, it was that.

"There must be another way." His voice was barely a rasp; his throat was too dry to speak. Merrick shook his head again.

"I have done everything in my power to stop it. The solstice is only a week away."

Alaric's mind spun. He made a promise he could no longer keep. He swallowed hard.

"Then she must leave."

"Connell will not stand for it."

"Why did you tell me, uncle? If not to help her?"

Merrick let out another weary sigh and sat on the edge of the woodpile. The men stood at the edge of the forest and the birds had begun to awaken for the day. They twittered happily in the trees. A light frost covered the ground announcing winter's imminent arrival.

"I only wanted you to know."

Alaric let out a frustrated growl. "You wanted me to know I provided Connell with a human sacrifice to the goddess! What good—"

A gasp behind him froze the words in this throat. He spun around in time to see a streak of black hair as Odessa sprinted away from him and into the protection of the trees.

"God damn it," he cursed as he tore off after her.

****

The air tore from her lungs as she raced through the woods. Branches clawed at her face and brambles snagged the hem of her cloak. She had to get the hell out of here. Alaric's words rang over and over in her head. Connell…human sacrifice…goddess…

The old stories raced through her as her feet trampled the underbrush. There were reasons her people stayed away from the forest. There was truth in the rumors after all.

Her lungs burned as she struggled to go faster. Her legs were heavy and clumsy, her body slow and out of shape. Other than her daily walks, she had no need for exercise. She did no heavy lifting or had any need to exert herself.

She was slow and soft. The tears seeped silently from her eyes, but she didn't have air left for crying. This was what happened to people who dared to change their fate. What sort of goddess led her here? Why did Narah require her death?

The footsteps were right behind her before she heard them.

"Princess, stop." Alaric's low growl was at her back. His breathing was steady and even where hers was ragged. She didn't look back but instead willed her legs to go faster. Her limbs were like jelly and her legs were scratched from ankle to knee. She had no idea which way to go or how to make it home.

"Odessa, please."

She stopped abruptly, and he nearly crashed into her back. She spun to face him, panting and sweating. A trapped animal.

He looked nearly as bad as she felt. His skin was still pale from his injury, the cut on his throat was an angry red line. He wore only the thin shirt he slept in, pants, and his boots. She was in her shift and cloak; she had only been stepping outside to find him. Now they both stood in the frosty woods with their breath turning to steam between them.

He eyed her warily like she might turn and run again, but she had no energy left. Maybe she was more useful to everyone as a sacrifice. Gods knew she had done nothing of worth while she lived.

"Is this your idea of protecting me? You promised me…" Her voice broke, and she brushed the tears away from her eyes. She was so tired of crying in front of him.

"I didn't know." His voice was rough, and he cleared his throat, but he didn't say more.

She pulled her cloak tighter around her. It was freezing in the shade of the trees; their bare branches cast long shadows across the frost-covered ground. He cast a glance over his shoulder as though afraid they had been followed.

"We have to go back."

She startled them both with the laugh that erupted from her mouth. It was a harsh cackle, cracked and brittle. She gasped and wrapped an arm around her stomach, laughing until the tears started again.

Alaric watched her; his forehead creased. He shifted from foot to foot.

"You want me to come back?" she asked between gasps. "Shall I lay down on the slab and wait for the solstice? Or do I get to sleep in your bed for a few more days?" She heard herself, heard how unhinged she sounded, and it only made her laugh harder until her laughs became great aching sobs.

Alaric stepped toward her, but she stumbled back, holding her hands out in front of her as though she could stop him. As though she could hold back this enormous man from doing whatever he pleased with her. But he did stop. He didn't move from his spot as she took another step back.

A light snow had begun to fall, the flakes swirling between them on the wind. Her cheeks and fingers stung with the cold. She was barely dressed. Her chest squeezed in panic. She would be lost in these woods for hours before finally succumbing to the freezing temperatures. Surely, she would die here, one way or another.

"You are not equipped for the journey," Alaric said, reading her mind. "I will help you, but not now. We must go back." Again, he glanced over his shoulder and shifted his weight.

He still hadn't moved, so she crossed the space between them and put her hand in his. She put her trust in the only person she had and prayed she wouldn't regret it. He nodded and led her back to the village.

Chapter 18: Unsavory Choices

The clouds had lifted. Tonight would be clear enough to travel. Alaric ducked back into the house. It had been two days since his uncle told him the truth of Connell's plans. Tonight, he would lead Odessa through the woods and back to the relative safety of the castle. He swallowed hard past the hot ball in his throat. Her life there had not been a good one. But they were out of options.

He grabbed his pack, planning to ready himself for the journey when Arowyn caught his attention. The girl sat quietly at the table, picking at a piece of bread. Her face was ashen, and a sheen of sweat glistened on her brow.

"Are you feeling well, little wolf?" He stepped beside her and placed a hand on her forehead. She was hot to the touch.

She gave him a weak smile and nodded. "I'm alright."

But she clearly wasn't. His heart dropped, dread and panic swirling through his veins. They had been so careful, had stayed away from their sick clansmen. The sickness traveled from person to person, like seeds on the wind. Layla had come to help with his arm. She must have brought it with her.

He blew out a heavy sigh, but his heart continued to hammer in his chest. Not Arowyn, please not her.

"Looks to me like you need more sleep. Come on, back to bed." He forced lightness into his voice and a smile onto his face.

Scaring her wouldn't help anything. The fact she didn't protest and crawled back into bed was her most damning symptom. She had played through a broken wrist when she was five and somehow managed to be the only family member not affected by the tainted meat that had the rest of them laid up for days.

Now she lay quietly under her blankets. Alaric ran a hand over her sweaty forehead and turned before she could see the worry in his eyes. He put the kettle over the fire to make the child some tea, and his mind raced with all that needed to be done.

The house was empty and quiet for once. He thanked the goddess for that. It was one of those clear late fall days, crisp but warm in the sun, and his brothers were out taking advantage of the weather.

"Arowyn!" Rieka burst through the door with a basket full of eggs. "You said you would help! I got pecked by every hen…"

Her voice trailed off at the sight of Alaric's harsh gaze. She glanced toward the bed and saw her sister, pale and asleep. Her own face blanched and tears filled her eyes. He stepped toward her and took the basket from her hands. She burrowed into his side, and he patted her soothingly on the back.

"Hush now," he whispered to her, stroking her dark hair. She was small and slight in his arms, and his heart squeezed painfully in his chest at the thought of leaving her.

It was only for one night. His aunt would come to look after them. If he didn't get Odessa home, her death would be on his hands. He swallowed hard, breathing in deeply through his nose and sighing out of his mouth. He did not have the luxury of time to sit and worry.

Alaric crouched so he was at eye level with his sister. The girl already had to bear so much hardship, he hated putting more in her lap. But everywhere he looked was a dead end.

"Listen to me." His voice was calm and deep, and it pulled Rieka's attention to him. "She will be fine. Arowyn is a fighter. A few days in bed and she will be chasing the hens to avenge you in no time."

Rieka smiled through her tears at the image.

"I need you to go get Aunt Iya."

The girl grimaced, and Alaric stifled a laugh. Iya was no one's favorite aunt, but Layla had sick children of her own to care for and Yara had a new baby at home.

"She will help us." She had to. She was family. "You can stay and help her. Weylyn and Faolan can stay next door for now."

This got her attention. Her chin quivered anew. "But where will you be? And Odessa?"

He sighed and pinched the bridge of his nose. He couldn't tell her the whole truth. "The princess needs to return home."

"But we fought to keep her! And you said she wants to stay!" His sister's lip trembled, and fresh tears fell from her eyes. The fact she loved Odessa so much did nothing to ease his already battered heart.

He grabbed her small hands in his. "Listen. There are many things I cannot tell you right now. But trust this, all my decisions are made with you in mind. Everything I do is for you." His throat burned with emotions he had no time for today.

She nodded and wiped her eyes with the back of her hand, straightening to her full four and a half feet. Her determined face was so like their mother's, his words caught in this throat. Last time it was Rieka in the sickbed and him as well. Their mother nursed them both back to health and then succumbed to the disease herself only a week later. She had used all her strength on them and had nothing left for herself. In the days and months that followed, Alaric wished she had let him go instead.

He cleared his throat again, shaking the thoughts from his head. "Go on now." His voice was gruffer than he meant it to be, but his sister wasn't fooled. She leaned forward and planted a soft kiss on his cheek before scurrying out the door to retrieve her aunt.

The kettle steamed fiercely over the fire, and Alaric poured the tea.

****

Odessa paced the length of the small house, waiting for the sun to set. She had done nothing but wait and worry for the past two days. Her options had been whittled down to two unsavory choices: stay here and die or return home and face her father. For a brief, dark moment she had considered staying, but she was like every other living creature—she strove toward life over death, even when that life was a grim one.

She sighed and sat on the edge of the bed, running her hand over the soft fur blankets covering it. The memory of Alaric's warm body next to hers flickered through her mind, and she wished she had more time with him. Her feelings for the man were too strong, too sudden, and too absurd to be true, and yet she felt them

127

anyway.

The first man to treat her kindly outside the castle walls and she falls in love with him. She heated with embarrassment. First Nolan and now Alaric. When would she stop handing her heart to every man brave enough to look at her?

A soft knock on the door interrupted her thoughts. With a last glance around the cozy space, she strode to the door. In the short time she had been here, this little house had become home. Another mistake.

Alaric filled the doorway when she opened the door, his face pale and drawn. Had he changed his mind?

"Ready, princess?"

She winced at the name and pulled her cloak around her tighter. "I am, but I'd like to say goodbye to your sisters before we go. I won't take long." She rushed to finish as a frown crossed Alaric's face. They needed to leave quickly, of course, but she would hate to leave the girls without a quick goodbye.

"That's not possible." He shifted and glanced over his shoulder.

"Why not?" Something was wrong. The smooth skin between his eyebrows stayed creased as he contemplated what to tell her. And more importantly, what not to tell her. But she intended to get the truth from him.

He breathed out sharply. "Arowyn is not feeling well. I don't want to disturb her."

"She's ill? Why didn't you tell me until now?" She twisted her hands in the fabric of her cloak. Sweet little Arowyn was sick. How could she leave now?

"My aunt is with her, as is Rieka. There's nothing

you can do."

Odessa nearly cried with frustration. There's nothing you can do, could be the title to her life story at this point.

"Kalon has amazing healers. Maybe there's a way—"

He shook his head, cutting her off before she could finish. "You need to leave. You know Connell's plan for you." His eyes never left her face, so she had no trouble seeing the pain he tried to hide.

"Maybe there's a way to change his mind! Maybe I could help the clan in another way!" Her desperation rose with every word from her mouth. She didn't want to return home. If he would just listen…

"I can't let you do that."

Her hands clenched into fists at her sides, and she trembled with impotent rage. He was sending her away. He wouldn't listen.

"What if I refuse to leave?"

His eyes widened, the shock that she could possibly be so foolish was written across his face. She could be as damned foolish as she wished! She put her hands on her hips and tilted her chin up to meet his unbelieving gaze.

Odessa watched the emotions war for control of his face. Shock quickly turned to anger which transformed into stoic resolve with a hint of sadness. His usual face, then. He let out a long sigh like he did when dealing with the children.

"If you refuse, I will throw you over my shoulder and carry you back."

She opened her mouth to speak.

"Don't you dare say a word." His voice was low

and menacing now. She had pushed him too far. "You do not belong here, princess. You never did, and I was a fool to bring you here."

Odessa blinked at his harsh words, cursing her heart for feeling every one of them.

"I will not have your blood on my hands. You will return home to your castle and live. I will take care of my family. You needn't worry about us any longer."

She swallowed the hot lump in her throat, refusing to let the tears fall. He watched her, waiting for a response, but she had nothing left to say. He turned on his heel and stalked out into the yard, and she followed. Once again, having no other choice.

Chapter 19: Home

The walk was long and cold in the dark. And Alaric's stoic silence beside her did nothing to help improve the conditions. By the time her father's castle, gleaming stark white in the moonlight, came into view, Odessa's hunched shoulders were aching, and her body shook from the cold.

She wore Weylyn's clothes and his cloak in case they were spotted leaving the village, but they had been walking for hours undisturbed except by the occasional bat or owl. Whatever fate awaited her at home, she was at least safe from the clansmen who wanted her dead. Unfortunately, of all the emotions churning the supper in her stomach, relief was not one of them. She could only imagine what her father would do to her now that she was home. She took a deep mouthful of the fresh forest air. It may well be her last.

Before the idea of her renewed confinement could press her lungs painfully in her chest, she turned to Alaric to bid him goodbye.

"I will go alone from here. It is dangerous for you to come closer..." the words faded away into the night as she caught Alaric's stare. Before he had the chance to blink it away, she found a new emotion in his eyes, longing.

He stepped toward her and brushed a stray hair behind her ear. He kept her cheek cupped in his hand,

and she soaked in the warmth. His hand may be the last that touched her. Her throat closed with emotion, and a tear escaped and clung to her lashes.

Alaric pressed his forehead to hers, his hand gripping the back of her neck, holding her close. She inhaled his woodsmoke scent one more time. She rested a hand over his rapidly beating heart. She was wrong earlier. This man was nothing like Nolan. And his next words proved it.

"I'm sorry." The first words from his mouth in hours broke the tense silence between them. He cleared his throat. "I'm sorry this is the only way to keep my promise to you."

She shook her head gently against his, wanting to tell him this wasn't his fault, but he kept going before she could speak.

"Your knight, will he protect you?"

He had loosened his grip and she pulled back enough to look at him. His body was one long line of tension, from his shifting feet to his tightly clenched jaw.

What would he rather hear? That she didn't know if Nolan wanted anything to do with her anymore or that he would take her into his arms as soon as he saw her and keep her safe? Another impossible question with no answer.

"I don't know." Her words were small and sad in the vastness of the forest around them. Her fingers ached from the cold, and she wrapped them in Alaric's fur vest, pulling him close again. "Go back to your family knowing this, I will be safe. The worst the king will do is lock my doors again."

Alaric's eyes darkened, his body tensing further

under her hands. She gripped him tighter, forcing him to look at her.

"I will be alive and well." Her voice had grown thick with emotion, and she nearly choked on the word well, but he needed to hear it before he would leave her. He had his own family to care for. It was time he stopped worrying about her.

He ran his hand down her marked cheek, tracing the color with his fingers. He brought his lips to hers and brushed them lightly against her mouth. She circled his neck with her arms and twined her fingers into his hair.

She stretched to reach his mouth, bringing their bodies flush together. Alaric moaned at the contact and her lips hungrily met his. The ice in her bones melted at his touch. He devoured her, his tongue sliding into her mouth as she opened for him. His arms wrapped around her waist, his hands grabbing and searching. Her top half was covered in Weylyn's vest and furs, but he ran his hands over her legging-clad behind and groaned into her mouth.

The sound vibrated through her and destroyed any resolve she had to resist the man in front of her. He backed her against the trunk of a wide, smooth-barked tree, filling her senses. She took him in, every last bit of him, storing the pieces away.

He gripped her hips and lifted her; her legs wrapped around his waist. The solid heat of him hit her core, and she whimpered. He pulled back and kissed down her neck, his breath rapid against her skin. Every numb part of her sparked to life under his touch.

He grasped at the buckles of her vest, fumbling and cursing against her throat. She moved her hands to help him, tightening her grip around his waist with her thighs. The vest opened and he slid one hand inside, caressing her over the thin shift underneath the fur. His other hand returned to her backside, pressing her tight against the tree with his body.

Odessa arched into him as his thumb slid across her breast, grazing the peak and sending sparks shooting across her skin. He groaned against her neck, nipping and biting. She gasped and grabbed him tighter, her hands grasping and seeking. Too many layers of clothes stood in her way. She wanted his skin pressed against hers, she wanted more, she wanted all of him.

A rustle in the leaves behind them stilled Alaric's quest across her body. He glanced over his shoulder, but the woods were dark and quiet. He turned back to her, his eyes nearly glowing in the moonlight. The scene around them fell back into place. The shadowy trees of the sacred wood, the fields stretching out toward the castle, and the white palace on the hill.

Alaric's heart raced against her chest, but he gently lowered her to the ground. He leaned his forehead against hers once more, his breath hot and ragged on her cheeks. When he pulled away, he took his warmth with him. Odessa tugged the vest back together and wrapped the cloak around her tighter.

His gaze held hers for a moment longer, a glimmer of tears in his eyes. He nodded and swallowed hard. Stoic calm returned to his features, and she was returned to their first meeting in this very spot. It seemed a lifetime ago when it was only a matter of weeks.

"Be safe, princess."

She blinked the tears from her eyes, and he was

gone, the shadows of the forest swallowing him up. There was nothing left for her to do but go home and face the consequences of her ill-fated attempt at freedom.

She left the safety of the trees and trudged across the moonlit fields. The ground was frozen and unyielding. She left no footprints in the dirt as though she didn't exist at all. A snowy white owl flew low over her head, and she envied its freedom.

Her breath curled in front of her as she dragged her heavy limbs up the last slope toward the castle walls. She didn't have wings, or options, or hope. Her face was not easily hidden or forgotten. There was no hiding for her. She learned her lesson.

A voice called from the top of the wall, and she lowered the hood of her cloak.

"I am Princess Odessa. I have returned." The words burned her throat and turned her stomach, but she squared her shoulders and prepared to enter her father's home. The hood stayed at her back.

Shouts rang out along the stone wall and the heavy wooden door finally creaked open to allow her entrance. The guard at the gate peered at her face in the lantern light. Odessa didn't flinch even as a cold sweat trickled down her back. Thanks be to the gods, the man didn't spit at her feet, but he averted his eyes as soon as his gaze caught on the shadowed side of her face.

He dipped into a perfunctory bow. "Princess, welcome home."

She stepped past him, swallowed the hot lump of emotion in her throat, and strode toward the castle doors to summon the king.

****

135

Alaric watched from the darkness of the forest until he saw Odessa's distant form reach the castle walls. The gates opened and stole her from his gaze. His lips were bruised from her kisses and the heat of her body was imprinted on his. What in Narah's name was he supposed to do now?

He blew out a long sigh. What was he thinking kissing her like that? He had only one answer. When he pictured Odessa returning to her knight, something hot and jagged pierced his gut. He wanted nothing more than to send her back to Nolan with his taste on her lips. It was a ridiculous notion. One he wasn't proud of.

He raked a hand through his hair to stop it from trembling.

A distant howl brought him to his senses. He waited for the response, but none came. A wolf without a pack. His shivers had nothing to do with the cold. He looked out into the field Odessa had crossed. A white wolf sat watching him with golden eyes. Icy breath caught in Alaric's throat, and he dropped to his knees on the frost-covered ground.

Again, his prayers were heard, and again he didn't understand the answer. Narah was here with him. With Odessa. But what did she want from him? Was sending Odessa home the wrong choice? What else could he have done? He knew in his heart his goddess did not call for Odessa's blood, so what was it about this woman?

He growled in frustration, and the wolf howled in response. The hairs on Alaric's arms stood on end. The back of his neck prickled with awareness. He turned to the sound of footsteps, but he was too late, too slow. The men were upon him before he could rise from his knees and in the moment before everything went black, he realized Narah had tried to warn him.

Chapter 20: Prisoners

News of her return raced ahead of her through the castle halls by an unseen circuit of gossip and official messenger. By the time she reached her father's chambers, he was already awake and waiting.

"The king requests your presence," the guard at the door informed her and she nearly laughed out loud. Obviously, her father grasped for control of the situation even as she returned home with no help from him or his men.

"Does he now?"

The guard looked up in surprise at her mocking tone, but his eyes darted away.

"I can't turn you to stone, you know. Feel free to tell the others." Her tongue had loosened after her time in the forest. She refused to cower in front of this idiot who could not even look upon her face! She raked her fingers through her tangled hair and ran a steady hand across the front of her vest. Her cheeks flushed warm at the memory of Alaric hastily undoing the buckles and reaching inside, stroking her so sweetly…but now was not the time for such thoughts.

The guard had turned a sufficient shade of scarlet at her rebuke, and he mumbled apologies as he stepped aside to let her in.

"Thank you. You are a brave and noble man indeed," she said dryly and strode into her father's sitting room.

The king had clearly been recently pulled from his bed. His gray hair stood at a steep angle on his head, and his cheek was creased with lines from his sheets. He had aged since the last time she'd seen him. Her life here already seemed to be so long ago.

Odessa's newfound confidence withered under his appraising stare. Even in his dressing gown with his hair askew, he made her feel inadequate. His gaze landed only briefly on her face before settling somewhere safer near her shoulder.

"Father." She sank into a curtsey, but with no skirt to hold she felt foolish. She straightened and waited for the man to speak.

He ran a hand over his large stomach, smoothing the silk of his robe under his plump fingers, making her wait. She took a deep breath in through her nose and out her mouth as she had seen Alaric do when the children were fighting. The trembling inside her calmed.

"How is it you have returned on your own?" He raised an eyebrow as though he were suspicious of what he could clearly see in front of him, as though she had tricked him.

"I no longer wished to stay." He did not need to know she had been terribly wrong to trust the Clan of the Wolf with her safety. Too many emotions threatened to topple the precarious grip she had on her situation. Now was not the time to sort out her feelings for the clan. Later when she was alone, she would make sense of the anger and sadness wrapped around the affection and attraction she had felt for Alaric. But not now.

She faked the stoic calm Alaric taught her and raised her chin.

Her father narrowed his eyes. "And they let you go?"

"Yes." The lie slipped easily from her lips.

He watched her even as he stood and conferred with the guard at the door. His eyes never left her body. Did he think she would disappear from his sight if he looked away? Did her father truly believe she held some sort of power because of the birthmark on her face? The idea was so startlingly preposterous, laughter threatened to escape her lips once more.

Her entire life, she assumed he hated her because her birth caused his beloved wife's death, but the fear creeping into his eyes as he stared at her told a different story. What was her father afraid of? And how could she use it to her advantage?

She did not have long to consider this new dynamic before two more guards entered the room. Both men were tall, one dark and one fair, but neither looked in her direction.

"These men will escort you back to your room, daughter. We wouldn't want you to wander off again." There was a threat behind his caring words, and it was obvious to everyone in the room. These men will lock you away, daughter. We wouldn't want you to escape again.

But Odessa didn't put up a fight as the men led her out of the door and through the winding corridors of her father's wing. It would have been futile to try to escape from two enormous castle guards. And she knew it was coming anyway. Returning home meant returning to the shadows, but now a new light had been shed on her current situation.

Her father locked her away not out of anger, or shame, but out of fear. And she could work with fear.

****

The dull ache in his head ceased throbbing long enough for Alaric to crack open one eye. He groaned and closed it again. The vibrating in his skull intensified as he tried to figure out what to do next. Waves of sharp pain radiated from his injured arm as he shifted on the bare sleeping bench.

He draped his good arm over his face, blocking out the morning light streaming through the window above the door. Every part of him was sore, and he wished for sleep to overtake him again. Thoughts of his siblings threatened to steal the air from his lungs, so he pushed them aside. They were in the capable hands of his aunts. It was the best he could do for them, something he should have insisted on years ago.

He ignored the ache that had taken up residence behind his breastbone since leaving Odessa in Kalon. There were plenty more pressing issues for him to worry about. He had no time to dwell on his foolish feelings. The princess was gone from his life, and the sooner he could extract her from his head, the better.

Never mind that his lips still tingled with the memory of hers, or that his tongue could not forget the sweetness of her mouth. Her phantom touches ran over his sore and tired body, the way she had clutched and grabbed at him, pulling him closer. He flushed hot at the memory. He was not proud of his behavior in the woods, but he couldn't find it in himself to regret it. In fact, his only regret was not doing it sooner.

The door swung open and startled him out of his

pain-induced revelry. His head swam as he struggled to sit; a wave of nausea washed over him.

"Don't get up on my account." A low voice growled from across the room.

Alaric groaned. He sat on the edge of the hard cot and scrubbed a hand down his face. The edges of the room blurred, but the man came into focus. Alaric didn't need to see him to know who had captured him, and the cold, calculating look on Connell's face did nothing to ease his worry.

"You were tasked with one thing." Connell paced the room, like a caged animal, but Alaric kept his eyes on the ground. If he followed him with his gaze, last night's supper would be spewed across the floor of the empty house.

"And not only did you fail, but you turned against your clan. You betrayed your own people to aid the princess of a foreign king."

"Had I known your plans for her, I never would have brought her here." His voice was nothing more than a scraping rasp against his throat, but Connell stilled in his pacing. He narrowed his eyes in disgust.

"They are not my plans. The goddess wills it."

Alaric pushed himself to his feet. The room swayed around him, but he held his ground in front of his chief. The older man stepped closer, invading Alaric's space.

He swallowed the anger rising into his throat. "Do not hide behind Narah."

"You saw her face!" Connell hissed; spittle landed in his beard. He was unraveling before Alaric's eyes. "She was light and dark like the moon. You said it yourself, Narah sent her here. Our people are dying, and you gave away the one thing that could save us."

For the first time, Alaric saw the fear in his chief's eyes. The people demanded an end to the disease ravishing their village, and Connell had no answers.

"You misread the sign. Narah would not demand her blood."

Connell's face twisted into an ugly sneer; his fear quickly covered by anger.

"What was the marked princess put in your path for, Alaric? To warm your bed?"

He cursed the heat rushing to his face at Connell's assertion. How foolish he had been to harbor those exact thoughts.

"She needed shelter, and I provided it."

The Wolf chief scoffed and turned away from Alaric to continue his pacing. Alaric eased himself back onto the edge of the cot and hung his head in his hands.

"Narah needs a sacrifice." Connell's words were no longer meant for him but muttered as the man ran a hand through his silver-streaked hair. His feet stopped in front of Alaric, and he forced himself to raise his head once more.

A slow smile spread across Connell's face.

"Your eyes."

Alaric blinked.

"One light and one dark."

He watched in horror as the man worked over the idea in his head.

"You may provide us with a sacrifice after all."

Panic shot through Alaric's body, and he stood on trembling legs. The clan had never sacrificed a warrior before. Surely, none of the elders would agree. But if they determined Alaric had betrayed the clan, they could banish him for life. Either way, his siblings would be alone.

"My family…" his voice broke, and he forced a hard swallow over the lump of fear in his throat.

"Your family is safe." Connell turned back to look at him. "But your littlest sister is ill. Pray you haven't sealed her fate by freeing the princess. You may have to trade your life for hers." With that he stormed from the house, slamming the door hard enough to send dizzying pain slicing through Alaric's skull.

He shuffled to the fire pit and threw a few logs onto the hot coals. The house was one of the few unoccupied homes in the village, and it was cold enough inside to see the breath in front of his face. He opened the front door and peered out into the bright morning.

"Morning." The familiar voice came from the side of the door. There weren't many voices in the village he wouldn't have recognized, but this gruff greeting happened to come from an old friend.

"Evander," Alaric greeted him. The two had grown up and trained together as boys. Something loosened in his chest at the sight of his friend.

"Seems you've gotten yourself into a situation." A slow smile crossed Evander's bronzed face. He leaned against the side of the house with his arms across his broad chest. "I'm under strict orders not to let you leave." He slid his eyes to meet Alaric's.

"And you intend to follow his orders?" Alaric squinted in the bright sun, the light splitting his head into two equally pounding halves. Evander was shorter than he was, a point of contention when they were younger, but he was swift and strong. Alaric on the other hand could barely open his eyes and was essentially down to one usable arm.

"Of course. I've no need to get on Connell's bad side."

Alaric gave a stiff nod. It didn't matter anyway. He would never get far without Connell knowing about it. It was a small miracle he was able to return Odessa safely last night before his clansmen caught them.

"Was it you who hit me in the head?" He ran a hand over the back of his skull where a tender lump had formed.

Evander let out a small laugh. "No, wasn't me."

"It was unnecessary anyway. I would have come willingly."

His friend lifted a shoulder, but something like pity crossed his face. "Why did you do it?"

"I had to."

Evander continued to study him, but Alaric didn't elaborate. Gods only knew how many people were aware of Connell's plan, and at the moment he didn't see any benefit to being the one to announce it. The sudden sickening realization that Evander might agree with it, made him even more resigned in his decision to stay quiet. He had no desire to find out if his friend supported such a heinous idea.

Finally, Evander's face softened. "I will check on them for you later."

"Thank you." The tension in his shoulders relaxed a bit more, and he turned back into the house. In the dim interior, he laid himself gently on the cot and closed his eyes. Connell's threat played over in his mind.

Arowyn was sick, and instead of being by her side, he was imprisoned by his own people. He couldn't regret helping Odessa. Even now he was convinced it was the right thing to do. But his failure to protect his family burned hot in his stomach.

If he believed giving his life would save Arowyn, he would slit his own throat at Narah's altar and be done with it. But he didn't believe it. His death would do nothing but add to the list of people who had left them. And Alaric couldn't bear to do that.

He dug the heels of his hands into his closed eyes causing sparks to appear behind his lids, trying in vain to clear his mind. There had to be a way out of the mess he had made of everything. And he had four days to figure it out.

Chapter 21: Fairy Tales

Odessa stared listlessly out her window toward the forest. She leaned her forehead against the cold glass, letting the chill seep into her. If only she could numb her thoughts as well as her skin. They ran on a continuous loop of failures and regrets.

But even as she berated herself for being so foolish, other images came to mind. Memories of Alaric's hands on her body and the press of his lips on her skin. And other memories too, of his smile and the way he blushed whenever she caught him looking at her.

What became of him when he returned to his village? She had been so preoccupied with her own fate that she had failed to worry about his. How would the clan react to her being gone? She prayed Alaric would not be punished. His little family needed him. Odessa's heart ached every time she thought about Arowyn sick in bed, and the helplessness of it all was driving her mad.

As much as her blood ran cold at the memory of the clan's plans, she also couldn't help but miss her little home and the relative freedom that came with it. It had been two days since her return, and she hadn't been allowed out of her chambers at all—not that she was surprised.

She lifted her head from the window and gazed

around her room. The sun streaked cheerfully across the worn floorboards, thoroughly at odds with her mood. The room was exactly how she left it a month ago, but she was different. Her skin itched to get out of here, but her father had men stationed outside her door at all hours of the day and night. She had checked.

The thrill she had gotten from seeing the fear in his eyes on the night of her return was soon forgotten. Whatever her father's reasons were for keeping her locked away, he was wrong. She had no power here.

Her door opened without a knock, and she stood in time to see Nolan enter. Her poor confused heart raced, stuttered, and tripped against her ribs. Old feelings mixed with new ones, turning her into a nervous wreck, but he was alive, and she was grateful.

"Nolan, you are well."

His eyes raked over her as he gingerly made his way toward her. His movements were stiff, and he winced in pain every few steps. Guilt swamped her and closed her throat to any more words.

His gaze flicked to hers. A grim smile touched the corners of his mouth but didn't reach his eyes. "Perhaps not 'well'. But I am alive."

"Nolan, I am so sorry. I never meant—"

He held up a hand, stopping her apology. He lowered himself carefully into a chair by the fire and gestured for her to do the same. His silence was unnerving.

Finally, he looked at her, and this time he held her gaze in his. Her heart thrummed against her chest.

"I felt a real affection for you, Essa. I paid you visits when no one else would. I spoke with you and shared your bed. But it was never enough. I wasn't enough for you." His eyes burned hot in his ashen face.

She opened her mouth to protest, but he went on.

"When you went missing without so much as a goodbye or a note, I searched the kingdom for you. I braved the forest and faced the savages for you." His face was tight with pain, and he gripped the arms of the chair so tightly his knuckles were white.

"I didn't ask you to come." Her voice was nearly a whisper, but he winced when she spoke.

"You disappeared! You left me without a word!"

The truth of his words hit her so hard she was breathless. He stared at her now with so much hatred, every excuse she had, no matter how valid, died on her lips.

"I led my men into battle to bring you home safe, and what did you do, Odessa?" He narrowed his eyes at her but held her gaze. All the times she had wished he would look at her and truly see her, she had never wished for this.

"You defended that barbarian," he answered for her. "He was as good as dead, and you stopped me. I nearly died for you, princess. Does that mean nothing to you?"

"I…" The words were a jumbled mess inside her. She had never meant for Nolan to be injured, but she also could not regret saving Alaric's life.

"I needed to leave," she began, finding her voice. "You of all people should have understood. It was wrong of me not to leave you a note, but I hadn't planned on what happened. At the time I thought it was fate."

Nolan sneered.

"But now I know that was a foolish thought. I was

foolish." She swallowed hard. "But I cannot be sorry I saved a man's life. He is a good man, Nolan. With a family who needs him. I never intended for you to be hurt."

"He is a savage. No better than the wild animals he lives amongst."

She shook her head. Even now, knowing what the clan would have done to her, she couldn't allow Nolan to speak of them that way.

"Did he touch you, princess? Did you let him do the things I have done to you?"

She stood abruptly, her face burning with shame. "You should go."

Her curt response only stoked the fire behind his eyes. He rose slowly and stepped closer. His once beloved face twisted with bitterness. She no longer recognized it.

"It doesn't matter what he did to you, Essa. I forgive you." He smiled a sickening smile. "We will start fresh."

He reached into his pocket and pulled out a small gold ring with a red stone in the center. He took her cold hand in his and pushed the ring roughly onto her finger. The shock had barely registered before he spoke again.

"Your father has agreed. We will marry tomorrow. Then we leave for the countryside as husband and wife."

The room tilted beneath her feet. She blinked at his smiling face. She had wanted those words for so long, but not now, not like this.

"Be happy, princess." He squeezed her hand tight in his. "You are finally getting what you want."

He grabbed her roughly toward him and pressed his mouth to hers. Her lips ground into her teeth and his breath was hot and angry against her face. He pulled away as abruptly as he had started the kiss and turned on his heel.

Nolan stalked toward the door, leaving her reeling. Her breakfast threatened to rise up into her throat at any moment.

"I will see you in the morning." He opened the door and disappeared down the hallway.

Odessa sank back into the chair, heaving and sucking in air. This was not happening.

****

She didn't have long to wallow before a soft knock at the door disrupted her spinning thoughts.

"Yes?"

The door opened a crack and a small face peeked around the edge. Faye's eyes widened and her face lit up when she saw Odessa. The guard at the door muttered something but Faye dismissed him with a flick of her wrist. A true princess through and through.

"I am here to see my sister. Surely you will not deny me a visit?"

Whatever the poor stumbling man at the door said, Faye nodded and rushed into Odessa's chambers, her skirts swishing around her feet.

"Odessa! I was so worried about you!" Faye flung herself into Odessa's lap, and she could do nothing but wrap her arms around the small girl and hug her tight. It was more contact than the two had ever had, and Odessa found tears stinging the corners of her eyes. She inhaled the girl's sweet strawberry scent and smiled for the first time in days. If only being home were more of this and less of her father's threats and Nolan's anger.

"I'm alright. No need to worry." She held the girl out at arm's length to get a better look at her. Her hair was braided in a dark ring around her head. A halo of wispy hairs had escaped the braid and framed her face. Faye grinned at Odessa, and she was immediately reminded of two other small girls, one of which was horribly ill. Had it been Faye sick in bed, her father would have the best healers by her side.

"They said you were captured by the Wolves! Was it terrible? You must have been so frightened!" Faye settled at Odessa's feet in front of the fire. She gazed up at her and for once Odessa felt like she had done something interesting. She had an adventure. A small smile lifted the corners of her mouth.

"Well, it wasn't all bad."

"Really? My friend, Daphne says they are more beast than man and covered in hair!"

Odessa's face warmed at the memory of Alaric's beard tickling her neck as he kissed her against the beech tree at the edge of the wood. Her fingers curled at her sides remembering what it had been like to grasp the coarse strands of his hair. She shook her head. Those were not things fit to tell the young child at her feet, but a familiar longing for a friend to share her thoughts returned to her chest.

She sighed out a long breath. Faye waited expectantly for more of the story. And it was rather nice to have a willing listener. "Actually, I met a little girl who reminded me of you."

Faye's eyes widened in disbelief.

"And she wasn't hairy at all," Odessa added with a grin.

Faye burst into giggles, and Odessa's heart swooped in her chest. "Let me tell you about the houses. They were straight out of a storybook!"

She pushed Nolan's words from her mind, spinning the ring so she wouldn't have to see the glinting stone, and she told Faye the tale of her adventures with the Wolves. At the time, it seemed wise to leave out the ending. Odessa didn't want to scare the child, after all.

Chapter 22: A Lovely Husband

Odessa was awoken at an ungodly hour by two servants hauling an enormous wooden tub into her room. They deposited it with a huff by the fire. Sylvie followed close behind.

"Rise and shine, princess. It's your big day." Sylvie's voice was filled with energy and good cheer, and it grated against Odessa's frayed nerves. It must have been only an hour or two ago when she finally fell into a fitful sleep. The sun was barely above the horizon. She groaned and yanked the covers over her head.

"Come now, don't be nervous. I'm sure Sir Nolan will make a lovely husband. Me and the other girls are very happy for you."

Odessa peeked out from her hiding place and found Sylvie's sweet smiling face leaning over her. It wasn't the woman's fault she was stuck in this situation, but her kind words only poked the sore spot inside of her.

A month ago, she would have been beside herself with joy. To marry Nolan and get as far away from this dreaded room was her only wish. But now her lungs squeezed painfully with every breath. Every time she shut her eyes, she saw his face twisted with anger. How could she possibly marry that man? And why had her father suddenly decided she was free to leave?

She offered a weak smile to Sylvie who still

hovered over her. Making the woman's job harder would do nothing but make Odessa feel worse. She tossed off the covers and hung her legs over the side of the bed.

Sylvie beamed. "Very good, my lady. I'll leave you to wake up, and I'll help fill the tub." She leaned in a bit closer and sniffed. "My word, the woodsmoke smell won't leave your hair. We'll take care of it." She patted Odessa lovingly on the knee and bustled out the door.

Now what? She rubbed her puffy eyes, trying to rouse herself into action. What a laughable thought. Action. What possible action could she take? A yawn overtook her, and she shuddered with exhaustion. She hung her head forward and rested it in her hands. Her hair covered the sides of her face like a curtain. Sylvie was right. It smelled faintly of woodsmoke and pine, and the scent made her insides ache. She had bathed when she returned home, as well as taking plenty of sponge baths in the village, but she couldn't bring herself to wash that scent from her hair. By now she was sure it was a greasy, tangled mess, but she didn't care. She hadn't planned on anyone seeing her this way, but now she was to be a bride.

The word made her insides tumble and swoop, and she raced for the porcelain bowl she used to wash her face. She emptied her stomach into it and stood up gasping for air. She had to get out of here! Her mind raced and her eyes darted around the room, looking for an escape, looking for any way out.

Perhaps while the maids were busy filling the tub, she could slip out among them, past the guards, and back to the forest. *Back to Alaric.* They could run away together—someplace far where no one would care about her face, or who she was—where Nolan and her father would never find her.

Short gasps escaped her lips. She couldn't draw enough air into her lungs and black spots floated in front of her eyes. Her legs trembled, and she reached for the table holding the bowl to steady herself.

Sylvie returned with a large bucket of water, took one look at Odessa, and nearly dropped it.

"Oh! Please, my lady, sit and rest."

She left the bucket by the tub and hurried to Odessa's side. Wrapping a warm and protective arm around her waist, she led Odessa back to the bed. A wave of affection for the woman threatened to upset her emotions even more. Odessa clung to her familiar hand.

"You lay back and rest, princess. It will all be fine. No need to be nervous." She patted Odessa's hand and helped her back under the covers. For a moment, Odessa imagined this was how a mother would speak to her when she was ill. Her chest tightened, and she swallowed the hot lump in the throat. She was a twenty-four-year-old woman. When would she stop wishing to have her mother by her side?

She closed her eyes, not allowing the tears to fall. Sylvie hustled back to work filling the tub. Odessa let the sounds of the water sloshing against the sides and the soft whispers of the maids calm her frantic heart.

She had to be rational. Things could be worse. She had loved Nolan, not too long ago, and he had shown her kindness over the past year. Perhaps being married to him would not be a terrible fate. And a home in the country actually sounded quite lovely.

But even as she thought the words, they rang hollow in her mind. Nolan may have been kind to her once, but now he was angry and bitter. He only wanted her when someone else had her. He had never attempted to free her before that. She feared his desire for her now was only some sort of twisted revenge against her.

She was wrong to leave without telling him, but she no longer loved him. She may have escaped the Wolves' sacrificial block, but her heart remained behind, already marked for another. How could she live a life with one man while always dreaming of the other?

She didn't notice the tears on her cheeks until Sylvie wiped them tenderly away and announced her bath was ready. Regardless of what she wanted, by the end of the day, she would be Nolan's wife.

****

Sylvie had a mirror brought in, and Odessa stood in front of it scowling at her reflection. The dress she wore was ill-fitting and squeezed too tightly around her bosom. The cream-colored satin pooled around her feet. The dress was far too long. She smoothed her hands down the front of it, wondering who had worn it before her. One of her sisters, she imagined. She hadn't been allowed to attend either of her sisters' wedding ceremonies or the lavish parties that followed.

Her wedding, she had been informed, would be a quiet affair, attended only by the king and queen and royal officiant. Simple and elegant, Sylvie called it, trying to put a positive spin on the oddly rushed nuptials. But Odessa was not surprised. The ceremony would be secret and hidden like everything else in her life, and then she would be whisked away by Nolan, out of her father's way for good.

157

How had the exact thing she always wished for become the thing she feared the most? She touched the stained side of her face, remembering the way Alaric's fingers would brush across both sides of her. She was light and dark like his goddess. Shouldn't that mean something? It meant something to him.

A thick white veil hung over the back of a chair. Today her face would be covered completely, not because she was a bride, but because she was cursed to hurt all those who came near her. The rumors suddenly rang true.

Shouts and footsteps crashed through the halls beyond her door. She turned from the mirror to find Sylvie, eyebrows drawn, grimacing toward the door.

"Whatever could that be about?"

Odessa gave a slight shrug, but fear prickled at the back of her neck. Tonight was the solstice. Was it possible the Wolves had come for her? They would never be able to breach the castle walls. More footsteps followed the first group. It seemed her father's entire guard was rushing through the corridors. Dread seeped into her gut.

Sylvie forced a smile and patted her hand.

"I will go and see what all the commotion is. Don't worry about a thing." She slipped from the room and Odessa followed, pressing her cheek against the door. She could barely make out the tense whispers between Sylvie and whoever was assigned princess-guarding duty for the day. She couldn't hear enough to make out anything useful, and from what she could gather, the guard was just as confused as Sylvie.

Odessa glanced back at the mirror and found her startled reflection looking back at her. Her pale cheek had gone nearly white with worry, but her neck and chest had broken out in blotchy red patches from nerves and stress. Her hair looked absurd piled high on her head in loops and curls in the style of the kingdom. She smelled of lavender and rosemary. Her stomach turned.

After the pounding footsteps and initial shouts, the hallway had gone ominously silent. Odessa paced her room, avoiding the mirror and the stranger she found there. What was going on?

She didn't have to wait long to find out the answer. A heavy fist pounded on the door. It swung open without waiting for her response.

Two of her father's men, Andrew and Nico, stood waiting for her.

"Your father requests your presence, princess."

Odessa nodded, not bothering with the veil, and followed the men down the hall. They strode ahead of her on long legs, making her scurry to catch up. Their footsteps echoed through the empty passageway. The eerie stillness filled her with panic. She could barely breathe in this damn bridal gown. She'd be lucky if she didn't faint at her father's feet.

Andrew stopped abruptly in front of her father's chambers and pulled open the heavy door. Odessa was not prepared for what she found inside.

The door closed with a thud behind her, and she was left alone with her father and stepmother. The queen sat in a heap on the floor, her gowns billowed out around her. She was already dressed for the wedding, but now her elaborate hairstyle sat askew on her head, and she spun her tiara nervously between her fingers. Her eyes were swollen and red. Odessa's blood ran cold. There was only one thing in the world that could rattle the queen this badly.

"Faye." The name left her lips in a strained whisper.

Her father swiveled his head away from where he stood gazing into the fire. He narrowed his eyes at Odessa. "Your sister has been taken."

All the air left her lungs and her ears buzzed. Taken?

The king noted the shocked look on her face. "I assume you know nothing about it?"

What was he accusing her of? "Of course, I don't! What is going on?"

Her stepmother sniffled miserably from the floor.

"The Wolves have taken her."

The room spun. She would not survive the crushing pain in her chest. "Why?" The question was torn from her throat.

"To replace you."

To replace her? Oh, dear gods, no! Not Faye, not sweet little Faye! Every cell in Odessa's body screamed in frustration. Faye was not light and dark like Narah. What did they want with her? This could not be.

"I don't understand."

Her father prowled toward her. A grim smile on his lips. The queen's eyes tracked him from her seat on the floor. The crown spun round and round in her hands.

"It seems you were valuable to the clan, after all, daughter. And when you left, they needed a different marked princess."

Faye's small purple birthmark flashed in Odessa's mind. Was that why they took Faye, because she was marked too? This couldn't be happening. She reached out a hand to the back of her father's velvet-covered chair to steady herself. He watched her every movement. How much did he know? Did he know what would happen to Faye tonight if they didn't get her back?

"Are you sure they took her? Maybe she got lost. Or wandered into the village."

"I have eyes and ears everywhere in this kingdom. Faye was seen walking near the edge of the woods. She was taken by clansmen before my guards could reach her."

Odessa's mouth hung open in disbelief. It was her fault. All of it. She never should have told Faye anything about the clans. The girl had always been curious but sheltered. Why did she choose now to explore beyond the castle walls? And who was in charge of watching her?

"Her nursemaid has been taken care of." Her father's words sent shivers up her spine. She did not ask what he meant.

"I am gathering men to attack at dawn."

"No!" Odessa's shouted answer startled the queen out of her grief-stricken stupor. The king's eyes widened in surprise at her outburst.

"No? I should not send men to rescue my daughter?"

Odessa desperately shook her head, struggling to form the words from the cacophony of thoughts swirling through her mind.

"I hoped you might have insight into the clan after spending so much time with them. But if you have nothing to contribute, you may return to your chambers." The king lifted a hand to dismiss her, but she didn't budge. Her fingers dug deep into the back of the chair.

"Dawn will be too late." She forced the words out past her panicked breathing.

"Too late?" Queen Louise's voice rose from the floor, trembling but strong. "What do you mean too late?"

Odessa stood firm under the gaze of her parents. Parents who couldn't seem to bring themselves to love her. But they did love Faye, and right now their eyes were clouded with fear. She could barely force herself to utter the words, but they needed to know.

"She will be dead by morning. They planned to kill me on the solstice. I can only assume they took Faye to replace me in their ceremony." She focused on her hands as she spoke, and when she looked up her stepmother's face was ashen, her mouth open in shock. Her father's face in contrast had turned bright scarlet.

He closed the space between them, and once again she became a target for his fear and anger.

"You..." he seethed. Spit flew from his lips and landed in his beard.

"Father, please." He flinched at the name from her lips. She had killed his wife and now she would be the reason his beloved youngest daughter lay on the sacrificial slab under the cold moon. Nothing she could say would break through the rage he felt toward her. Except for maybe one thing. She slammed the ring Nolan had given her into her father's palm.

"I have a plan."

Chapter 23: For the Good of the People

Alaric paced the small space, taking the same route he took every day he had been trapped in this house. Round and round he walked, circling the center fire pit. His thoughts followed a similar path, round and round his mistakes and failures. Occasionally, a sharp burst of pain when he thought of his baby sister weakening more each day, would break through his numbness. The breath would leave him, and he would be forced to sit until the panic subsided.

Today, the sun shone brightly through the windows above his head illuminating the dusty table and floors. It was the solstice. What would become of him? Connell hadn't been back and other than a few updates about his siblings from Evander, he had no idea what was happening outside these walls. Walls that closed in on him more and more each day.

The door pushed open, startling him.

"Uncle!"

"Alaric." The man quickly closed the door behind him and grabbed him by his good arm. Deep creases lined his face and the dark smudges under his eyes were worse even than the last time Alaric saw him.

"What is it?"

Merrick sighed and ran a hand down his tired face. "I tried Alaric. I truly did." His uncle sat heavily in the only chair. Alaric rushed to his side.

"Tell me, uncle. What's going on? Am I to die?" He shook Merrick's shoulder jostling the man from his dazed state.

"No. Not you."

Relief was a flash of light, quickly covered by darkness. "Who?"

Merrick swallowed hard, shaking his head as though he still could not believe it himself. "I truly believe Connell's gone mad," he muttered. "I've been trying to talk sense into him all week, but he won't listen. And he's convinced others. So many others." He dropped his head in his hands.

Alaric squatted in front of him and squeezed his arms, forcing his uncle to look at him.

"Please, tell me what's going on."

Merrick's soft brown eyes focused on him. "We lost ten more people in two days, Alaric. The sickness is stronger this time."

Alaric nodded, staying outwardly calm while his heart threatened to leap from his ribs.

"Connell is determined to have a sacrifice. He says it's the only way to appease Narah and stop the sickness."

His uncle stopped, his eyes filling with tears. Alaric shook him hard enough to rattle the man's teeth. "Who! Who dies tonight?"

"The little princess." Merrick's voice was not more than a whisper, but the name jolted through Alaric's bones. The little princess. Odessa's sister. Connell meant to slaughter a small girl tonight on Narah's altar.

His heart stopped and then rammed into his chest.

"No. No, no, no. This cannot be. He has gone mad, uncle!"

Merrick moaned, dropping his head again. "I tried. I tried." He repeated his lament over and over as Alaric rocked back on his heels.

"Tell him to take me."

His uncle's head shot back up. "What?"

"Me. He can have me. Tell him to leave the girl alone. I will go willingly. Please, uncle. Tell him."

Merrick shook his head even more vehemently than before. He looked old and haggard. Alaric hated to see him this way. This was what Connell's hysteria was doing to the clan. There must be other ways to fight this sickness, other cures to explore.

But if the people wanted a sacrifice, he would offer himself.

"Listen to me. As long as my siblings are well cared for, I have done everything I need to do here. I have served my purpose. Care for them like they were your own, and I can leave this earth."

"Alaric…"

"Tell him. Tell Connell."

Merrick gazed at him with haunted eyes. Alaric didn't budge from his crouch in front of him, never wavering. At last, his uncle nodded and rose from his seat.

"I will give him your message, but if you think I will argue for your death, you are wrong."

****

"Where is she?" Nolan burst through the doors into the king's study. King Orion raised his bent head and arched a silver eyebrow. Nolan made a hasty bow but didn't slow his stride toward the king.

"What have you done with my wife?"

Orion leaned back in his chair and clasped his

hands over his stomach. Nolan bit back his emotions. This was his king after all. But his breathing was ragged, and his pulse drummed loudly in his ears.

"She isn't your wife, yet. And she won't be. She's gone."

"Gone?" Red flashed in his vision, and he pressed his eyes closed, squeezing them shut.

The king's voice was calm when he spoke, but he tapped a nervous foot on the floor beneath the desk. Nolan listened to the incessant clicking of the man's boot against the stone. He ground his teeth and opened his eyes.

"She has gone back to the Wolves." Orion's fingers were clenched so tightly together over his middle they were white. "It was the only way to bring the little princess back to me."

Nolan steadied himself on the edge of the king's desk. He glanced out the window over the king's shoulder. He could just make out the tree line that marked the edge of Asherah's wood. The sunny afternoon had quickly turned to a rosy dusk and out there somewhere Odessa rode back to the barbarians. His hands clung so tightly to the edge of the desk his fingers ached from the pressure.

He managed to bring his gaze back to the king. He swallowed all the words clamoring to escape. His throat burned with the need to scream at his king.

"We had a deal." His voice was even but his insides boiled. "What about the prophecy? What about getting Odessa as far from the clans as possible?"

The king shrugged, but the gesture was anything but casual. Every line of his body was tense.

"The stakes changed."

"You gave your word."

Orion stood and slammed his hands on the desk. He leaned forward and his face was inches from Nolan. "She is my daughter. I could not leave her to her death."

"They both are." Nolan held the king's cold stare. His breathing was heavy as though he had just finished a training duel. The king could have him dragged out of here and imprisoned for his insolence, but he didn't. Nolan was the only person who knew the depths of the king's fears.

Orion straightened to his full height. "It is done."

Nolan opened his mouth, but Orion raised a hand to stop him. "You'd better remember your place." Both men stood, seething in the silence between them, but Nolan knew better than to continue questioning his king. The man would only allow so much.

"If all goes well, we will have an alliance with the Wolves before the night is over. Something neither forest kingdom has attained. We would have this over Melantha forever. The clans cannot unite against us if the Wolves stand with us. I acted on behalf of the entire kingdom! You have no right to question your king!"

"Of course, your majesty," Nolan ground out, dipping into another hasty bow before rushing from the room. His mind spun with questions as he strode back to his chambers. An alliance with the Wolves, but how? And what would become of Odessa when she returned to the clan? But perhaps most importantly, how would he possibly get her back this time?

He had to get out of this foolish wedding attire; the white tunic mocked him for his trust in the king's promises. If Orion would not protect his marked daughter, Nolan would. He tossed the tunic onto his bed and pulled on a black one instead. He hissed in pain, moving quicker than his arrow wound allowed.

God damn it! He had been so close to having Odessa back in his arms and all to himself again. He wouldn't rest until she was his wife. The wife he deserved. Was he not entitled to her love after all he had done for her?

He pulled on a dark black cloak and strode out to ready his horse.

Chapter 24: Sacrifice

Connell denied his request. At sunset, Alaric was escorted from his prison into the sacred grove. The clearing was quiet and still; the night air was cold and biting. Every adult member of the clan had gathered. Alaric's heart ached at the sight. They were so much fewer in number than even a few months ago. The faces around him were etched with the sorrow and the deep, debilitating fear of losing the people you love.

The girl lay peacefully asleep on the stone slab in the middle of the small circle of trees. She had been drugged and the knife well sharpened. The sacrifice would be bloody but not violent.

Alaric attempted to shake Evander from his arm, but his friend's grip did not loosen.

"What do you think I'm going to do?"

Evander glanced around the field at the gathered clansmen, his eyes landing on where Connell stood under the sacred oak.

"Chief's orders."

Alaric noticed how Evander's gaze never rested on the little princess but instead skirted around the clearing. The crowd gave off the same energy, nervous and uneasy like a pack of wild horses during a lightning storm. It wouldn't take much to send them all running.

He had attended many solstice ceremonies since becoming an adult member of the tribe, and they were always solemn affairs. An animal sacrifice was made in offering to the goddess Asherah of the wood in thanks for her protection and with the hope, the sun would return soon.

Never in his lifetime had the clan sacrificed a human and certainly never to their clan goddess, Narah. She was the goddess of the hunt, of wolves, and the moon. She did not require the blood of an innocent girl!

His eyes remained on the princess. He watched her small chest rise and fall. Her face was so similar to her sister's...

He struggled to free himself, twisting away from Evander, but the man grabbed his injured arm and pulled it behind his back. The pain brought him to his knees in the freshly fallen snow.

"You make this harder for both of us," Evander panted in his ear.

"Good," he growled but remained kneeling. There was nowhere else for him to go.

The crowd shifted uneasily around him. People he had lived with his entire life pretended not to see him. He had betrayed his clan. And Connell had made sure they all damn well knew it.

The Wolf chief came to stand beside his sacrifice. He raised the knife above his head and began the ancient chant. The clan joined in until the forest was vibrating with the voices of his people. Their words echoed in his bones, but unlike in years past, Alaric did not raise his voice in hope for the coming year. He could see no way out of the darkness that threatened to encompass them all if blood was spilled tonight. Narah had turned her back on him.

He kept his gaze focused on the feet of the people

around them. The contents of his stomach threatened to spill on the snow in front of him. When the chant ended, he looked up. He had nothing left to offer Odessa except to bear witness to the tragedy unfolding in front of him. He would not leave the little princess to suffer her fate alone.

The moonlight glinted off the knife as Connell brought it down to his side and stepped toward the sacrificial slab. The people held their breath.

A howl rang out through the night. And the Wolf chief dropped the knife.

****

The howl tore from Odessa's throat, wild and unbidden. She hadn't planned to do it, but what other response could one have to seeing their baby sister about to be slaughtered? She tugged the white, fur-lined cloak tighter around herself and stepped out of the shelter of the trees.

The chief had dropped his knife, and she breathed a small sigh of relief. He looked at her wide-eyed as though she were a ghost. A ghost or a goddess…

"Narah," the people whispered and dropped to their knees in front of her. All except Connell, who continued to stare. Her legs trembled beneath her borrowed wedding dress. She hadn't meant for this! She did not wish to impersonate their goddess, only to retrieve her sister.

Odessa looked out over the crowd, at the tops of the heads of the clanspeople. Not one head remained unbowed, except for one. Alaric stared at her in disbelief. He strained against the man holding him, trying to get to her. She shook her head, willing him to stay put.

171

"I'm not Narah." Her voice wavered as she spoke. "Please. Stand."

Her words broke Connell from his stunned silence. "Of course, you are not the goddess. You are nothing more than the Northern princess."

People flicked their eyes to her, assessing her anew.

"I've come for my sister." She rolled her shoulders back and spoke with a confidence she did not feel.

Connell sneered.

"I will trade myself for her," she added before he could refuse. The chief's eyes widened in surprise. "It is me you want. I am marked by Narah. My sister has nothing more than a small blemish on her face. You are making a mistake."

She heard Alaric's pained groans from the crowd, but she kept her eyes on Connell. His gaze drifted from her to Faye and back. A line of sweat rolled down her back and froze to her skin. She swallowed hard.

Her only contingency plan involved the two guards waiting farther back in the woods. If anything went wrong, they had explicit instructions to save Faye at all costs and leave Odessa to her fate. Connell's gaze flicked over her shoulder, spotting her father's men. The man was shrewd, and Odessa could clearly see him assessing his options. She guessed there were at least one hundred clansmen in this field, but none were armed. If she let her father's men loose, the casualties would be high.

"And if I agree, your men leave with the little princess?"

Odessa nodded. Even if she had any, the words would have stuck in her dry throat. She understood his meaning of course. If the guards left with Faye, Odessa would be left alone with the clan. Panic threatened to overtake her. Fear flooded her bloodstream and every bone screamed at her to run. But there was nowhere for her to go.

Connell narrowed his eyes, making her wait for his decision for so long she feared she would suffocate.

"I agree to the trade."

A pained shout reached her from the back of the crowd, but if she looked at Alaric now, she would lose her grip on the small tether that still held onto her emotions. Instead, Odessa glanced back at Andrew, and he stepped forward to claim Faye. Most of the clan had returned to their feet, and Andrew eyed them warily as though they might spring at him at any moment. If she was being honest, Odessa wasn't entirely sure they wouldn't.

Looking out at the faces, she recognized very few from her time spent in their village. The sickness and her precarious position among them kept her isolated. But she had felt loved and accepted by Alaric's family, and when she looked at the crowd again, all she saw was fear in their eyes.

Andrew scooped Faye into his arms. Odessa ran a hand over the girl's hair, and she smiled in her sleep. He handed her up to the other guard and remounted his horse. As the hoofbeats echoed through the forest, Odessa turned back to Connell's hard stare.

He had the knife in his hand, and he gestured toward the stone slab with his other. "I promise to make it quick, princess."

She stepped toward the stone. Close enough to see Connell's wide eyes, his pupils blown huge and black.

His face was pale in the moonlight and beads of sweat glistened on his forehead despite the freezing temperatures. His fevered gaze never left her face, and she couldn't help but notice how the knife shook in his hand.

Odessa swallowed hard and took the one chance she had.

"I want to offer you a deal."

The chief blinked and some of the mania left his eyes. "A deal?"

The crowd shifted, shuffling in the cold.

"Yes. I've come to propose a marriage alliance with the Northern kingdom."

A collective gasp rose from the clan, but if Connell was shocked, he didn't let it show on his face.

"The terms of the trade were your life for your sister's. Do you go back on your word, princess?"

Odessa struggled to maintain her composure under the man's fierce glare. Her legs threatened to give out beneath her.

"Of course not. If you do not like my terms, then I will uphold my end of the trade. But you may find I am worth more to you alive than dead."

The crowd was excited now, murmurs and whispers filled the night. What would she propose? Could the Kalonian princess actually help them? Odessa felt the wind shifting in her favor.

"What is it you offer us?"

The people quieted to hear what she had to say.

"I will marry into the clan as a show of goodwill from my father. In return for keeping his daughters safe, he offers the Clan of the Wolf his best healers as well as protection from Melantha. He only asks if the time should come when Kalon needs the Wolves they will return the favor."

Connell narrowed his eyes. "We will not fight the king's wars."

"My father doesn't expect you to. He has a large army. He only asks for the Wolves to stand with the North if he asks them to." Her father had been explicit about this part of the bargain. Odessa's only concern had been to get Faye home safely, but the king wanted assurance that the Wolves would stand with the North. It had never been done before, and she worried she had overstepped the Wolves' patience.

The crowd came alive at her words and questions were pelted at her from all directions.

"When will the healers arrive?"

"Why should we help the Northern king?"

"The clans stand alone!"

"Can the healers save my baby?"

"What about my father?"

"Enough!" Connell raised a hand above the crowd and waited for silence. It took several minutes for the people to settle. As he stood waiting, four people stepped forward to join him in front of the stone slab.

Odessa recognized the other elders from her arrival here weeks ago. Connell turned to them reluctantly and they formed a tight circle of bent heads. Apparently, the elders weren't willing to let Connell make a decision about this on his own.

Her gaze fell to the edge of the clearing as she waited for their verdict. Alaric remained on his knees; his arm twisted viciously behind his back. His forehead was creased in pain, and she watched the rapid rise and fall of his chest. She tried to give him a small smile to tell him not to lose hope, but her cheeks were frozen from the cold or perhaps the fear.

As their eyes stayed locked across the snowy field, Odessa admitted to herself saving Faye had not been her only purpose in returning. If her plan worked, she would gain something too. The husband she wanted and the freedom she desired.

Connell cleared his throat, and the crowd fell silent once again. Odessa's eyes snapped back to him. The breath burned in her lungs as she waited for his answer.

"The clan accepts your proposal."

The earth rocked beneath her feet as relief swept through her. Thank the gods! She lived! At last, she truly lived!

"You will stay here with the clan until we find you a suitable husband." Was that disappointment flashing in Connell's narrowed eyes? It didn't matter. He had been overruled. And now just one more thing…

"Narah has already chosen a husband for me." Connell's stare burned into the side of her face, but now she looked at only one man as she spoke. "He is light and dark. Alaric is marked for me."

The man holding him back finally released his arm, and Alaric staggered to his feet. The crowd between them parted, voices rising louder and louder now, a sea of burning questions and cautious hope. But Odessa couldn't hear any of it over the blood pulsing in her ears.

She stumbled toward him on numb legs, and he was upon her, his arms around her, and she collapsed into him. Safe, at last.

****

"Damn it, Odessa!" Nolan cursed into the still

night. He finally had a clear shot at the barbarian for the first time all evening, but too quickly Odessa was in front of the man, blocking him. Nolan's grip on his bow tightened; his half-frozen fingers burned with the need to let the arrow fly. But he couldn't risk missing his target and hitting his betrothed.

He lowered his bow and watched the scene in the field. From atop his horse hidden far behind the tree line, he had seen Faye carried away by two of the king's men, but he couldn't for the life of him figure out what Odessa had said to make it happen.

It didn't take him long to piece together what the clan wanted her for. The knife, the stone slab, the chanting. It was obvious the clan had returned to its savage ways and planned to sacrifice a princess. He would be damned if he allowed that to happen.

But somehow Odessa had stayed the chief's hand and now she stood in the midst of the clan, a princess among wolves, and it was the chief that strode from the clearing. She must have accomplished what her father sent her to do and formed an alliance, but what were the terms?

Slowly, the people broke off into small groups and returned to their homes in the village. As the field emptied, Nolan was awarded a better view of Odessa and the barbarian. The man scooped her up in his arms and carried her to the trail back to the village. What was he doing with her?

Odessa was so small and fragile in the beast's arms. Was he stealing her or saving her? From where Nolan sat in the cold forest, it was impossible to tell.

Chapter 25: Safety in an Unsafe World

Odessa didn't remember Alaric carrying her or the walk back to his home. Her body, unable to deal with the intense emotions of the past two days, had fallen into a deep sleep.

When she awoke in the middle of the night, she was back in the little house, and Alaric was dozing in a chair beside her bed. She peered at him from under the pile of fur blankets. He was to be her husband. She had chosen him and now he was hers. But what if he didn't want her?

The enormity of the situation crashed down upon her. She managed to save Faye and for that, she would be eternally grateful. But she had also made a deal with the clan. One that involved her staying here and living among them. How would they treat her? What if they never accepted her?

A new thought sent a fresh round of terror through her veins. What would stop her father from weaseling out of his end of the bargain? He had Faye back. He didn't care at all about Odessa. She squeezed her eyes shut and prayed to whatever goddess saved her last night to continue her protection.

Alaric shifted beside her. His neck was bent at a horribly uncomfortable angle. It would be stiff in the morning.

"Alaric," she whispered into the darkness.

He sat up, blinking, and focused on her face. "You're awake." His voice was gruff and thick from sleep.

"I'm sorry to wake you." She sat and wrapped a blanket around her shoulders. "You looked uncomfortable. I can make room for you in the bed. If you'd like." Her cheeks heated at her boldness. The last time they shared a bed he had barely touched her, even though she wanted him to. But the way he had kissed her in the woods near Kalon before returning home made her believe that perhaps he wanted her, too.

He glanced at the bed and furrowed his brow. "I'm fine here."

Her heart sank at his curt words. She had declared him hers in front of the entire clan, but now he could barely look at her. Her insides burned with embarrassment.

"You should get some more rest."

"You're angry with me?" Her question was so quiet she wasn't sure he heard her until he finally met her eye.

He ran a hand down his face, breathing in and out deeply. But when he returned her gaze, he did not look any calmer.

"You could have been killed," he growled. "You nearly were. I sent you away from here to protect you and you came back!" He grew louder with every word.

"I had to!"

"You had to?" He flung the words at her, standing abruptly. He towered over where she sat on the bed, but she refused to be intimidated by him.

"Yes! My sister was in danger!" She rose from the bed, dropping the blankets. Her too-tight wedding dress squeezed her bosom and made her breathing even more erratic.

"Loosen these ties before I faint again!" She spun and presented him with her back. For a moment no one moved, and the only sound was Alaric's harsh breathing behind her. A tremor ran through her body as she waited, until finally, his fingers ran along her spine, loosening the laces of her dress. She took a deep inhale for the first time all day.

"Oh…thank you." When she turned back to Alaric, he was studying her with a still creased brow. She pressed her thumb into the space between his eyebrows, smoothing out the worry she found there.

"I tried to stop them." His voice was nothing more than a choked rasp.

"I'm sure you did."

"Gods, when I saw you in the clearing, I thought for sure I was hallucinating. You were so…" He cupped her cheek with his hand. "So…terrifyingly beautiful."

"I never meant to scare you. I only did what I had to do. You would have done the same."

He gave a small nod, not able to argue further. Of course, he would have risked his life for any one of his siblings, and she had done the same. He couldn't fault her for it.

Alaric dropped his hand from her face and shifted on his feet. Their impending marriage weighed heavy on her mind, but nerves fluttered in her gut. How did one broach the subject of a marriage with someone they hardly knew? A marriage required for safety in an unsafe world?

"Your father's healers…" Alaric's words broke through her thoughts. "Will they be able to help?" The worry lines were back between his brows. Of course, he was thinking of his sister and not the desperate marriage alliance Odessa had proposed.

"I do. They are the best in the land, revered for their cures." Her fingers itched to reach out and touch him, to comfort him, but suddenly he seemed miles away.

He cleared his throat. "You should get some sleep. The elders want us married in the morning."

It was the first he had spoken of it and the word sounded choked and miserable in his mouth. He didn't want to marry her. He merely acted as he usually did, to protect his family and his people. If his clan insisted he marry the cursed princess, he would do it.

Odessa brought a hand to her marked cheek and swallowed the tears threatening to spill over. She had saved her sister the only way she could. Alaric would not be a bad husband to her, of that she was certain. She tamped down her disappointment at his lack of enthusiasm for the plan. It had been foolish of her to think he would be happy. But she was free of her father, free of her prison, and she was determined to make the most of this second chance.

"I will send word to my father as soon as it is done."

Alaric's eyes searched her face a moment longer before turning toward the door.

"I wanted to ensure you were alright, but now I should check on Arowyn and allow my aunt to return to her own family."

He hadn't told her what happened to him between her escape and her return, but the dark shadows under his eyes and the way his shoulders sagged in exhaustion told her enough. She didn't ask but instead let him go, leaving her alone in the small house once again.

Odessa removed the wedding dress and folded it neatly at the end of the sleeping bench. She slipped back beneath the warmth of the furs and attempted to get some rest. Tomorrow was her wedding day. Again. With any luck, this one would end with a marriage.

Chapter 26: Cleansed

The steam rose up from the center of the bathhouse, obscuring his uncles from view. Alaric sat sweating on the wooden bench across from them, a length of linen wrapped around his waist. The trip to the bathhouse was supposed to cleanse him of his bachelorhood and prepare him for marriage, but he wasn't sure it would be enough.

His uncles were quiet, which was not entirely unusual, but weren't they supposed to impart their wisdom for a happy married life? None of them seemed to have anything to say about their nephew marrying a Kalonian princess.

Merrick cleared his throat, and Alaric found his face through the steam. "She is brave, your future wife." His uncles, Rhys and Rawlin, nodded in agreement.

The men who had married his mother's sisters were all similar in temperament, steady and calm like the still waters of the lake the clan fished in the summer months. They were all the opposite of his own father and he often wondered what led his mother to choose the hot-headed man.

Rhys shifted his bulk on the bench, the largest of the three, his big belly hung over his linen cloth. "Her face surely is a good omen."

No one bothered to mention it was this same face

that nearly got the woman killed. Apparently, in less than twenty-four hours, the clan had smoothly transitioned to believing Odessa was more useful to them alive. Alaric clenched his fists at his sides. None of them had looked at her like he had. None had seen her as the sweet, strong woman he knew her to be. She was nothing more than a symbol to them.

And now she was to be his wife. His stomach swooped in anticipation. His mind raced over their moments together, the stolen kisses and fervent embraces. But how many of her actions had been out of a desperate need for his protection and how many had been because she wanted him? He was thankful for the heat of the sauna. His uncles did not need to see him blush like a boy.

"She will make you a good wife." Rawlin wiped a massive hand across his brow, brushing away the sweat. "And her healers will save our people."

The words hung between the men, hovering in the steam rising off the heated rocks. No one spoke of their sick family members, their sons, and daughters that lay at home in their beds writhing with fever dreams. The weight of their lives sat heavily on Alaric's shoulders.

The sweat coated his chest, dampening the hair. A dunk in the cold tub outside the steam house would seal his new life. But he was anything but ready to tie his life to the princess. Dueling emotions warred inside him. Fear and worry for his family, nervous anticipation at becoming a husband. How could he ever keep them all safe?

He leaned his head back against the wall of the little hut, filling his lungs with the humid air, thinking about his life's sudden change in direction. Odessa had turned his world upside down more than once already. What would it be like with her as his wife?

A dawning revelation had his insides uncoiling for the first time in weeks. Odessa had done more than save her sister last night. She had saved him as well. Connell had no choice but to release him when Narah's chosen one chose him. A calm washed over him, a peace he hadn't felt since before his mother died filled his chest.

Odessa was not here to add one more person to his list of people he had to protect. No, she had come back to help him as she promised. He sighed and straightened on the bench. His uncles watched him with furrowed brows. Did they worry he would back out? Did they think he would let his family down like his father had so many times?

Alaric rolled back his shoulders and stood in the small space. He would be a good husband to Odessa and maybe someday their arrangement would be more than political. He would see to it that she never regretted her decision to place her trust in him.

"Uncles, I am ready."

The men grunted in relief. It was time.

****

Odessa had never been in such a tight space with so many naked women in her life. Or so many women at all, clothed or otherwise, for that matter. At most when they were young, her sisters would visit her for tea in the afternoons after sneaking away from their tutors, or she would have an awkward run-in with her stepmother and Faye in the halls of the castle. But there was no one in her life with which she enjoyed such ease. She watched with envy as Alaric's aunts chatted, and teased, brushing hair from each other's faces with such casual and unconditional love causing a familiar ache to throb in Odessa's chest.

The three imposing women, Layla, Iya, and Yara sat across from her in the little steam hut. Once they were settled, all three women studied her with slitted eyes. Odessa kept an arm wrapped around her chest and was thankful for the length of linen covering her lower half. Nevertheless, she felt completely exposed. She was certain the woman could see straight through her, right to the tangled ball of nerves at her center.

Even as their company made her fidget in her seat and made her hand drift self-consciously to the marked side of her face, her needy, hungry heart was happy for their presence. If she had to choose between returning to her chambers alone or facing these formidable women every day, she would, without hesitation, choose the latter.

Layla, who had stitched Alaric's arm after the battle, tossed a copper braid over her bare shoulder. She gave Odessa a small smile. That was encouraging, at least. Odessa wiped a hand across her sweaty brow. Were they trying to cook her alive?

"So, you are to marry our Alaric," Layla began, leaning forward to add another ladle full of water onto the hot rocks, the loud hiss filling the small space. The steam clouded the air between them. "He is a good man."

"Yes, of course." Odessa nodded, her damp hair sticking to the sides of her face. How much longer would she be subjected to this torture chamber? She was meant to be cleansing herself of her maidenhood to prepare for becoming a wife, which was preposterous considering she was no maiden. But it didn't seem wise to question the clan's traditions on her first official day as one of them.

"But you..." Iya chimed in menacingly. She was the oldest of the sisters. Her hair was silver, and her face deeply creased in a permanent scowl. Odessa braced herself for whatever came next. "You are a princess. Blessed by the goddess. Spared from death." The older woman arched a gray eyebrow, assessing Odessa with eyes the color of freshly tilled earth.

Odessa waited for the rest of her speech, the part that would surely follow about her cursed face and her cursed luck. The elders believed her when she said she was more valuable alive than dead, but would these women believe it too?

Iya wrapped her arms across her full chest, her eyes never leaving Odessa's face. "How will you adjust to life in our small village?"

Odessa nearly laughed out loud at the unexpected question. A life in this small village was more life than she ever expected to live! A husband and a home of her own. Perhaps children one day...her stomach fluttered at the possibilities. Living here would be an adjustment for sure, but not for the reasons the woman thought it would be.

"I have a lot to learn, but I plan to be a good wife to Alaric. I think my life here will be a good one."

The three women sighed out as one. Yara leaned forward and grabbed her free hand, squeezing it in her own. The youngest of the sisters, her dark hair was swept off her neck in braids crisscrossed atop her head.

"And we welcome you."

Odessa returned her smile, choking back tears at the woman's kind words. It wasn't an apology for the treatment she had received at the hands of the clan, but it was a start. Odessa breathed out a small sigh of relief. This one small gesture of acceptance was more than she had ever received from her own father, and she grabbed onto it with both hands.

"Now..." Yara sat back with a grin. "You don't need us to explain what happens on the wedding night, do you?"

Odessa's eyes widened. "Uh...no...that won't be necessary." If her face hadn't already been bright red from the heat, she was sure it would be crimson now.

Layla threw her head back and laughed, smacking a naked thigh with her hand.

"Thank the gods for that," Iya muttered, leaning her head against the wooden wall behind her. "That boy has enough to worry about."

Chapter 27: A Marriage of Equals

For the second time in twenty-four hours, Odessa took his breath away. She stood outside his Aunt Layla's house, wrapped in the same white cloak she wore the night before. But now her hair was intricately braided in the way of a bride, and a crown of holly sat atop her head. She was half Kalonian and half Wolf, and she was all his. His heart thundered in his chest.

The sun dipped low in the sky, sending long shadows across the snow-covered garden. He strode to his uncle's house to claim his bride. Odessa's face raised at his approach. Her lips curved into a smile, and he missed a step, nearly tripping over his own feet.

"Careful, brother." Weylyn patted him heartily on the back, laughing as he came up beside him. A quick retort was on the tip of Alaric's tongue, but he held it back. Seeing his brother with a smile on his face was a rare enough event that he didn't want to ruin it, especially after what he had put the family through in the last week. Faolan walked along Alaric's other side, his eyes on his own feet. The boy hadn't said much since Alaric returned home, announcing both his freedom and impending marriage. It was not lost on any of them that this wedding was a rushed and urgent affair.

Typically, clan weddings lasted for days with feasting and drinking long into the nights. But Alaric's wedding was happening before any of them could prepare for it. There would be no celebration, only a hastily written message to Odessa's father indicating the deed was done. Alaric was acutely aware that Arowyn's life depended on this alliance and the healers it would bring to the clan.

Rieka squeezed his hand in her small one and brought his attention back to the present moment. His wedding day. Gods, how did he get here?

The small family stopped in front of where Alaric's aunts and uncles were gathered. Arowyn remained home in bed with Iya looking after her, but the rest of the family would bear witness to the wedding vows. Alaric released Rieka's hand and smiled at his sister's solemn face.

"All will be well," he whispered to her, and she rewarded him with a small smile. He prayed it was the truth.

"Alaric, your bride awaits." Merrick's voice cut through his worries.

"Yes, uncle." He grabbed the older man's offered hand in his and pulled him in for a hug. Each of his uncles followed suit and then he was assaulted by kisses and kind words from his aunts. It pained him that his cousins remained home, fearful of the sickness that spread so easily from person to person. He never imagined his wedding would be so sparse and fraught with anxiety.

Alaric stepped out of Layla's embrace and into the circle of pine boughs his aunts had crafted in the garden. Odessa stood in the center waiting for him. He took a deep shuddering breath and met her gaze. The unwavering trust he found there stole his voice. This was not the first time she put her life in his hands, and he was determined not to fail her this time.

"Hello, princess." He took her hands in his. They trembled in his grasp. He held them tighter, warming them with his own.

"Hello." Her full lips tipped up into a smile.

Her smile encouraged him. "Do you know how this will work?" he asked, realizing she may not know anything of the clan's marriage rituals.

She shook her head, so he went on. "We will exchange vows and rings. There will be no officiant, only witnesses. We only need to make promises to each other, no one else."

Her brow creased with worry. His heart tripped. Was she having second thoughts? Then what would they do? He had no desire to force a woman to marry him, but he was painfully aware of how few choices they had.

"What is it?" He spoke softly, ignoring the others waiting impatiently in the garden. Odessa was his only concern.

"I don't have a ring."

Relief flooded through his veins. That he could fix.

"I have rings for each of us." He reached into the small pouch hanging from his waist and pulled out two silver bands. They lay nestled together in his palm, glinting in the last light of day as he held them out to show her. Odessa would wear his mother's ring and he would wear his grandfather's, having no desire to keep any part of his own father near him.

Each ring was carved with twisted knots around the band. They were simple and sturdy. They didn't belong on the hand of a princess, but they were all he had.

"They're lovely." Odessa ran a finger around each ring, and it was only now that Alaric realized she never wore jewelry of her own.

"Are you ready?" His blood thrummed in his ears. How could either of them be ready? They barely had time to recover from the solstice and now they were being thrust together with lives hanging in the balance.

But if he was being honest with himself, this was what he had wanted all along. Ever since he saw Odessa at the edge of the wood, he knew he belonged to her. Narah hadn't marked her for the clan, she had marked her for him. The fact that they had made it to this place was nothing short of a miracle. And he wasn't about to let it slip through his fingers.

"I am." Odessa's voice was steady, and her gaze locked with his. The way she looked at him gave him hope that she felt it too, that this was about more than alliances and survival. This was about them.

The air grew colder as the sun dipped lower in the sky, painting the snow around them violet. Their breath mingled in steam clouds between them as Alaric took Odessa's hand once more. Delicate flakes of snow drifted down, landing in Odessa's dark hair. The light on the melting crystals gave the impression of stars in the night sky. She tilted her face up to his and once again he fell in love with both sides of her, the light and the dark. He vowed to himself he would cherish them both.

He cleared his throat and began the vows.

"I give to you all that I am and all that I have, freely and with joy.

I pledge my life to you from this day on, for as long as we both wish it.

Together we will walk the road of life side by side. The journey will be sweeter if we make it hand in hand.

I pledge to you my living and dying,

My tears and my laughter.

I pledge my strength when you are weak and my admiration when you are strong.

Together we will make a home, a family, a life.

You are the stars in my sky and the light of my days.

This is my wedding vow to you.

This is a marriage of equals."

He brushed the tears from her cheeks with his thumb and helped her recite the vows back to him. When she spoke the last line, he slid his mother's ring onto her finger. She took the larger ring from his hand and slid it onto his finger, sealing in the vows they had made in front of his family.

Before he could stop himself, he grabbed her face in his hands and pressed his mouth to hers. The silence around them was deafening as she kissed him back, wrapping her hands in the warmth of his furs and pulling him closer. There was no cheering or yelling of encouragement as there had been at the many clan weddings he had attended throughout his life. Instead, there was only the sound of hoofbeats as his uncle raced off to deliver the message to the king. That and the sound of Alaric's thumping heart. Perhaps the princess could love him back after all.

****

"She's sleeping." Alaric slipped back into the little house after checking on Arowyn and found Odessa in nearly the same spot he had left her. She glanced at him from her seat by the fire where she was warming her toes.

"The rest is good for her."

He nodded, not sure if it was true or not, but there wasn't anything they could do for her now. Gods willing the Kalonian healers would be here by morning.

"You're still wearing your cloak."

Odessa peeked at him from under the fur-lined hood. "I'm frozen." She rubbed her hands along her arms to warm them, but she smiled at him through her discomfort.

Alaric shucked layers of his own furs until he was down to his wool tunic. He added more wood to the fire.

"You will have to get used to the cold now that you're my wife." He had meant to tease her, but the word wife hung heavy between them.

Odessa looked away and studied her feet. "I suppose I will." She spoke softly, carefully, her passion from the ceremony transformed into shyness now that they were alone. Did she regret her decision?

He moved to the cooking platform, filled two mugs with leaves for tea, and put the kettle to boil over the fire. He needed to do something with his hands. There was more he should say to comfort her or make her at home here, but he had no idea what they were. Words had never come easily to him and the current moment was no different.

Alaric poured the steaming water over the leaves and handed a mug to Odessa. The earthy scent wafted toward him as he sat at the table across from her. He watched as she wrapped her delicate fingers around the mug and sighed as she inhaled deeply.

"I feel warmer already." She smiled at him over

her mug and the pride and happiness he felt at her statement was absurd. He made the woman tea, not exactly a tale the storytellers would relay down the generations. Even still he smiled back at her, relaxing into his chair.

She blew across her tea to cool it and took a small sip. Her thickly braided hair hung over her shoulder and the holly crown still sat on her head. He was meant to take it off when they consummated the marriage. His face heated, imagining all the things he wished to do with his new bride.

Alaric had spent many wedding nights with friends and cousins shouting and singing drunkenly outside the newlyweds' door while they enjoyed each other inside. But it was quiet outside the little house. Another reminder of the strange situation he found himself in. The clan required no proof the marriage had been consummated and the letter was already sent to Kalon.

He flicked his eyes back to Odessa's face and wished he could read her thoughts. It would certainly make things easier. He would rather cut off his own tongue than have to ask his wife if she wished to officially share his bed.

Odessa shrugged out of her cloak. She wore the same white dress she wore last night. It dipped low in the front and hugged close to her body, revealing a tantalizing amount of skin. The sleeves were long and belled out at her hands, and he knew from last night the dress laced up her back with silk ribbons.

He remembered the feel of them slipping through his fingers, imagined untying them now, pictured the way the dress would look pooled on the floor. He groaned. Odessa's head jerked up.

"Are you alright?"

Alaric cleared his throat and attempted to clear his mind. "Yes. Fine."

She tipped her head to the side, considering him and her lips curled into that small knowing smile again.

"It was a beautiful ceremony."

He blinked. Ceremony? Right, the wedding. Their wedding. Gods, the flushed skin on her chest was distracting. Especially the way the pink continued between her breasts. A trail he would like to follow. With his tongue.

She raised an eyebrow.

He cleared his throat again. "It was. Even if it was a bit smaller than usual."

"Are weddings usually large affairs here?" She leaned back in her chair taking away the view he had been enjoying.

"Oh yes. They often go on for days. Is it not like that in Kalon?"

Sadness shadowed her face for a moment before she spoke. "They last for only a day, but that is about all I know. I've never attended one."

Guilt washed over him for asking. He should have known. His fists curled at his sides. If he ever came face to face with her father, he would have a very hard time not slamming his fist into the man's face. And imagine the problems that would cause.

"Wearing this wedding dress is about as close as I've ever come to a Kalonian wedding. It must have belonged to one of my sisters."

She was still talking, but Alaric heard none of it. He stopped listening when he heard the words 'wedding dress'. Something had struck him odd about the dress, but he hadn't figured it out until right now. She was wearing a wedding dress. When she arrived here last night, she was already dressed for a wedding. But why? Did she think they would be married on the spot? Did it matter what she wore to such a hasty wedding? Or had she already been dressed for a wedding when she found out about her sister being kidnapped?

"Anyway, it doesn't fit very well, but I guess it worked out alright—"

"Princess,"

She looked up at his abrupt interruption. "Yes?"

"Why were you wearing a wedding dress yesterday?"

"I…uh…" She must have seen something in his face because she was no longer able to form a coherent sentence.

"Tell me. Were you intending on marrying someone else, yesterday?" His voice was a low growl in his chest and a distant part of himself felt bad for scaring her. But another part of him, a part he was not proud of, was glad. It was one thing to be backed into this marriage, but to be given a second-hand bride! How foolish he had been to believe this marriage could be anything more than it was: a way for Odessa to save her sister and herself.

He leaned forward across the table. Her eyes had gone wide and panicked like a deer cornered by a hunter. "You must understand…I had no say in the matter…"

"Who was it, Odessa?"

She hesitated. "Nolan."

Her knight! Of course! He stood abruptly, knocking into the table and sloshing the tea over the sides of the mug.

"Please, listen to me! I didn't want to marry him! I don't know why my father changed his mind, but suddenly he wanted me married off and gone." She stood too and followed him across the small space until she stood in front of him, so close he could feel her warmth. Lavender and rosemary wrapped around him. If he could just take her in his arms, if things could be simple for once!

But sharp, prickly emotions rolled around inside him. Embarrassment and jealousy fought for his attention. Only a day ago, his wife was ready to marry another man. A man far better suited for her. If it hadn't been for the actions of his clan, she would be safe with her knight right now. Anger tightened his throat and shame heated his cheeks. He needed to get out of here.

"I need to check on my sister." He reached for his cloak, but Odessa grabbed his arm.

"No, you don't."

"I do." He spoke through clenched teeth in a tone that usually sent his younger siblings running but Odessa didn't back down.

"You need to stay here and talk to your wife."

That word again. Wife. What was he supposed to do with this wife? This wife belonged with a different man.

"You talk." He managed to grind out the words.

"Okay, fine. But you need to listen." She waited with a hand on one hip until he nodded in agreement. He dropped the cloak onto the bench by the door.

"Marrying Nolan was not my choice. I had no desire to be anywhere near the man, but you might recall it was you who sent me back to Kalon. It was you who refused to listen to me when I said there might be another way." With each accusation, she poked a dainty finger into his chest.

"I told you we could convince Connell to use me in a different way to help the clan, but you wouldn't listen. You sent me back into the hands of my father."

Alaric opened his mouth to protest. He had only been trying to save her life! She held up a hand to silence him. He ground his teeth together until his jaw hurt.

"And once I was home, my father and Nolan came to an agreement. I was to marry Nolan and be whisked off to the countryside where I could cause no further problems. And that is exactly what would have happened, had your clansmen not come and abducted my sister!"

He grimaced. He was not proud of his people for falling for Connell's lies, but a trickle of relief flowed through him as well. Nolan did not deserve her.

"It was me who formed the plan to save her. It was me who negotiated the alliance." With each word she stepped closer until his back was against the wall, and she was pressed against him.

"And it was me who chose you." She paused and held his stare, her chest rising and falling rapidly. "And do you know why I chose you?"

Alaric swallowed hard and shook his head. This delicate princess had him pinned to the wall, and there was nowhere he'd rather be.

"Because I wanted you." She stretched up onto her toes and reached her arms around his neck. Her fingers tangled in his hair as she pulled him closer. He leaned his forehead against hers, and she whispered against his lips.

"Do you want me, too?"

Chapter 28: Together

Alaric hesitated for a heartbeat, and then two. The moment dragged out between them. Odessa's question filled the space with possibility. She'd confessed everything including the real reason she came back here. Of course, she needed to save Faye, but her own selfish reason intertwined with the selfless one. She needed to be free of her father, she wanted her own life, and she wanted Alaric.

His forehead still leaned against hers and at some point, his hands had found their way to her hips. Another breath more and she would die on the spot from waiting. But the next breath never came. His lips crashed onto hers and stole the air from her lungs.

He pulled her closer, his fingers digging into her hip bones.

"Of course, I want you," he groaned, pulling away from her lips only long enough to growl the words. "I've wanted you since the day I found you in the woods." His lips ravaged hers, licking and biting until she opened for him, and his tongue stole inside, caressing her until she matched his groans with her own.

Alaric's hands traced the outline of her body, running over her hips and waist, before settling firmly on her bottom. He squeezed her flesh and his moan of approval vibrated across her lips. His hands worked their way up her back and found her laces. He tugged and pulled until he tore away from her with an exasperated sigh.

"Who tied you into this thing?" He spun her around and continued yanking on her laces so hard she had to fight back the giggles threatening to spill from her mouth.

After another several tense moments of muttered curses from behind her, Alaric dropped the ties and turned her back around.

"Do you care much for this dress?" he asked, his face flushed.

"Not at all." Odessa bit her bottom lip to contain her mirth at his frustration.

"Good."

Before she had a chance to process what he was doing, Alaric grabbed the dagger hanging from his belt, turned her back around, and sliced through the silk laces in one smooth cut. He slammed the knife onto the bench and easily loosened the cut ties.

Oxygen flooded into Odessa's lungs as her body expanded to its normal size. The relief only lasted a second before it quickly returned to desire. Alaric's hands skated across the skin of her back as he parted the dress and let it slip off her shoulders. He lifted her heavy braid and draped it over her shoulder, exposing the sensitive skin of her neck. She shivered as his lips kissed and nipped at her nape, traveling lower to where her neck met her shoulder. He sucked the delicate skin there until she gasped his name.

Alaric's hands gripped her arms, searing her through the thin fabric of her chemise. He turned her around once more. Odessa expected to be pulled into his embrace, longed for it in fact, but instead he kept her at arm's length. His eyes raked over her, leaving her body trembling in their wake. The thin silk undergarment she wore was practically transparent, and his gaze had gone dark with desire.

He still wore his tunic and tight leather trousers, making Odessa feel even more exposed in comparison. His wide leather belt sat low on his hips, and she reached out to unbuckle it. Her fingers trembled as she removed it and tossed it onto the bench next to the forgotten dagger. When she met Alaric's eyes again, his lips curved into a lopsided grin.

"That's a good start, princess." He tugged the tunic over his head, revealing the carved muscle beneath. A howling wolf was tattooed on his chest, and Odessa ran a hand across it. Alaric's skin pebbled beneath her touch.

"Did it hurt?"

He shrugged and she found her hands smoothing across his shoulders and over the ridges of his arms.

"Maybe. But not enough to remember after the whisky that came with it." He was still smiling, and the sight was so rare and beautiful, tears stung behind her eyes.

He stepped toward her and cupped her face in his hands. His kiss, when it came, was hungry and greedy. She met his hunger with her own, opening deeper for him, her body a frenzy of heat and need. She whimpered and purred with only a distant realization that those sounds came from her.

Alaric gripped her bottom once more and lifted her into his arms. She wrapped her legs around his waist and let herself be carried to the bed. The holly crown lay on the floor by the door, already forgotten.

Odessa let out a small squeak of protest as he pulled his lips from hers, but he left a trail of kisses across her nose and cheeks to soothe her. He lowered her gently onto the bed. She lay back into the pile of furs and blankets and gazed at the man above her. The smile on his face had been replaced with a look of sheer desire, and she was sure it was mirrored on her own.

She had never wanted anyone like this, not this strongly, not like she wanted sunshine, or sea-salted air, or honey licked straight off the comb. She wanted Alaric like she wanted all the delicious and wonderful things in life.

Being with Nolan had been desperation, not love. Laying with him had been an attempt to fill her empty heart and her empty life. But being with Alaric felt like reaching for the things she truly deserved, not scrabbling after the crumbs that were thrown to her. The way Alaric looked at her, truly looked at her, felt like freedom.

He crawled over the top of her, dragging his hot skin across her silk-clad torso. It was torture. "The first time I take you should be in our bed and not against the door," he growled in her ear. Heat pooled in her core at his words.

"The first time?"

She could feel his grin against her cheek. "You didn't think once would be enough, did you, princess?"

Suddenly, she didn't mind the endearment. Alaric worked his way down her body, trailing kisses in his wake. He bunched up her chemise around her hips and his lips brushed against her inner thighs, one and then the other. She squirmed under his touch, but he held her tight.

"I'm going to kiss you here." His words tickled her overly sensitive skin. She peered down the length of her body at where he kneeled between her legs. His hair had come undone and lay hanging at his shoulders. His skin was golden in the firelight and his eyes never left her face. She nodded once, unable to tell him how much she wanted him to do just that, to kiss her there. She had never imagined…

Oh, holy gods! Alaric bent his head and worshipped between her legs. The world tipped and Odessa squeezed her eyes shut at the sensation. She dug her fingers into his shoulders, needing to touch him. What was he doing to her?

The heat built and built until she was nothing but sensation.

"Alaric," she moaned, needing something, needing more, but she didn't have the words to tell him.

He made a gentle humming noise against her overwrought flesh, and she thrust wantonly against his face. He slid a finger inside her and another, never relenting with his tongue. Odessa's breaths were nothing more than ragged gasps as she climbed higher and higher towards that unreachable peak. She had never been this close before, never thought it was possible.

Alaric raised his head, replacing his mouth with his thumb, and circled hard and fast. He held her stare as she tumbled over the edge, bucking beneath his hand. Pleasure so intense it was nearly pain radiated out from her core. She moaned and writhed until he had wrung every last bit of it from her. Then he gently removed his hand and dusted kisses along her thighs and belly as she returned to her senses.

He slid alongside her and gathered her in his arms.

"I've never…I mean I didn't know…"

She peered up at him. "It was never like that." She thought he might tease her, but instead, a shadow crossed his face. Did she just remind him she had been with another man? She had no intention of discussing Nolan again even if it was to discuss his shortcomings in bed.

Alaric shook his head, his hair rustling against the pillows. "It should be. He didn't treat you right."

He didn't say more, and Odessa relaxed into him. His kisses soon erased Nolan from her memory. Alaric tugged her chemise up farther, removing his lips from hers only long enough to pull it over her head and toss it to the floor.

She ran her hands across his chest and around to his back. His muscles shifted beneath her fingers as she clung to him. Alaric sucked on her bottom lip as his hands traced every curve of her body as though he were trying to memorize them. He groaned against her mouth as she tugged on the ties of his pants.

His hands covered hers and he laughed, his breath tickling her face.

"Let me. We've destroyed enough clothing this evening." He stood, untangling himself from her and undid his laces, allowing his pants to slide over his hips. Odessa watched greedily from where she lay stretched out in the furs, her body still thrumming with desire.

He towered over her, his gaze raking hungrily over her body. There was something different in his stare now, something untamed and possessive behind his eyes. Something that said he was about to take what was his. It thrilled Odessa to see it. She wanted it, wanted him to claim her like no one else ever had.

Alaric climbed back into the bed, covering her body with his, kissing her sweetly, the kiss completely at odds with the look in his eyes. He pulled away and rested his forehead against hers.

"If we…" he hesitated. "What I mean is…"

He grimaced a bit as he shifted his weight, pulling Odessa's attention to the jagged scar running up his left arm. Not so much a scar yet, but a carefully stitched wound. It reminded her how short a time they'd known each other. Alaric opened his mouth to speak again, and she ran a hand encouragingly down his back.

"If we do this, it means you are my wife." He held her gaze. "Is that what you want? To be a true wife to me?"

"Alaric, I…"

"We will live together. This marriage will protect you. If that is all you wish it to be, I will accept that." He shifted again with pain written across his face. He rolled to his side next to her, unable to support himself on his injured arm any longer.

Odessa rolled toward him and leaned up on her elbow. His expression had changed again, and he looked young and anxious in the firelight.

"I told you how I feel. I chose you. I want you."

"So, you will be my wife then?"

She laughed a little. The marriage ceremony hadn't been enough to convince him they were truly married, but she understood his worry. She had the same one.

"You want me to be? You're the one who didn't have any say in the matter."

He cupped her face with his hand, running a thumb

across her purple cheek. It was strange how little she thought about it now, something that had filled so much of her thoughts before.

"I want you for my wife. In every way." His eyes had gone dark with desire again, and Odessa's heart beat erratically. She answered him by taking his mouth in hers and feasting on his sweet lips.

"Good," she murmured against him. "Because I want you for my husband." She wrapped a leg over his hips until she straddled him, kissing and biting down his neck and chest. He lavished attention on her breasts, the soft hair of his beard tickling her sensitive skin. Odessa straightened causing Alaric to groan in protest at being deprived of her breasts. She reached behind and wrapped her hand around his cock, pressing it against the soft flesh of her bottom. She rolled her hips back and forth until they were both panting.

"Princess," he growled. "Do that much longer and we will never get this marriage consummated." He traced a finger down the line of her neck to the tip of her breast. He rolled the nipple between his fingers. Odessa dropped her head back, her long hair grazing the hand that still stroked Alaric behind her.

She lifted her hips and eased herself onto Alaric's waiting cock. The moan that escaped her lips filled the small house. She had never been so bold in the bedroom, had never taken what she wanted. For a brief moment, a flicker of worry that Alaric would think less of her for such wanton behavior appeared in her mind, but when she opened her eyes and looked at him, he grinned at her.

"What?"

"I like the view."

She admired his ridged torso below her, his bronze skin damp with sweat. "Me too." Odessa leaned forward, and Alaric flicked a tongue over one nipple and then the other. The sensation shot directly to her core, and she quickened her pace, chasing what she needed.

Alaric drove into her, hitting a place inside her she never knew existed. She sighed his name over and over until her throat was raw and sweat trickled down her back. He held tight to her hips, thrusting up as she pushed forward, the pressure building once again. Together they moved, rocking faster until Odessa reached the peak again and tumbled over the side. Alaric held tight to her as he found his release and Odessa collapsed in a heap on top of him.

His heart raced beneath her ear as she lay on his chest. He stroked a hand gently over her hair, pushing the sweaty strands from her face as she slowly came back to herself.

"That's once," he whispered.

She lifted her head to look at him and found the grin she already adored. Being his wife would not be hard at all.

Chapter 29: Broken Promises

Nolan hadn't slept in nearly two days, not since he saw that barbarian haul his beloved Odessa off to his forest shack. The sun had barely crested the horizon, but Nolan was already itching to go find the king and demand more answers. It was dangerous, he knew. He had already pushed the king far enough with his questions, but he couldn't sit idly by and let Odessa be sold off to the clan. She was his and he would have her.

He waited until the dull gray light of dawn penetrated the darkness in his room before stalking out the door in search of Orion. When he found him in his study, the man looked as though he had slept about as much as Nolan had. Dark circles were smudged beneath the king's eyes, and his gray hair stood at odd angles on the man's head as though he had been tugging at it.

The king looked up wearily when Nolan entered and let out a long-suffering sigh. Nolan chose to ignore it and strode forward to where the king sat by the fire.

"Your majesty." He swept into a low bow. "Odessa has yet to return and I—"

"She's not going to." Orion's curt words stopped Nolan in his tracks.

"Ever?"

The king ran a hand down his beard. "The alliance is set. She has married into the clan. I just received word."

"Married?" The word sank into his bones where it would fester. Married into the clan? Had the king lost his mind? "How could you?" The words were out of his mouth before he could think better of it, but the king didn't call for his guards. He only stared wearily at Nolan. He suddenly looked older than his sixty years.

"My daughter has caused me nothing but pain for the past twenty-four years." A shadow crossed his face at the memories. "Sometimes I think it would have been best if I had left her for the spirits of the forest to take when she was a babe."

Nolan swallowed. He never believed the stories of the forest spirits. He knew what happened to babies left by their parents near the edge of the woods. He shuddered.

"But her mother never would have let me rest had I done that. She barely lets me rest as it is now. Even though I try. Even though I gave that girl everything a child could want or need."

Except love. Or freedom. Nolan didn't dare speak the words out loud. He watched as the king shifted in his seat, glancing behind him as though someone was there whispering in his ear. Nolan saw nothing except the slight blowing of the curtains behind them. Odd since the windows were closed.

The king shook his head, his attention returning to Nolan. "It was the best course of action. For the kingdom. And for Odessa."

It was one of the few times Nolan had ever heard the king speak her name, and it sounded odd on his lips.

"After all, it was her idea."

Her idea? Nolan felt the king's gaze on him as his anger boiled over and scorched his insides. He thought the king had sent her away, forced her into this alliance, but it was her. Odessa chose to leave him. She chose that savage over him. After everything Nolan had done for her, after everything the clan had done to her! His hands clenched into fists at his side, and he trembled with the effort to keep his rage inside. This was his king. He forced himself to remember that when all he wanted to do was throttle the man and scream at him for letting her go.

"You formed quite the attachment to my daughter." The king still studied him, realizing for the first time how deep Nolan's feelings ran.

All he could do was give the king a quick nod in agreement.

"You should have come to me sooner." Orion sat back in his chair, his hands over his stomach. Nolan bit the inside of his cheek to keep from saying all the things he wished to say to his king, to the man who kept his daughter locked away and yet continued to pretend he only had her best interests in mind.

"I would have been happy to have my cursed daughter off my hands. But what is done cannot be undone."

Nolan tasted blood. How dare he pretend he would have allowed Odessa to marry! He had forbidden it!

"Let her go, Nolan. And leave me in peace." The king raised a hand, dismissing him and Nolan forced his feet to move.

His strides were long and furious as he made his way back to his rooms, his footsteps echoing loudly through the still empty halls. The king's words chased each other around in his mind. Odessa was married. Odessa chose another. Odessa chose the barbarian.

Orion's insinuation that he would have happily married his daughter off to Nolan earlier only made his anger burn brighter, mingling with his regret. She had asked him only weeks ago to go to her father, and he had refused. That was the day, the moment she decided to leave. Because of him, because he wasn't enough for her.

He reached his rooms and nearly tore the door off its hinges as he entered. He needed something to break, something to throw, but he kept his chambers bare and utilitarian. The porcelain ewer and bowl were the only things he could find that would shatter nicely. He hurled them at the stone wall but felt no relief as the shards hit the floor.

There had been a time when he was the only friend Odessa had, when she clung to him, worshipped him even. All her attention had been for him, all her love had been for him. And now she had taken it from him. How could he survive without it?

Nolan sat on the edge of his bed and hung his head in his hands. A small rational part of him whispered it was time to move on. Odessa had made her choice, and he had to respect it. But a louder part, a primal, bruised part, shouted that it wasn't fair. The king was a liar who went back on his word, and Odessa was nothing better than a whore, selling her body for the good of the people.

What about him? He was meant to be her savior, her knight, and she had taken that from him. He lifted his head and his gaze wandered to the tree line in the distance. If Orion wouldn't help him, he would handle the situation himself.

And he would be damned if he sat back and allowed what was rightfully his to be taken from his grasp.

Chapter 30: Morning's Gift

Light slanted in through the windows and warmed the side of Odessa's face. She burrowed further under the blankets, not wanting to wake yet. She shimmied closer to the firm body next to her, laying her hand on his broad chest. Her fingers traced a trail through the soft hairs there, and Alaric murmured incoherently in his sleep.

Odessa smiled to herself running kisses along his arm to his shoulder and then rested her head there, drifting in and out of dreams. She had done it. Rescued Faye, freed herself, and married the man she wanted. It was hard to believe this part wasn't the dream, but Alaric's heart beat steadily under her hand.

He rolled toward her and kissed across her marked cheek until she fluttered her eyes open.

"Good morning, wife."

She couldn't help the grin that crossed her face. "Good morning to you, husband."

Alaric returned her smile, and her insides fluttered. She would never tire of seeing it. In the early morning sun, she could see the copper and golden streaks running through his dark hair. His eyes with their two colors were rimmed with long lashes. She reached out a finger and ran it down his long straight nose. She traced his full lips until he sucked her finger into his mouth and nibbled on the tip.

He pulled her closer and the long, hard length of him pressed against her belly.

"I have something for you."

"Oh?" She raised a mischievous eyebrow, and he laughed his rare throaty laugh.

"Not that." He untangled himself from her and rose from the bed, not bothering with clothes. Odessa watched him walk over to the hook that held the leather pouch he always kept with him. He rummaged through it while she enjoyed the view.

Alaric hurried back to bed with something clutched in his hand.

"A morning gift," he explained, warming himself again by pulling her close.

"What's a morning gift?"

"It's our tradition for the husband to give his wife a gift on the morning after their wedding," he explained, one hand running up and down her back in a thoroughly distracting manner. "If I was a wealthy man, I could give you land or sheep or jewels. But I'm not."

A flush of embarrassment crossed his face.

"I don't want land." She kissed his nose. "Sheep make me sneeze." She kissed his cheek. "And I have no use for jewels." She kissed his mouth, urging his lips open until he kissed her back, sweeping his tongue into her mouth.

"You are what I dreamed of," she told him honestly when she pulled away, her lips tingling with desire.

"You dreamed of big barbarian men in that castle of yours, princess?" His grin was downright wicked, and Odessa nibbled his bottom lip.

"Yes." Her voice was nothing more than a whisper,

but instead of kissing her further, Alaric pulled back and took her hand. He pressed something cold and metal into her palm. She raised it above the blankets and looked at the small key on a silver chain.

"It is the key to my home, our home."

The tears burned the back of her throat as he kept going.

"It belongs to you now. It always will. This is your home and no matter what happens between us, it will always be yours. It's tradition."

She couldn't speak, could only press the key tightly into her palm. A key. To her home. Who needed jewels when Alaric had given her the only gift she had ever wanted? Freedom. Freedom from her father, freedom from her curse, freedom even from him if she wanted it.

"Thank you." She managed to choke out as the tears began to fall. Alaric kissed them as they fell, following them down her neck and across her collar bones.

"I never want you to feel like you have to be with me. I am a guest in your home." His words whispered across her breasts as he traveled across her body. "Never forget it." His mouth on her stomach traced kisses from hip bone to hip bone.

He smiled at her and she grabbed him by the shoulders, pulling him up to her face.

"I'm happy to share my home with you," her voice wavered on the words my home, but she kept going, "and my life."

He nodded, swallowing hard, suddenly as emotional as she was. He took the key from her hand and put the chain around her neck, securing it in the back. It hung between her breasts, a comforting weight directly above her heart.

She didn't know what force or goddess or luck had brought her this man, but she was very glad it did.

****

"You got married without me!" Arowyn's voice was strong and clear as she accused Alaric of leaving her out of the festivities. He had just walked in the door and had to grip tightly to the door frame to keep from dropping to his knees in thanks at seeing his sister awake and speaking. It had been over a week since his wedding and the arrival of the healers. He wasn't brave enough to hope for such amazing results this soon.

"You're awake, little wolf!" He closed the door softly behind him and hurried to her bedside. Rieka was close on his heels. Arowyn's lopsided grin nearly killed him. How often had he wondered if he would never see it again?

"Auntie says I'm much better now." Arowyn lifted Alaric's hand and pressed it to her brow. "See, the fever's all gone."

Her forehead was cool to the touch, but Alaric looked to Rieka for confirmation. All of his aunts had returned to their own homes for the moment.

"It's true. Iris gave her a tonic to drink every day, and her fever broke overnight," Rieka reported, ever the little woman of the house. Seeing the confusion on Alaric's face, she went on, "Iris is one of the Kalonian healers. She's very kind. And so beautiful. Her hair reaches nearly to her bottom, and it's braided in hundreds of tiny braids!" She stroked her own hair dreamily and Alaric had to shake her out of her thoughts.

"So, she is well?" It was too good to be hoped for.

He looked back to Arowyn, still pale from her illness, her face thinner than it once was, but her eyes were bright and clear. Perhaps she truly had come through the worst of it.

"Iris says she must continue to rest—"

"But I'm not tired!" Arowyn cut in, and Rieka scowled at her. It was oddly comforting to see the two of them argue, and Alaric smiled to himself. Nothing could be more normal than his siblings' bickering.

"She says you must, Arowyn! For at least another week." Rieka stood with her hands on her hips, the stance full of authority.

Arowyn opened her mouth to protest further, but Alaric brushed the hair from her face and placed a kiss on her forehead, distracting her for the moment. As the baby of the family, she loved to be pet and coddled. He could imagine the face Rieka was making behind his back.

"So, you really did marry the princess?" Arowyn asked, her earlier complaint resurfacing.

"I did." Alaric ran a hand down his face, not wanting to say much more. The circumstances surrounding his marriage were complicated, to say the least, and not anything he wished to explain to his sisters.

"Is it true she came to save her sister and defeated Connell and was chosen by Narah to help us?"

He sighed. Apparently, he wasn't going to have much of a choice.

"And who told you all of that?"

"I heard auntie talking."

Of course. How could he ever expect to shield his sisters from the truth? Not in such a small clan and with such chatty aunts.

"It is true she came to help her sister, and the elders agreed it would be best to make a marriage alliance with the North. Thanks to Odessa you are well. Which is all that matters."

He stood, ready to leave before his sisters could interrogate him further. "You should get some more rest. I'll come back later."

Alaric patted Rieka on the head, but before he could escape the girl asked, "Do you love her?"

He let out a slow breath, unsure of how to answer this innocent question. The intensity of his desire to say yes shocked him. But a part of him still didn't believe Odessa was his. He was afraid to say it out loud, this admission of love. If he said it and she left, then what? It was still hard to believe she would stay forever. An outsider had never lived amongst the clan before, at least not that he could remember. Better to let his sisters believe the marriage was for the good of the clan and nothing more. They better not get too attached.

"I… she will be a very good wife for me."

Rieka's forehead crinkled. Her hands were still on her hips, and it was as though his mother was back. She always knew when he was lying.

"Well, I am glad to have another sister," Arowyn proclaimed from her bed and again Alaric was struck with the unfamiliar joy at seeing his family happy.

"We have enough sisters already!" Weylyn said as he and Faolan burst through the door, bringing a blast of cold with them.

"You're back!" Arowyn squealed.

"She must not get overexcited!" Rieka scolded, and Faolan ruffled her hair as he brushed past her to get to his bunk.

"Aunt Layla said it was safe to come home!" Weylyn tossed his sack onto his bed and went to sit beside Arowyn. "Look at you, better already!"

She beamed at the attention. "Iris said I am her best patient."

"Iris, huh? Faolan was hoping to fall ill so Iris would take care of him next." Weylyn laughed until Faolan tossed a pillow at his head, the boy's face turning bright red.

"That's enough. Your sister still needs her rest." Alaric tried to sound firm, but his joy at seeing his family back together had seeped into his voice.

"Don't you have a wife to attend to?" Weylyn smirked.

"That's right. Where is the fair princess?" Faolan asked, happy to have the attention turned away from him.

"She's probably burning your supper," Weylyn teased, and even Rieka and Arowyn giggled. Alaric leaned against the door, allowing his siblings a good laugh on his behalf. They deserved it.

"I think I smell smoke!" Arowyn toppled over in glee at her own joke. Rieka slapped a hand over her mouth to hold in her laughter, but the boys made no move to cover their own mirth. Alaric felt no need to defend his wife to these silly fools. Their teasing only proved they already accepted her as one of their own.

"Oh, very funny. Don't be jealous because I live amongst royalty now." Alaric swept into a low bow that had his siblings booing and throwing pillows at him. He chuckled and tossed them back.

"Go home already!" Weylyn shouted and the

others agreed.

Alaric lifted a hand in goodbye and went out into the cold, his heart full of his family's good cheer. The day was bright and for once he was not weighed down with worry. He looked at the house across the garden and for the first time truly thought of it as home. If this was why Narah put Odessa in his path, he would be forever grateful.

He didn't get far before he spotted his wife walking toward home. His wife. The words added to his happiness. Odessa walked quickly, her face shadowed by her fur hood. She didn't like the cold. Alaric's own face heated as he considered all the ways he could warm her.

Odessa still wore the sumptuous white cloak she brought from Kalon, but her hair was braided away from her face in the way of the clan, and under the cloak, she wore the simple wool tunic the rest of the clan wore. If she missed any of the luxuries she had at the castle, she never showed it. Could she possibly make a life here with him? Surely it was different from what she was accustomed to. Even if the king had treated her unkindly, the cloak proved he had not deprived his daughter of material comforts. How could Alaric ever match what a king could provide?

The princess's hurried steps soon brought her close enough for Alaric to see her creased brow, but as soon as she looked up and saw him watching her, her face broke into a brilliant smile. Perhaps he could compete with the king after all.

"How's Arowyn?" she asked before she had even reached him. She was out of breath from walking and her pale cheek was flushed pink to match the marked side.

Alaric smiled. "She is well enough to fight with her sisters and to tease me about my new wife."

Odessa's grin mirrored his own. How wonderful it was to share life's unexpected joys with someone.

"I'm so glad! I will go in and visit her in a moment." She stepped closer and wrapped her arms around Alaric's neck, stretching on her toes to place a chaste kiss on his lips. More unexpected happiness filtered through him, unwinding the anxious knots in his muscles and his mind.

"I paid a visit to Layla. Asena and Sairsha are doing better as well." He loved that she had already made herself at home with his family. If Odessa wasn't scared off by his well-meaning but overprotective aunts, she could weather anything.

"I'm glad to hear my cousins are recovering."

Odessa nodded, continuing her story. "I spoke with the healers as well."

He kept his arms wrapped around her as she talked. It amused him how much she liked to tell him about her day. And in stark contrast to listening to his siblings' constant opinions and arguments, he found listening to his wife to be quite pleasant.

"Apparently, this sickness is something they'd seen before in Kalon. It went through several of our villages last year. In fact, they think it's possible the Kalonian soldiers passed it on to the clan." The crease in her forehead returned. "So, in the end, it was the least my father could do, since it was our fault the sickness arrived here at all." She blew out a long sigh, and Alaric held her closer.

"However it came, I'm glad it's gone. Thanks to

you." He placed a kiss on the tip of her nose. "You're frozen!"

She softened in his arms and a flush of pride ran through him at the fact that he was the one who could calm her.

"Yes, but I knew you would warm me up."

Heat rushed through his veins, and he leaned down to cover Odessa's mouth with his own. She gave a soft moan against his lips before pushing him away.

"Everyone will see us!"

"Everyone? Who?" Alaric gestured around him to the quiet road and the sleepy houses. The only witnesses to their brief show of affection were the birds in the trees. And even they were too cold to be out of their nests.

Odessa grinned again. "Let me check on Arowyn, and then I will come home to you."

Alaric's heart soared. *She will come home to me.* The words chased away his earlier doubts.

"She's fine. I saw her with my own eyes." He tried to grab her hand to pull her to his chest again, but she eluded his grasp.

"Give me a few moments with her! What kind of sister would I be if I didn't check on her?" The teasing had faded. Odessa had claimed his family as her own, and there was nothing he wanted more.

He gave a quick bow in her direction causing the smile to return to her face. "As you wish, princess. But don't be too long. I would hate for you to catch a chill." He turned and walked back to the small house with Odessa's sweet laughter following behind him.

Chapter 31: Winter Offerings

Winter settled over the Wolf village and wrapped them in a peaceful blanket of white. Odessa was glad for the chance to settle quietly into her new life. The healers were able to cure most of the sick clan people except a few that were beyond help, their bodies already too ravaged to fight any longer. The healers left the clan with cures and tonics to use for any future cases. With every report of another clan member's recovery Odessa's muscles loosened, her body unwound its tight hold on her emotions. Her plan had worked.

The snow made leaving the house nearly impossible, so she didn't have to see much of the rest of the clan. Other than Alaric's siblings and the occasional visit from an aunt or cousin, Odessa didn't have to face many other people. And for that, she was also grateful.

While she felt safe and happy with her new husband, she had not forgotten the circumstances that brought her here. Sometimes she could push it from her mind for a day or two in the snug comfort of her house, but eventually, the night of the solstice, Faye's little body on the stone slab, Connell's glinting knife, would all come rushing back to her. She would pause in her work, her hands deep in the warm dough or her fingers clenched tightly to her knitting needles, and she would breathe in through her nose and out through her mouth until the panic subsided.

It had only been a few weeks since her hasty wedding. She prayed the memories of the terrifying night before it would soon fade. And in the meantime, she was thankful for her cozy house, the door to which she held the key, and her newfound family.

It was against the walls of her little home the wind now blew the driving snow. Another storm had descended upon the forest, blanketing the village in more snow and ice. Odessa listened as it whistled past, happy for the warmth of the fire crackling in the fire pit. She stirred the stew again, determined not to burn it this time. It smelled alright. Perhaps she had finally got it right.

Alaric burst through the door bringing a blast of cold wind with him. He closed the door behind him, muttering to himself. His cloak was covered in icy snow, his cheeks red from the cold.

He stamped his feet to remove the snow from his boots and looked up at where Odessa still stood by the pot.

"Everyone's fine next door. Plenty of food and firewood to last them a few days at least." Alaric brushed the last of the snow from his hair and came to warm his hands by the fire. He placed an icy kiss on Odessa's cheek.

"Smells good." He leaned over the pot and inhaled deeply.

Odessa smiled. "I hope so. I'm determined not to burn it."

Alaric stepped back and grinned at her. "I do know how to cook. I could do it."

She huffed and stirred the pot again. Alaric swept a

stray hair behind her ear with his frozen fingertip. Odessa shivered. "It only seems fair that I cook. You do all the hunting."

He leaned in and left a trail of kisses along Odessa's jaw. Her grip on the spoon as she held it over the pot was weakening. "In the spring, I will teach you how to hunt."

The words themselves were not particularly romantic or tender, but he was willing to teach her, to give her the skills to survive on her own, and that meant everything to her. She dropped the spoon into the pot and wrapped her arms around Alaric's neck. He gazed down at her, and the moment was so lovely, so profoundly ordinary in a way she never expected to have, she had to remind herself she wasn't dreaming.

"What's this?" she asked, noticing the parcel tucked inside Alaric's vest.

He pulled it out and handed it to her, making himself comfortable at the table. Odessa tore through the brown paper and pulled out a knit shawl. It was beautifully done, dyed a deep purple with a black stripe along the edge. She wrapped it around herself and was immediately warmer.

"Where did it come from?"

Alaric shrugged. "I found it outside. Lucky, I did too. After this storm, we wouldn't have found it until spring."

"Who do you think left it?" Odessa ran a hand across the careful stitches. Why would someone leave such a beautiful gift?

"Not sure. Could be anyone. I suppose it's a thank you." He reached out his arms and pulled her onto his lap. He was quickly defrosting, and his body was warm

227

and welcoming. Odessa relaxed into him.

"A thank you for what?"

Alaric lifted the hair from her neck and kissed and sucked the delicate skin. Odessa giggled and squirmed in his lap, but he tightened his grip.

"For all the lives you saved, princess," he whispered in her ear.

"Oh." She was suddenly too warm for the shawl. She shrugged it off and laid it on the table. Alaric's hands were on her hips, and he turned her so she straddled him in the chair.

"That was kind of them." She murmured onto his lips. He kissed her slowly, gentle at first, then with little nips and bites, like they had all the time in the world. She supposed with all the snow piling up outside, they did. And no disruptions.

"We'll have to find some way to pass the time. It will be a few days before we can get out again," he said, reading her mind.

"I have been meaning to practice my cooking."

Alaric groaned into her neck, and she giggled. "That's not what I had in mind." His voice was low and growly, reminding her of why the clan was named after the wolf. Shivers ran through her body. He pulled her closer so she could feel exactly what he had in mind.

Alaric grabbed tight to her bottom, and she rocked forward, making them both groan. He sucked on her neck, the rasp of his teeth against her skin sent heat through her entire body. If things were ever uncomfortable between them, or new, or awkward, they always had this. This heat. This desire. It was there from the start, and their marriage had only made it grow stronger.

She was not an inexperienced virgin on their wedding night but being with Alaric was nothing like being with Nolan. His affections came without a price. Any worries that she had traded one prison for another, had faded as soon as Alaric placed the key in her hand. Every day since, he had proven he cared about her enough to let her make her own choices. And she loved him for it. Maybe it was time she told him.

Odessa rocked forward again, this time leaning forward to nibble on his ear. He hissed and sighed, gripping her tighter, kneading the fleshy parts of her.

"I love you." The words were no louder than an exhale, but Alaric stilled beneath her. It wasn't until she said them out loud that she realized she had never said them before. To anyone. Perhaps he didn't feel the same, but she was still glad she said them. She wanted him to know.

She pulled back far enough to look at him. His earth and sky eyes studied her. The silence stretched out between them, and the heat rushed to her face.

"You don't need to say it back. I only wanted you to know."

Alaric shook his head. "No...I..." He cleared his throat and tried again. "It's only I didn't expect you to feel it so soon. I assumed you would need more time..." The creases between his eyebrows she hadn't seen in days, returned now as he fought for the right words. Odessa suddenly wished she was anywhere but in his lap. There was nowhere to hide from his searching gaze.

"I didn't expect you to feel the same way about me as I feel for you. Not yet anyway." He cleared his throat again as his words sunk in. He felt the same about her.

229

She leaned her forehead against his, relief flooding her veins.

"Could you say it?" she asked, quietly, emotion clogging her throat. "I've never heard it before. Not directed at me anyway."

His eyes filled with tears, and she kissed them away as he cried them out of empathy for her. He wiped hers away with his thumbs as he cupped her face.

"I love you," he rasped. The words vibrated through her, and when their lips met again the kiss was messy and tear-salted and perfect.

"Now about passing the time," she said, sniffling and wiping the last of the tears from her face.

Alaric grinned and lifted her with him when he stood from the chair. He carried her to the bed, where clothes were quickly shucked and tossed to the floor. Odessa snuggled deep under the fur blankets and let Alaric prove his love to her over and over as the snow fell outside and the stew burned over the fire.

****

The gifts didn't stop. In fact, they kept coming all winter long. Alaric stooped to pick up the latest offering before going inside. The smell of fresh-baked bread wafted from the small basket he found outside the door.

Odessa glanced up from the table where she and Faolan were tossing dice. Rieka and Arowyn were draped across his bed, their mouths full of something he was sure would leave crumbs between his blankets.

"Faolan is teaching me to play." Odessa's voice was full of cheer despite the crowded house. Or maybe because of it. She seemed to thrive on the chaos and noise of Alaric's life. After years of being alone, she soaked up every bit of his messy family.

"What did we get this time?" Arowyn was off the bed and peeking in the basket before Alaric could even get his cloak off.

"It's not for you." He held the basket out of reach with one long arm and ruffled his sister's hair with the other. She scowled at him.

"Odessa said we can have some." Rieka was closing in now too, circling the table like a scavenger.

He set the basket on the table with a thunk. Odessa peered in.

"It's bread." She sighed at the delicious smell.

"Bread?" Arowyn scrunched up her nose. "I was hoping for more of those little cakes we got last time."

"Again, the gifts are not for you." Alaric leaned over and planted a kiss on Odessa's cheek. "They are for Odessa."

"I don't mind sharing." Odessa tore a chunk of the warm bread and handed it to Arowyn and another for Rieka. Faolan reached in and grabbed his own.

Alaric sat in the chair next to his wife and allowed Arowyn to crawl into his lap even though she was getting much too big for it. He watched his family enjoy the latest gift. At first, he thought the presents were a kind welcome for his wife, a thank you and an apology wrapped into one. But lately, the gifts made him uneasy. The way they were left on the doorstep instead of given directly to them, the way they hadn't stopped despite Odessa having been here for nearly two months now. It almost reminded him of the offerings left for Narah under the sacred tree, almost as if the clan had begun to leave offerings for his wife...

He tore off a piece of bread and pushed the worries from his mind. Things were going too well for the little family, and he had a way of looking for the negative. For too long he had to be prepared for the next tragedy that would befall them. Maybe now he could simply enjoy the gifts.

"Where's Weylyn?" he asked, eager to change the path of his thoughts. "Next door with the house to himself?"

"He's out," Faolan spoke with a mouth full of bread as he tossed the dice across the table. Odessa frowned. Apparently, Faolan was winning.

"Out where?"

Faolan gave a shrug. "My guess is it's a girl."

"What makes you think it's a girl?" How was it possible his younger brother was off with some girl? Although, when Alaric was fifteen... He grimaced and Odessa giggled as though she read his mind.

"He's happy when he gets back."

"He comes back whistling," Rieka added with a grin.

"It's probably Daciana." Arowyn tossed the dice for Odessa and squealed with delight at her luck.

"Daciana? Why would you say that?" Alarm flared up inside Alaric. Daciana was the last girl he wanted Weylyn to be seeing.

Arowyn turned back to him, her eyes bright and mischievous. "I've seen her sneaking around outside and a few minutes later, Weylyn leaves." She smiled, pleased with her skills of deduction.

Odessa glanced at Alaric. His concern must have been written across his face.

"Who's Daciana?" she asked, turning her attention from the game.

"Connell's daughter." Rieka stood by Odessa's

side, absentmindedly braiding pieces of her hair.

"Yes, exactly." Alaric stood, setting Arowyn onto the floor. "Alright now, you all can go spend time in your own home." He grabbed cloaks and toys littered around the small house and handed them to his siblings. They grumbled and shuffled toward the door, Odessa doing nothing to speed the process along. She kissed and hugged them goodbye as though they weren't just going next door and wouldn't inevitably all end up back here by supper. But she looked so damn happy doing it, Alaric couldn't bring himself to say anything to discourage her.

When the children were gone, Odessa turned to him, her back against the door.

"Why are you so worried about Weylyn seeing Daciana? Is it not allowed?"

Alaric sighed and slumped back into his chair. Odessa crossed the room and put the kettle over the fire for tea.

"I'm not worried."

"You are."

He let out another breath. "Fine. I am. Connell doesn't need another reason to hate this family, and Weylyn groping his daughter in the woods isn't going to help."

"What makes you think he's groping her?"

"I remember being fifteen."

Odessa let out a small laugh. "I see." She placed a mug in front of him and he inhaled the soothing aroma. She sat next to him and took the rest of the bread from the basket. When she lifted it a small piece of paper fluttered to the ground.

Written in cramped script were the words, For

Narah, and nothing else. Alaric's earlier fears flooded back in. The gifts were an offering. Did the people believe Odessa was the goddess? His mind flashed back to the scene in the field on the solstice, her fur cloak and two-sided face, her head tipped back howling at the moon. Surely, the people knew his wife was not the goddess Narah?

So few people had actually met her. The winter had been long and cold, and Odessa kept to herself. If the solstice was the only memory people had of her, not to mention the healing that took place in her name afterward, it was no wonder they were leaving gifts at his doorstep.

"What is it? Your face has gone pale." Odessa lifted the paper to look at it. "For Narah? I don't understand."

"They are leaving offerings for you."

"Offerings?" Her eyes had gone wide as the realization of what he was saying sunk in. "They don't think I am her? Do they?"

Alaric shook his head. He didn't know what to think. But whether they thought she was the goddess herself or simply goddess-sent, Connell would not like it. The man feared anything that might diminish his power over his people. If he knew the clan had begun revering Odessa, then Weylyn and Daciana were the least of their problems.

"I don't know."

Odessa dropped the note as though it burned her fingers. The look of shock on her face slowly transformed into anger.

"First, I am cursed, evil, and wicked. And now I am blessed by the gods, a savior to your people?"

Frustration laced through her words. "Is it too much to ask to be seen as myself and nothing more?" Her eyes were filled with tears when she looked at him, but she refused to let them fall, instead wiping them away roughly with her sleeve.

Alaric took her hand in his, wishing he could do something to ease her pain.

"Let them see you in the spring. The people will come to recognize you for what you are."

"And what am I?" Her voice cracked and Alaric left his chair to kneel at her feet.

"You are Odessa. And that is enough."

And it was enough for him. He loved Odessa for everything she was, for the way she always burned supper, for the way she loved his siblings as fiercely as he did, for her light that managed to survive her dark childhood. But another thought prickled at the back of his mind. One he wasn't ready to voice, one Odessa wasn't ready to hear. A part of him still believed Narah put Odessa in his path that day. He could find no other explanation for it. He prayed for an answer and Odessa came. Was it so wrong to think his wife was fated to be his? Fated to help his people? And if she was, would it be so wrong for her to claim the title of goddess-blessed, to let his people thank and appreciate her?

Under the fear and worry about Connell's reaction, something else began to grow. Pride. Pride in his wife for being courageous and smart, for saving his people, for choosing him. But when he looked into Odessa's face, he knew these were things she did not wish to hear right now. So instead, he kissed her fingertips and worshipped silently at the feet of his goddess.

Chapter 32: Snowdrops

"I found them! I found them!" Arowyn tore into the front garden where Odessa stood chatting with Alaric's cousins, Asena and Sairsha.

"You found what?" Odessa laughed as Arowyn crashed into her, barely slowing down in all her excitement.

"The first snowdrops! I spotted them!" The little girl's face was pink from excitement and cold. It was mid-March and winter had finally started to loosen its grip on the forest, but the air was still chilly and the wind harsh through the bare trees.

"Snowdrops! How lovely."

"No! Not lovely! It means it's time! I have to find Uncle Merrick." And with that, she raced back out of the garden and down the road.

Odessa looked to the women for clarification.

"Snowdrops mean it's nearly time for the annual gathering of the clans. Happens every spring." Asena was the spitting image of her mother, copper hair and all. She leaned against the wooden fence around the garden, watching Arowyn skip away. The way Layla had spoken of her daughters when they were ill led Odessa to believe they were young children, when in fact they were eighteen and nineteen years old.

Sairsha was round where Asena was tall, and quiet where Asena was loud. Her hair was a deep brown with flickers of red in the sunlight. She remained crouched in the garden where she had been advising Odessa on what to plant and when.

Odessa wiped her hands on her apron and let the early spring sun warm her face.

"What happens at the gathering?" she asked.

"If you ask the elders, the gathering is meant to celebrate the forest's awakening from its winter slumber." Asena grinned. "But if you ask the mothers, the gathering is the perfect place to find a husband."

Sairsha groaned and rolled her eyes. "And to gossip."

"Oh, yes. Plenty of that." Asena looked at Odessa with sympathy in her green eyes. "I'm sure you'll be the talk of the gathering this year."

Odessa winced.

"Don't worry her, sister." Sairsha shoved Asena leaving a dirty handprint on her sleeve. "It's nothing to be concerned about." The girl tried to reassure her, but Odessa's stomach rolled with nerves.

"What do the others say about me? The other Wolves, I mean." Ever since her conversation with Alaric about the gifts from the clan, she wanted more information. What did the people think of her?

Sairsha became suddenly interested in the dirt around her feet, but Asena met Odessa's question honestly and without hesitation.

"They think you were sent by Narah to protect us."

"I see." So, Alaric's fears were not unfounded. "But surely you don't think that do you?"

Asena studied her face, and Odessa brought a hand to her cheek. The girl shrugged. "I'm not sure. But I know this, if it weren't for your healers, I'd be dead."

"Don't talk like that!" Sairsha's gaze shot to her sister's.

"It's true." Asena turned back to Odessa. "Whatever brought you here, I'm glad it did. And I know my cousin is too," she added with a grin. "Don't worry. The gathering is always a good time. Plenty of food and drinks and certain Raven Clan boys."

At this teasing, Sairsha's face turned a deep scarlet.

"And do all the clans worship Narah?" Odessa knew so little about the other residents of the forest.

Sairsha answered this time, happy for the change in subject. "Narah is worshipped by all the clans, but the Wolves hold her higher than the others. Each clan has its own god or goddess who offers them extra protection."

Asena rolled her eyes at her sister's speech, but there was more. Odessa wasn't done with her questions.

"I thought the clans didn't get along."

"It depends," Sairsha answered with a shrug, but Asena's face darkened, her sunny demeanor instantly shadowed. "But all feuds are put aside for the gathering," Sairsha added with a pointed look at her sister.

"I will never put aside what the Foxes did to our brother." Asena folded her arms across her chest, and Sairsha blew out a frustrated sigh.

"The clans have faced each other many times in battles and raids over the years. It is often difficult to forget," Sairsha explained.

Odessa nodded, waiting for the sisters to elaborate, but both stood silent in her garden now. "And the clans intermarry?" she asked in an attempt to lighten the sour mood that had descended on her guests.

"Sarisha is hoping they do!" Asena laughed, breaking the tension, but relented when she saw her sister's horrified face. "I'm only teasing." She turned back to Odessa to explain. "Intermarrying is rare, but it happens. Alaric's own father was a Fox. Did he not tell you?"

Odessa shook her head. Alaric was happy to tell her the details of any family member, and many stories had been told over the long winter, but he never spoke of his father. In fact, none of the children did.

"It's not surprising." Sairsha nudged her sister in the side with her elbow to silence her, but Asena went on. "He wasn't a kind man. Or a useful one at that. Spent most of his time drinking. Typical Fox."

"We should go and help Ma." Sairsha tugged on Asena's arm with an apologetic look at Odessa. Asena relented and leaned in to hug Odessa goodbye. Sairsha did the same and the two were off together strolling arm in arm toward home.

Odessa sighed and looked back at the garden that was currently nothing more than half-frozen dirt. She wasn't shocked by the girl's admission about Alaric's father. She knew plenty about fathers. But Alaric had never spoken about it, and that only proved how much he was still hurt by it.

She picked up her small basket and strode around the house to gather the eggs from the hens. The peaceful day had been uprooted by the news of the gathering and the gossip of the clan. Perhaps it didn't matter what the clan believed about her. Whether Narah brought her here or not, she was here now, and eventually, they would accept her. Alaric's family already had. The more the people saw her, the more her lack of divinity would become clear.

As for the story about his father, Alaric would decide when he was ready to talk about it.

****

Nolan shifted, his feet sinking into the cold mud. His head swiveled back and forth with every rustle and crack of a twig. Even with all his senses scanning the woods around him, the Wolf chief appeared in front of him without warning. He stepped out from the long afternoon shadows, and Nolan made sure to hide his surprise.

"What is it you want?" The chief growled, cutting right to the heart of the matter.

"I have a proposition for you." He was surprised the chief himself had come to meet him, assuming he would have someone else do his dirty work.

Connell grinned a wolfish grin. "There seem to be many propositions coming from Kalon this winter. Do you wish to marry into my clan too?"

At the reminder of Odessa's marriage, Nolan's fists clenched at his sides, and his insides burned with a slow and steady rage. One that had kept him warm all winter while he made his plan.

"No. Not another marriage. I hear you have a princess you don't want. I'm offering to take her off your hands."

The chief paused, considering Nolan's words. "What makes you think I don't want her?"

"I hear your people have begun to worship her. How long before they answer only to her? How long before she is named leader of the Wolves and you are nothing more than her pet?"

Connell's eyes flashed silver in the dying light, his

hand hovering over the dagger in his belt. Nolan was right. The chief feared for his position, just as Nolan hoped. A muscle ticked in Connell's jaw. Finally, he spoke.

"What do you propose?"

Nolan's mouth twisted into a smile. It was time he claimed what was rightfully his. His king was nothing more than a coward, ruled by fear of a weak and deceitful woman, so Nolan would take matters into his own hands. He would take Odessa back, and if he couldn't have her love, he would settle for her submission.

"Grant me access to the village during your gathering. Make sure you keep her husband in line. I don't want him following us. And I will make sure you never have to worry about the princess again."

Connell nodded once in agreement, turned on his heel, and disappeared back into the shadows.

Chapter 33: The Gathering

Odessa stood in the front garden watching Arowyn run in circles around her. Rieka stood leaning against the fence, yawning dramatically every minute or so. Faolan had left nearly an hour ago, and Alaric had gone into the big house to drag Weylyn out by his ears if necessary. Or so grumbled as he stalked away from Odessa and into the house.

It was the first day of the clan gathering and the entire village had been awash in anticipation for a week now. It was the Wolves' turn to host, both an honor and a burden judging by the reaction of the clanspeople. It was early April and the chill had only begun to lift from the forest air. Odessa shivered in the early morning light.

Alaric burst from the house, muttering fiercely and a red-faced Weylyn followed behind.

"Let's go," he barked, grabbing Odessa's hand and striding from the yard.

She ran a thumb over the inside of his wrist, rubbing gently until he slowed his pace and his furrowed brow softened. He smiled down at her.

"Sorry." His shoulders lowered away from his ears. "But wrangling them is like herding chickens."

Odessa laughed, filling the quiet village with the sound. The family was late. Not that there was much to be late for. Alaric had explained to her the night before the first day was mainly for getting settled, getting reacquainted, and sizing up the competition for the next day's games. But even still, the village was empty. All of the Wolves must already be in the clearing where the gathering would be held.

"Oooo…Weylyn you look so pretty… Daciana will love it…" Arowyn teased, yanking on her brother's hair.

"Hey!" he yelped and chased her around Alaric and Odessa as they walked through the center of town.

"You're getting mud on my dress!" Rieka dodged her siblings and looked in dismay at her dirty hem.

"There's mud everywhere! Don't blame us!" Arowyn called as she raced past, Weylyn hot on her heels.

"Has anyone seen Faolan?" Alaric asked, apparently just realizing they were short a child.

"He left hours ago." Rieka inserted herself between Odessa and Alaric, forcing them to let go of each other's hands and take hers instead.

"At least one of us is on time." Despite his sour mood, Alaric looked incredibly handsome in his finest tunic. It stretched over his broad chest and muscled arms. The sun found the gold in his brown hair and glittered across it. Being beside him, even with a child or two in between, helped ease the fluttering nerves in Odessa's stomach.

Arowyn and Weylyn slowed as they reached the trail through the trees to the open field. As the field came into view, Odessa gasped at the sight. Hundreds of clanspeople filled the grassy area. The Wolves had made camp closest to the trail and several familiar faces greeted her. Beyond that, the other clans were setting up tents and lighting fires to burn off the remaining chill of the morning.

Merrick came to meet the family, clapping Alaric on the back in greeting. Soon they were surrounded by aunts and cousins, and Odessa found herself pulled into embrace after embrace. Her heart lifted with each hug, with each happy greeting, the feeling of being a part of something filled her to the brim.

From beyond the circle of Alaric's family, other Wolves stared at her in curiosity. She gave a shy smile to some and received smiles in return. Which ones had left gifts at her doorstep?

Connell's glowering stare caught her attention before he stepped up to the wooden platform erected for this occasion. She hadn't seen him since the solstice and her skin pebbled with goosebumps that had nothing to do with the chilly air. He looked as though he'd be happy to have another go at slitting her throat. Odessa tucked herself closer to Alaric's side.

Connell stood on the platform with his daughter at his side looking out over the crowd. Odessa noticed the girl's gaze searching the crowd as well until it landed on Weylyn. A pink blush crept up her cheeks. Odessa smiled to herself. Faolan was right after all.

The clanspeople milled about greeting each other, enjoying being out in the fresh spring air. Odessa was introduced to person after person, all claiming some sort of relation to her husband. Most offered smiles or kind words, but others dipped into shallow bows, and a few, much to her horror knelt at her feet and kissed her hand.

Alaric shifted at her side as another clanswoman stooped in front of her.

"Please," Odessa's voice was nearly lost in the sea of people around them. "Please. There's no need to kneel."

The woman took her hand and placed her lips on the back of it. "Because of you, my son lives." Her eyes were filled with tears when she gazed at Odessa. Her stomach flipped over in panic. She looked to Alaric for help, but he simply nodded in goodbye to the woman when she stood to leave.

"We can't let them do this," she hissed.

He looked down at her, puzzled. "We can't let them thank you?"

"You know that's not what they're doing."

Alaric opened his mouth to say more, but before he could the sound of a horn blasted through the crowd. Connell blew it again and the people reluctantly quieted. By the third blow, he held the attention of all four clans.

Odessa was glad for the distraction. She couldn't allow anyone else to show their thanks in such a way. Regardless of what these people believed, she was not the goddess, nor was she sent by one.

Her gaze roved the clearing in an effort to distract herself. Each clan had claimed a corner of the great field, and the trees of the forest grew tall on all sides. If it weren't for the flags they flew over their campsites, she would never have been able to tell them apart. Above their own fires flapped the green flag with the same howling wolves she was greeted with the day she arrived; the ones carved above the doors of the meeting house.

Closest to the Wolves were the Foxes, their tents skirting the edge of the tree line. They too gathered around fires with their families, waiting for the day to begin. She had no way to know which people were Alaric's relations. Many of them had his same brown hair with glints of red and gold among the strands. It seemed any of them could be related to her husband.

After the Foxes came the Bears. They had traveled the farthest, coming from the southern edge of Ashera's wood. Their land bordered Melantha, and Alaric told her tales of the damage the southern kingdom had brought upon the clan. Even from a distance, Odessa could tell their numbers were smaller than the rest.

On the far side of the field, the Ravens set up camp. Odessa had hoped to meet their infamous chief, a woman famous for her ruthlessness on the battlefield with hair and eyes as black as night. Odessa loved listening to Alaric's tales about the Raven beauty. Perhaps later he would introduce her.

Whatever differences the clans saw between each other, Odessa was unable to discern. She had heard stories before of blackened faces and bearskin coats, but perhaps those things were saved for the battlefield.

Instead, when she looked around all she saw were people. Not much different than the people she had seen in Kalon. Not much different from the people who had shunned her, spit at her, and locked her away.

And now, somehow, she was supposed to believe these people saw her as something good? As a hero? She couldn't stomach it. The change in direction was too abrupt, too complete. She was the same person here as she was at home. Nothing had changed except for the stories the people told about her. How could she rely on something so fragile for her safety?

Connell's voice interrupted her frenzied thoughts.

He shouted a welcome to the other clans and the clans shouted back, their voices vibrating the very earth she stood on. Connell's daughter, Daciana, no longer stood beside him, and Odessa turned just in time to see her, and Weylyn disappear into the trees. She considered telling Alaric but decided against it. No need to cause more bickering between the brothers.

The crowd around her began to shift as Connell finished his welcome. As the people moved, she was no longer blocked by the Wolves. It only took a moment, but everything seemed to slow, as though she could have predicted it before it happened but could do nothing to stop it.

A man from the Clan of the Fox spotted her and froze. Several more Foxes looked in her direction, wondering what captured the man's attention. She raised an instinctive hand to her face as more and more clanspeople turned to look. Alaric's hand was a steady weight on her back, a reminder she wasn't alone.

The Clan of the Bear spotted her next, and one by one the people dropped to their knees. Someone shouted Narah's name, and more people dropped in supplication. Odessa's breath died in her throat. She couldn't think, couldn't speak, couldn't move. She stood watching helplessly as every clan of Asherah's Wood knelt before her. No, not her. Narah, goddess of the moon, light, and dark like she was. But she was not Narah. She was Odessa and she wanted none of this.

Before Alaric's hand could clamp onto her arm, before anyone else could speak, she tore from the field and into the safety of the surrounding trees.

****

It didn't take long for him to catch her. It never did.

Odessa slowed her run and turned to face him. Her chest heaved with ragged breaths and her heart thumped painfully behind her ribs. Alaric watched her for a moment, considering her before he spoke.

"Why did you run?"

The question was absurd. Why did she run? Why did he not already know the answer to that question?

"I am not the goddess." Her voice was choked with fear and anger. "I told you that from the beginning."

Alaric stepped closer, his familiar scent washing over her. This was her husband. The man she loved. Why did he not know her heart?

"I know." He ran a finger down her cheek and took her chin between his fingers. "But you saved us anyway. Let the people thank you."

"Thank me?" He flinched as she pulled away from his touch. "They think I am something I am not! I have lived that life once. I do not wish to live it again." She crossed her arms, her mouth set in a firm line.

Alaric huffed. "Do you truly believe you are so different from the rest of us?"

Odessa's gaze snapped to his, not expecting this question. He didn't let her answer.

"Do you think people don't judge me? Label me?" He stepped closer again, his body looming over her. "I am a barbarian, a savage, a warrior. But I am also too soft, too fearful, too worried about my siblings." His voice was rough and jagged, and he was close enough now his heat called to her even as they argued. "I am the son of a useless man and the husband of a foreign princess. You are not the only one trying to break free of people's ideas about you."

She struggled for a response. Surely this was

different! She hated the pain in Alaric's eyes, but she couldn't bring herself to comfort him. All she saw was the field filled with row after row of people kneeling in front of her. Her throat closed, and she took a step back gasping for air.

Alaric reached for her hand, but she pulled it away.

"I can't do this."

He shook his head in frustration. "It doesn't matter what they say you are. It was you who made the alliance. It was you who brought the healers! Did you not tell me the same thing on our wedding night? Goddess or not, Odessa, you saved them."

The truth of it hung just beyond her grasp. Fear and a bone-deep exhaustion stood in her way. She couldn't be what these people wanted her to be. She wasn't cursed but she sure as hell wasn't blessed either.

"Do you ever wonder if maybe she did send you here?" His question was so quiet she almost didn't hear it. "I prayed for you. That day. I prayed for an answer, and you came." He had never told her that before. His eyes pinned her to the spot, sky and earth, asking her if she believed as he did. She swallowed the hot lump in her throat.

"And your face…" The word died on his lips as her mouth dropped open.

"My face." Her hand went to her cheek, for the second time today after so many weeks of not caring about her marking. The tears traced hot tracks down her cheeks. Alaric reached out a hand to wipe them away, but she kept out of his reach.

"I only meant…"

She backed away further until she collided with a tree. She stayed pressed against it, allowing its sturdy trunk to hold her up.

"You were supposed to be the one person who saw me for what I am. Who saw me." She drew in a shuddering breath. A horrible thought fought for purchase in her mind and once it was there, she couldn't shake it.

"You like it."

"Odessa…" Alaric's voice was a warning not to say things she couldn't take back, but it was too late.

"No. I see it now. You like it. You like that it was your wife who saved the clan. You want everyone to think you're married to Narah's chosen one!"

Alaric's eyes opened wide in horror at her words, but she kept going, throwing them at him.

"You wanted to parade me around at this gathering like your prize! No one will remember what a drunk your father was now that you have me by your side."

She had gone too far. She knew it before the words had left her mouth. Alaric went stone still, even his breathing slowed. Odessa stepped toward him.

"I shouldn't have…"

Alaric shook his head, stepping away from her. "This is what you think of me?" His brow was furrowed, and Odessa suddenly wanted nothing more than to make it smooth, to take his worries away, to coax that rare grin from his lips.

Why had she said what she said? Why had she lashed out at him as though he controlled what his people believed about her?

"Alaric, please. I didn't mean it. I'm upset and scared and I—"

He held up a hand, his shoulders sagging. "I thought you were fated to be mine." He gave her a sad smile. "But maybe it was a mistake after all."

Fresh tears welled up in her eyes. She was his. Why did it have to be fate? Why not a choice they made together?

"I am yours!" She reached out and wrapped her hands in his tunic, pulling him close. "I am yours, Alaric."

He leaned his forehead against hers. "I don't know how to keep you safe from this. The people believe you were sent to us, and so do I."

She closed her eyes and sighed.

"I love you, princess."

"I love you, too." And she did, but now her love was tangled up with other emotions, with her fear and confusion, with her lack of control. She survived a life ruled by rumors and superstitions once, she didn't know how to survive it again.

"I think I'll go back to the house."

"I'll come with you." His words were warm against her cheek, and it would be so easy to say yes. But she also needed time alone, time to think about what he'd told her. Time to figure out if she could reconcile their very different ideas on why they were together.

"No, you go back with your family. I'll be alright."

He pulled back and studied her, clearly not convinced things were well between them. Odessa raised a thumb and smoothed the wrinkles between his brows.

"I promise I'll be there when you come home tonight." She placed a soft kiss on his lips.

"I do love you."

"I know." She turned to go but not without one last glance behind her at the man she chose.

Chapter 34: The Weight of Words

Alaric returned to the field alone and rattled by his conversation with Odessa. Should he have gone home with her? He shouldn't have told her he believed Narah sent her here, that much was perfectly clear.

He ran a frustrated hand through his hair as he stomped back through the woods to the gathering. Of course, Odessa longed to be free of people's judgments but that was a luxury no one received. Why couldn't she embrace her new role? Surely it was better than being shunned.

He loved her regardless of who or what brought her here, and he wasn't at all certain he had convinced her. He hovered at the edge of the tree line, considering turning around and following Odessa home, but before he could decide for himself, his family spotted him and pulled him back into the crowd.

"Where's Odessa? Is she alright?" His Aunt Layla leaned in close as though she were going to whisper but she spoke loud enough for everyone around his family's fire to hear. The heads of his cousins and siblings lifted, listening.

"She wasn't feeling well."

Layla nodded, her mouth open, ready to ask more, but one look at Alaric's face, and her jaw snapped shut. He stood with his arms crossed, scanning the field. The other clans had gone back to setting up, and more and more fires appeared around the perimeter. He let out a long sigh, wishing his wife was beside him.

The Wolf Clan had set up in family groups on their portion of the field, eating and talking around their own fires. People broke off and visited others, exchanging food and gossip along the way. Even though they lived in the same village, it had been a long, cold winter. There were many faces Alaric hadn't seen in months.

As the morning wore on Weylyn wandered back to the family's fire, grinning from ear to ear. Alaric did not miss the red welt on his neck but had no desire to discuss it with the boy now. Instead, he gave him a hard enough tap on the back of his head to wipe the ridiculous smile off his face.

Arowyn and Rieka raced from fire to fire with the other children, shrieking and laughing like they hadn't had the chance to do in months. Alaric spotted Faolan at a neighbor's fire, his head bent low next to his best friend, Caden. The boys whispered together, and Faolan's cheeks turned a fierce shade of pink. Alaric ran a hand down his beard, realizing he would now have to have a talk with both of his brothers.

Merrick held out a mug, and Alaric gratefully took the ale and drank. Between the way Connell was glaring at him from several fires over, Weylyn's complete inability to be discreet, and his argument with Odessa, drinking ale before noon seemed perfectly necessary.

He tried to shake the dark cloud hanging over him and enjoy the early spring sunshine, but he kept replaying his conversation with Odessa over in his mind. Was she right about him? Did he want to show her off? Was he pleased when the clans knelt before her?

The thrill that ran through him at the thought betrayed his true feelings. Of course, he was pleased. But did he plan it? Did he hope to have his father's legacy and his own past sins wiped clean by marrying her? Perhaps that's what fueled his initial desire to bring her back to the clan, his need to prove himself always hiding right below the surface, his fear that he would fail his family never letting him rest.

Whatever plans he had for her, whatever triumphs he aimed to achieve by bringing her home were tossed aside as soon as he spoke to her. Loving her was inevitable and as vital to him as air. Blessed, cursed, it didn't matter what his people believed. He would gladly face the ire of all four clans if it meant keeping her at his side. No matter how the clans' feelings shifted, he wanted her. It was the one thing he was absolutely certain of. He needed to tell her. Now.

Alaric turned to leave just as his father's cousins arrived at the fire.

"Cousin!" Branton slapped a huge hand on Alaric's shoulder. He hadn't seen much of his father's family since the man died, and he had no desire to speak with them now.

"Branton. Afi." He greeted the men with a nod.

"Where has Narah's servant gone? We wished to meet her." Afi looked over Alaric's shoulder as though Odessa was hidden behind him.

"My wife wasn't feeling well. In fact, I was on my way to check on her."

The men ignored his efforts to move past them and instead kept talking. "We heard rumors of Narah blessing the Wolves, but we didn't truly believe it until we saw her."

"How did you manage to marry the goddess's handmaid?" Afi laughed.

"Come have a drink by our fire and tell us the story!" Branton draped an arm over his shoulder and dragged him toward the Fox's camp. Alaric nearly protested further, but perhaps Odessa needed some time to herself. He let himself be led to his cousin's fire and accepted the offered ale.

People gathered around eagerly to listen to how he came to be the husband of Narah's chosen one.

"I knew the moment I saw her," he began. The faces around him smiled and cheered his opening. He took another swig from his cup, fueling his story.

"Our people were in trouble. The sickness was back." Heads nodded in sympathy. "So, I prayed to Narah, as all Wolves do. The goddess has a fondness for us, just as Aden, god of fire, favors the Foxes."

The story shimmered and shifted inside him as he planned what to say next. His words had the power to change what the people around the fire thought, what they would say to others. Odessa's tear-stained face crossed his mind.

"I knew the moment I saw her face she was meant to be mine." The gathered crowd yipped and howled in approval.

Alaric grinned. Now was the moment. He could claim his wife was goddess-sent, blessed by Narah herself and sent to save the Wolves, or he could assert that his wife was nothing more than an ordinary woman. And yet, neither captured the truth.

"Odessa negotiated the alliance, she brought the healers, and she chose me for her husband." He shrugged and the crowd laughed, tossing crumbs at him.

He held his hands up in surrender. "That's all I know! The goddess does not speak to us any more than to anyone else." This version of events felt right. Perhaps his wife did not believe she was put in his path by Narah, but he would never believe she was ordinary.

Branton put a firm hand on his shoulder and squeezed. "Good for you, cousin! A toast to Alaric and his bride!" Mugs were raised in a toast to Alaric and Odessa's long and happy marriage. He only wished she were here to see it. To see that the people did not expect her to be the goddess or anything else except for herself. He should go home and get her, but the ale was flowing, and the stories were long.

Chapter 35: Taken

Odessa tramped through the underbrush back to the village, needing to be alone. Was Alaric right? Was she making too much of this? Her rapidly beating heart told her no, but her mind returned to Alaric's words, to the list of names people had called him, to the look on his face as he recounted them. She had spent so little time around other people she had never considered that she wasn't the only one living under the oppressive judgment of others.

She stepped through a cluster of bare branches and the outer ring of the village came into view. She hesitated. Maybe she should go back and stand proudly beside her husband, accept the people's thanks, and enjoy the festivities? The idea made sweat roll down her back and her skin prickle under her tunic. Or maybe she should go home and hide? Indecision kept her rooted to the spot.

Odessa was so tangled in her own thoughts she didn't hear the footsteps behind her until the hand was covering her mouth and the voice was whispering harshly in her ear.

"Essa," the familiar voice hissed, and her heart stopped.

She struggled against Nolan's hand, but his other arm was wrapped tightly around her body, squeezing the air from her lungs.

"There is no point in struggling, princess." Arms that had once held her in a loving embrace locked around her. "I'm bringing you back to where you belong."

She screamed against his hand, but the sound was muffled, and she was too far from the gathering field for anyone to hear. They wouldn't have been able to hear her cries over the din of so many voices anyway.

Nolan dragged her toward a horse waiting at the edge of the village. She kicked and thrashed making contact with his shin. He bit out a curse and lifted her off her feet. He dropped the hand from her mouth, and she shrieked with every ounce of strength left in her.

"Oh princess, I was hoping I wouldn't have to do this." Nolan placed her feet back on the ground and she glanced at freedom. She lunged away from him, but he was faster. He grabbed her arm and pulled her close. It was as though she watched from a distance as he drew the sword from his belt. She thought dimly that he meant to kill her, but it wasn't the blade he brought down on her head but the hilt. Pain spiked through her skull before everything went black.

****

It was dark by the time Alaric stumbled from the field and back along the path to his bed. His siblings had wandered home long ago, carried by aunts and dragged along by uncles. Tomorrow they would do it all again and Odessa would be by his side. He smiled to himself, eager to get home to his wife, eager to make it up to her.

He turned into his own front garden and stopped abruptly. The alcohol that just a moment ago swam sleepily through his veins burned off in an instant. A

258

figure leaned against the side of the little house, hiding his face in the shadows. Where was Odessa? Panic surged through him, waking every inch of his body.

"Who's there?" He glanced toward the big house, praying no siblings wandered out to check on the noise.

He probably shouldn't have been surprised when Connell stepped out of the shadows and into the moonlit yard, not after the way Odessa was treated at the gathering. Of course, the man would be upset.

Connell stalked toward him; his eyes narrowed. "She's not here."

"What are you talking about?" Alaric's hands twitched with the need to grab Connell by the throat and shake him until he explained himself.

"Your wife. She's gone."

Impossible. Terror gripped his stomach and twisted.

"What did you do to her?"

Connell sneered in disgust. "She didn't belong here."

Alaric grabbed the man by the tunic and nearly lifted him off the ground. His chest ached with every inhale and exhale. "What did you do to her?" Every word was a pained growl ripped from his throat.

"Let her go." His chief twisted out of his grasp and shook himself off.

"Let her go? She is my wife!" Alaric looked toward the house, willing Odessa to walk out, wishing he could take back everything he said to her during their fight, regretting every moment he spent today that wasn't with her.

"I advise you to let her go, Alaric. Or the clan will find out the true story of your father's death."

Whatever breath Alaric had left after hearing his wife was missing, was kicked out of him by Connell's threat.

"I'd hate to see how the Foxes would react to the news." The man stepped closer again, his cold gray eyes seeing straight to Alaric's biggest fear. "You know the penalty. You would be exiled. Your siblings would be alone." His laugh was like dry leaves in the wind. "The arrow wound was in his back, Alaric. He was a drunk. But you…" He tugged on Alaric's beard. "You are a coward."

Connell chuckled his joyless laugh again and backed away before Alaric could grab him. He turned, leaving Alaric alone in front of his house.

****

Alaric's legs had long ago gone numb, and the wet ground had seeped through his pants where he kneeled in the garden. Odessa was gone and his siblings were in danger. Hadn't he already lived this? Was he not allowed any peace? His plans to remain prostrate in the mud for the rest of the night were interrupted by the soft crunch of footsteps.

Daciana stood in front of him, her small hands clasped nervously at her waist. Her eyes darted around the garden. Alaric rubbed a hand wearily down his face.

"Go home, girl." His voice was no longer human, but more like the sound of a wounded animal.

She shifted slightly in the dirt but didn't turn to leave. Alaric brought his gaze to her face. She took after her mother, and Alaric was thankful. He had no desire to look upon any face that reminded him of Connell. The girl's rose-gold hair was tucked neatly inside her hood and her round face was soft and young in the moonlight. But her mouth was set in a determined line and her shoulders were rolled back, ready for battle. Damn these fierce women who refused to leave him alone.

He rose slowly, his limbs screeching in protest. "What is it?"

"I saw her. Your wife." Her voice was quiet but strong.

Alaric swallowed hard and nodded at her to go on.

"I was in the woods with Weylyn... I mean we went for a walk."

Alaric was sure if it was light, he would be able to see the blush work its way up the girl's cheeks.

Daciana cleared her throat. "Weylyn returned to the gathering, and I stayed back for a moment. I heard a scream."

His heart flung itself against his rib cage, howling to be released. A scream meant Odessa was taken against her will. A scream meant she was in danger.

"I snuck closer to the sound, and I saw a man carrying your wife. He put her on a horse and rode out of town. I'm sorry I didn't tell you sooner. I was afraid." The girl was talking faster now, the words spilling from her in a cascade of worries and apologies.

Alaric raised a hand to stop her speech. She gazed up at him with round eyes. He was wrong. She had the same gray eyes as her father, except where his were narrowed in hatred, hers were open and kind.

"Why are you telling me at all?" he asked.

"My father and I don't see eye to eye on a lot of matters." Her voice was even again, her face determined. Alaric would bet anything the other matters involved a certain brother of his.

"And it's not right. He was involved. I'm sure of it. My father has hated your wife since the solstice. It was meant to be his heroic moment and she stole it from him."

Alaric cleared his throat and the girl blinked, remembering his towering presence over her.

"I've heard him rant about the matter for months now. But it's not right. She should be allowed to stay. If she wishes."

Her speech finished she wrapped her hands in the ends of her cloak and worried the fabric between her fingers. The fight had gone out of her, and she suddenly looked young. Too young to carry around the sins of her father.

Alaric put a hand on her shoulder, and she met his gaze. "Thank you."

Daciana nodded once, ready to leave, but Alaric held her still.

"Tell me. What did the man look like?"

"His hair was light. Golden almost. It struck me as odd that someone so beautiful could do something so ugly." She shifted again and Alaric released her. Daciana confirmed what he already knew. His fists clenched at his sides. He hated to think of the knight with his hands on Odessa, but the man had loved her once. Surely, he wouldn't harm her?

"Thank you again. Your father will never find out what you told me. I swear it."

Daciana nodded with a grateful smile and dashed from the yard. Alaric watched her go, the blood slowly returning to his extremities. He wanted nothing more than to ride to the gates of the castle and demand his wife back from the bastard who stole her, but there were other factors to consider.

The big house loomed over him, a reminder of the souls it held inside. If he went after Odessa now, his siblings' futures would be threatened. His cowardice, his exile from the clan would hang over them like a curse for the rest of their days. His aunts and uncles would ensure they would never go hungry, but who would marry them? Who would sit beside them? Who would respect them once they knew the truth about Alaric?

He had to think. There must be a way. He strode to the smaller house, praying to Narah and anyone else who would listen, to keep Odessa safe until he could get to her.

Chapter 36: Threats

It was dark by the time they reached the castle, and Odessa's head throbbed with every jarring step of the horse. They had made one stop when she woke from her injury-induced stupor. Nolan allowed her to dismount and have a few sips of water before he tied her hands in front of her and hoisted her into the saddle once again.

He rode behind her, his legs tight around her. His sour breath on her neck made the bile rise in her throat.

"We're home, princess." His voice was light but held no warmth. The man she once loved had been twisted into a bitter, angry creature.

"My father will not be pleased." The words were sharp and uneven after a day of not speaking. "He needs the alliance as much as the Wolves do." She struggled to sit up straight, but her back blazed in discomfort.

Nolan cackled. "Oh, I think he will be. Especially after I tell him what I saw in the forest." He raised a hand in greeting to the soldier on the wall and the gates lifted for them. The horse seemed nearly as grateful as Odessa when Nolan pulled her to a stop and dismounted. He helped Odessa from her seat and her knees buckled as soon as her feet hit the ground. Nolan tugged her to a stand.

"We are going to have a little chat with the king,

sweet Essa. Then we will have our reunion."

The way he said her name made her skin crawl. Her mind refused to consider what he had in mind for their reunion.

He pulled her through the muddy yard and in through the castle doors. Her hood was off, and she watched in horror as every guard and palace servant turned away from her as she passed. She was invisible again and after months of being seen, it gutted her to be erased.

Alaric's words tumbled through her head as she was yanked from hall to hall, her hurried footsteps echoing in the cold space. No one was safe from judgment. Wasn't it better to be amongst people who saw her as a blessing? Why had she run from it?

She had no time to answer her own tortured questions before she was thrust through the doors of her father's study.

"What—"

Whatever question her father was about to ask, died in his throat upon seeing her. The king's gaze swung wildly between her and Nolan until it landed on Nolan and stayed there.

"I told you to leave it alone." His voice was ice and steel, but fear simmered behind his eyes. Again, Odessa wondered what was it about her that had her father so afraid?

"Your majesty." Nolan swooped into a bow and then strode toward the king, leaving Odessa hovering by the door. She glanced at it. Surely, there were guards standing outside. Not that it mattered. Where would she go? Back to the Wolves? How many times would she be passed back and forth by powerful men? A bone-deep weariness settled over her.

"The clans have gathered in the Wolf village."

"It happens every year, Nolan," the king snapped. "Get to the point. Why have you jeopardized our alliance with the Wolves?" His face had gone scarlet even as his voice remained steady.

Odessa braced herself for what came next.

"All four clans bowed down to your daughter."

The king's face went from red to white in a matter of seconds. His hands gripped the arms of his chair so tightly Odessa feared they might splinter beneath the force.

"They were only thanking me." She hurried forward. "Thanking us both, really. For the healers." Her father didn't bother to raise his gaze to hers.

"They were worshipping her as some forest goddess," Nolan broke in, stepping in front of her. "All four clans."

Nolan's last three words fell like pebbles into a stream, each one rippling out into Odessa's memories. Her father was afraid of the clan's uniting and for whatever reason he was afraid she would be the one to do it. Suddenly, so much of her life made sense. Why he wanted her locked away, why he sent men to retrieve her from the Wolves, why he insisted the alliance must include the promise the Wolves would back Kalon. For reasons she couldn't begin to imagine, her father thought she would be the one to unite the clans of Asherah's Wood.

Had she learned this years ago, or even months, she would have laughed at the absurdity. What power did she have to influence the clans of the forest? But the image of the clansmen on their knees in front of her was burned into her memory. This time instead of panic it brought power.

Her father rose from his seat and stalked closer to the fire. He leaned against the mantle and stared into the flames. Nolan shifted on his feet, waiting for his king's response.

When he looked up the fear was gone and something else burned behind his eyes. Impotent rage. And she was the easiest target.

"Get her out of my sight," he hissed. "I don't care what you do with her but make damn sure the Wolves never get their hands on her again."

"Yes, your majesty." Nolan's voice dripped with satisfaction. Odessa wrapped her numb fingertips inside the ends of her cloak.

"And Nolan, the next time we march to Melantha be sure to pay a visit to the clans along the way. Show them what happens when they go against a king." His eyes flicked back toward the fire and Odessa's mind flashed to an image of the Wolf village engulfed in flames.

"But they haven't gone against you! I told you—"

"Get her out of my sight!" The king's voice cracked through the room. Nolan yanked her arm toward the door and a gust of cold wind swept through the study. Papers on her father's desk fluttered and the old king's eyes opened wide like a spooked horse. The fire in the fireplace went out, and they were plunged into darkness.

The only sound was the king's harsh breathing. Nolan's fingers tightened around her bicep. A loud smack as her father's hand came crashing onto the desk elicited a startled gasp from her lips.

267

"I kept her alive as long as I could, damn it." Her father's voice was a low rasp. "I've had enough of your cursed daughter."

The wind blew again, and Nolan dragged her from the room.

****

They stumbled into the hallway, Nolan still holding tight to her arm. All the color had drained from his face.

"What was that?"

He shook his head, glancing back at the now-closed door of the king's study. "I don't know. It was as though he was talking to someone..." Nolan's voice trailed off when his gaze met hers and his face hardened against her once more.

"It's time to go."

"Where are you taking me?" Odessa dug her feet in, but the stone floor was polished to a slick shine. Nolan easily pulled her along. She tripped and he tugged her up. She twisted her arm, and he yanked her closer.

The halls were empty and quiet. Most of the castle had gone to sleep, but in a palace this big there was always someone around. Odessa searched in vain for anyone who could help her, but it was as if whatever strange wind blew through her father's study had already cleared these halls.

At the end of the corridor, the queen herself hovered in the shadows. Nolan didn't see her until they were nearly upon her. He startled and loosened his grip on Odessa's arm. He tucked her close to his side instead.

"Your majesty." He dipped into a perfunctory bow. "I was escorting the princess back to her chambers."

The queen arched a slender black eyebrow. "I did not realize the princess had returned." Her gaze raked over Odessa's appearance and a frown cracked her smooth face. She must look a mess after being dragged through the forest. Could the queen tell something was wrong? And more importantly, would she care enough to do something about it?

Nolan held her closer, and she felt the sharp tip of his blade in her side. Her heart stuttered in her chest. Would he dare to stab her right here, in front of the queen? If she were braver, she would find out. But her body trembled in fear, the acrid taste of it rising into her throat. Would Nolan truly use that blade on her?

"She had a bit of an ordeal with the clans, but she is safe with us now." The lie was smooth and effortless from his lips.

Queen Louise narrowed her gaze, her dark eyes flicking from Nolan to Odessa. "I see."

Odessa widened her own eyes, as though she could send a message straight to her stepmother's mind. If only.

"As you were." The queen gave a quick nod and Nolan steered Odessa around her, her hopes plummeting. Once she was out of this castle all would be lost.

She turned around in time to catch the queen's eye. Louise brought a finger to her lips and gave Odessa a knowing nod. Nolan yanked her roughly around the corner before she could make sense of the queen's gesture.

Nolan muttered to himself, nonsense about duplicitous women as he led her through the dark hallways and down the twisting back staircase. A new horse waited for them in the back garden, and Odessa nearly wept at the thought of returning to the saddle. Her body ached and she dreaded wherever Nolan was taking her.

"Please." She cursed the sound of her own weakness. "Please, Nolan. Can't we stay here?"

He shoved her toward the horse. "You heard your father. He told me to get rid of you. Which is exactly what I plan to do. But not before I have my fun with you." He sneered at her; his once beautiful face contorted in bitterness. "I was good to you, princess. I was good to you when no one else was and still, you left me. You betrayed me and humiliated me. And now it's my turn."

She no longer recognized the man in front of her. How could she have ever given her heart to this monster? Her stomach turned. Her knees nearly buckled. But she inhaled through constricted lungs. And she ran.

Odessa sprinted across the garden on leaden legs, her lungs screaming with the effort. Nolan's footsteps were right behind her. She zig-zagged blindly through the garden, trampling the early spring vegetables. The cook would be angry in the morning. The cook! Why would she care what the cook thought at a time like this?

Nolan cursed loudly behind her, but she didn't look back. If she could get around the corner, they would come face to face with the palace guards. The guards may not care about her, but Odessa was fairly certain Nolan wouldn't kill her in front of them.

A few more steps and she'd be there. She pleaded with her legs to move faster. She wished she'd worn leggings instead of skirts this morning. They twisted around her ankles, tripping her. She stumbled. Her body smashed hard into the stone wall of the castle. Nolan's shoulder dug into her chest knocking the breath from her lungs. Spots clouded her vision.

"Oh, Essa. Why do you make it so hard?" Nolan's voice was in her ear before she succumbed to the darkness.

Chapter 37: The Goddess

Every part of her throbbed with a dull ache. Odessa opened her eyes and the gray light filtering in through the grimy window slanted across her face. She squinted and struggled to sit; a sharp pain shot through her side. Her strangled gasp was the only sound in the room.

What was this room? She shimmied back until she leaned against the headboard of the bed and groaned quietly. Nolan must have broken a rib or two when he slammed her against the stone wall of the castle. Every breath reminded her of what he did.

She had never seen this place before; not surprising considering she hadn't seen most places. The room was small and spare. The bed on which she sat was covered in a faded quilt that matched the threadbare rug beneath it. A fireplace filled with ash, but no fire waited patiently against the far wall.

Odessa scanned the room for her cloak and boots, but Nolan must have taken them. The bastard knew she couldn't get far without them. What was she going to do? She could barely sit up without pain, she had no idea where she was, and a tramp through the forest without boots was futile at best and dangerous at worst.

A frustrated sob rose in her throat. She was so tired of being helpless. So damn tired. And where was Nolan? If he was going to kill her, he should just get on with it. A tear rolled down her cheek and she scrubbed it away. Enough. Enough tears, enough sorrow, enough self-pity.

She eased her way to the edge of the bed and gingerly stepped down. Her ribs ached in protest, and she bit her lip to keep from crying out. The coppery taste of blood brushed against her tongue. She crept closer to the room's only window. The floor beneath her feet was freezing. Spring had barely begun, and the mornings retained their winter chill. Her breath clouded the space in front of her.

Odessa yanked the comforter from the bed and wrapped it around her shoulders. Another shallow breath and she continued her slow trek to the window. She made it on trembling legs and clutched tight to the sill when she reached it. She wiped away the dust with the corner of the quilt and peered out at the familiar landscape. Nolan hadn't bothered to take her far. Her father's castle loomed in the distance and frost-covered fields glittered out beyond her newest prison. She guessed they were in an old hunter's cabin near the edge of the forest. Her window, however, only afforded her a view of Kalon and not the sacred trees.

At the thought of the woods and the life she left behind, Odessa could no longer hold back her tears. Her throat grew tight, and she struggled to swallow the hot ball of emotion lodged there. Even if she could find a way out and manage to walk her way back to Alaric, she would only be putting him in harm's way.

Her father's words echoed in her mind. He planned to teach the clans a lesson for daring to bow to her. What would he do to them? How much worse would it be if she returned?

She leaned her forehead against the smudged glass.

Images of Alaric danced through her mind. It would have been better for everyone if they had never met but she couldn't seem to regret their time together. She lived more in the last few months than she had in her entire life. She had known love and safety and belonging. It was more than she could have asked for.

Odessa didn't know how long she stood there remembering, but her feet were numb, and her side ached when she heard the first howl. Her gaze shot up and the howl rang out again. Her heart raced. Was it Alaric? Had he found her? She scanned the field for her husband but instead spotted a lone white wolf in the distance. Her coat glinted in the sunlight as she threw back her head and howled again.

The hairs on Odessa's arms rose to attention. The memory of the clan on their knees came to her mind as the wolf howled once more before it disappeared over the ridge. Odessa blinked. Had she imagined it? Perhaps. But she hadn't imagined the fear in her father's eyes at the idea of the clans uniting. It was the only way they stood a chance against the surrounding kingdoms. If she could be the thing to unite them, why shouldn't she?

Her knees buckled and she collapsed to the ground, her body no longer strong enough to hold her up. She laughed bitterly, the sound echoing back to her. How could she do anything to help Alaric if she could not even stand? She rested her head against the wall behind her. It had been over twenty-four hours since she had last eaten. She was battered and bruised. And heartbroken. She closed her eyes and waited.

A soft tapping on the window woke her and she struggled to her feet. A slender face greeted her beyond the dusty pane. The woman was a maid to the queen. Odessa recognized her immediately. She yanked at the window trying to open it, her ribs screaming in protest at the motion, but the old window wouldn't budge. She looked around frantically for something to throw through it but found nothing in the room beyond the quilt and rug. She growled in frustration and turned back to the woman.

The maid held up a hand, signaling to Odessa to wait. She spoke but Odessa could barely make out the words. She pressed an ear to the window.

"I will take a message," the maid repeated. "To your husband."

Odessa's heart rose in her throat and nearly choked her. What could she say? What few words could she relay to this woman—her only lifeline to the world—that would bring Alaric here? She thought of the clansmen, united in their reverence to her. She saw her father's fear and his anger. She imagined what havoc he would wreak on the clans. She couldn't let it happen. Not again. Not because of her.

She brought her mouth close to the glass, afraid to shout. She still didn't know where Nolan was or when he would return.

"Tell him, Narah calls her people to Kalon."

The woman stared at her with wide eyes before nodding once and disappearing around the side of the house.

Odessa's entire body shook with the weight of what she had done, and she stumbled back to the bed. She pulled the blanket around her ears and laid down to wait. With any luck, the clans of Asherah's Wood would march to Kalon in time for her to see it.

****

Alaric startled awake, nearly falling out of the chair he had dozed off in some time just before dawn. Before he could make sense of the knocking sound hammering through his skull, he was hit with the pain of his heart being torn from his chest all over again. Odessa was gone. He gripped the edge of the table and struggled for breath. How could he possibly face the day without her?

"Are you ready? I want to go!" Arowyn's impatient yell accompanied her pounding on the door.

He ran a shaking hand down his face, attempting to rouse himself, and shuffled toward the door.

"Is Odessa awake, yet? Can we go?" She peppered him with questions as soon as he opened the door, her freckle-covered face bright in the morning sun.

"She's tired today. Is Weylyn awake? He can take you." His attempt to keep his voice even and calm was failing. He cleared his throat.

Arowyn peered around him, but he blocked her view of the house with his body. The last thing he needed was for his siblings to discover Odessa was gone. Or at least not until he figured out what to do about it.

Arowyn scrunched up her nose. "Weylyn's still asleep, and Faolan left already. Rieka's at auntie's house holding the new baby, but I want to go back to the gathering! I need to prepare for my race." She looked at him with grave eyes. The children's footrace was very important to her. She hopped from foot to foot in anticipation.

He ruffled her hair, the copper glinting between his fingers. "Alright. Let me get dressed and I'll take you."

276

One more unsuccessful peek around his leg and Arowyn scampered off to wait for him in the garden. "Don't be long!" she yelled over her shoulder.

Alaric turned back into the house with a sigh. His empty bed stood as a glaring reminder of the person who was meant to be in it. Connell's threats still rang in his head. He needed to figure out a way to find Odessa without attracting the chief's attention. Once he was sure she was safe he would deal with the consequences of his crimes.

He pulled on a fresh tunic and laced up his boots. It was warm enough today to do without a cloak, but he put on a vest and tied his hair away from his face. He hadn't slept more than an hour and his eyelids were gritty and swollen. Hopefully, no one would think it was anything more than too much ale the day before.

Today was the day the clans would compete in various games and contests. A more civilized way to work through their grudges and rivalries. Not that it stopped the violent skirmishes that happened throughout the year. There was always a wrong to avenge. But not at the gathering. The gathering was sacred.

Normally, the games were Alaric's favorite part of the gathering, but this morning as he walked through the dappled sunlight of the forest to the gathering field, his stomach was tied in knots. A deep dread had settled into his bones. And without Odessa by his side, he was untethered. A light breeze could topple him.

Arowyn chattered away as they walked, her small hand in his, and he attempted to hide his mood. But after the third generic grunt in response to her questions, she seemed to be catching on.

"What's wrong? Today is your favorite day!" A crease formed between her eyebrows. He pressed his thumb there, smoothing it out. She was too young to have worry lines that mimicked his own.

He forced a mischievous grin. "Nothing, little wolf. A bit too much ale yesterday."

Arowyn nodded, but her face remained serious.

"Do you think you will win the race today?"

"I am the fastest Wolf by far," she boasted with a smile. "But did you see the Bears yesterday? Their girls are so tall."

"Height means nothing for a footrace. Too much wind up there to slow them down." He ruffled her hair again and she giggled.

Alaric's heart twisted in his chest at the way Arowyn beamed up at him. What would his siblings think when they found out what he had done to their father? Would Arowyn's face still light up when she saw him? Would Rieka preen under his compliments? Would Faolan seek him out for advice?

And Weylyn. It was Weylyn's reaction he feared the most. He remembered their father best, had been the oldest when he died. The man had not been kind to any of them, but he was their father nonetheless. Would Weylyn understand why he did what he did? Would he forgive it?

Connell was right. Alaric was a coward. He had no desire to uncover the answer to any of these questions. But he could see no way around it. He had to find Odessa. If Connell had thought he would simply let her go, the man was a fool.

They continued their walk, the field coming into view. The Wolves were in the same spot as the day before; their fires burning off the morning chill. Arowyn ran off to join her cousins in preparing for the race and Alaric watched her go, not nearly as eager to join his family. He had become adept at hiding his emotions over the years, but this morning he was nothing more than a hollowed-out shell. He wasn't sure he could hide that.

Especially not from his aunts. Layla hustled over, her concern written across her features. For a moment she looked so much like his mother, he nearly spilled his secrets to her before she even asked.

"Where is Odessa? Is she still unwell?"

"Just tired." His gaze roved everywhere, refusing to land on his aunt's face.

She made a small noise of disapproval but then broke into a smile. "Perhaps it has happened for you." She clapped her hands in front of her as Alaric wracked his brain for the reason she would be so pleased.

"Women are often exhausted when they are with child. Especially in the first few months."

Alaric's mind spun as his aunt prattled on.

"She needs plenty of rest. And I have a wonderful ginger tea that will help if she is nauseous."

He clapped a hand on her shoulder to stop her from going on. Layla was beaming at the dream of a baby when in reality his wife was missing. He hadn't questioned why he and Odessa hadn't conceived yet, he was just happy to have her by his side, but this story, this life that would never be his, that his aunt was spinning out before him was too much for him to take.

"It's not that, auntie." His voice was too loud, too abrupt. His aunt flinched.

"Oh. Well." Her brow creased in worry, an echo of

Arowyn's earlier expression.

"She is tired. That is all." He softened his voice and Layla nodded before hustling off to feed everyone around her fire.

Alaric shifted on his feet, feeling as though he may crawl out of his skin. This was a mistake. He couldn't stand here all day and pretend everything was fine. He needed to go. He needed to track down Odessa now. Connell's threats be damned.

He caught a glimpse of his cousins at the Foxes camp. Branton and Afi would have been boys when his father left to marry his mother, but they were kin all the same. How would they react to the news of his father's murder? If a Wolf killed a Fox in battle, that would be an honorable death. But to kill a member of another clan with no cause? The clans had fought over lesser infractions, but that was grounds for war.

Narah, help him! His actions put his entire clan in jeopardy again. At every turn, he made things worse. It would have been better if he had never met Odessa. The traitorous thought crept into his mind and took hold like a parasite. He looked around the field at his people, at the lives he would risk if he went after his wife.

But how many of them would be lost if she had never come? How much blame could he put on his own actions? He had only ever acted out of good intentions, out of the love of his family.

Another thought more wicked than the first replaced it. He wanted Odessa back at all costs. He would risk everything for her and for that he could not feel sorry. Perhaps he was not a good man after all.

Alaric spent much of the morning in a fog, struggling between his own selfish needs and those of his clan. He even tried to convince himself Odessa was better off with her own people, that Nolan would take care of her. But his body physically rejected the idea. He nearly lost the little breakfast he had been able to choke down.

Daciana saw Nolan take Odessa by force. She hadn't gone willingly. She was in danger. What was Alaric still doing here? He had to go after her. He would make peace with the Foxes once he found her. He slipped quietly to the edge of the forest, making sure Connell was distracted resolving a dispute at the archery competition before he disappeared into the trees.

He hadn't gotten far when he saw a figure in the distance. She wore an emerald cloak in the style of Kalon. She hesitated as she neared the field and Alaric ducked behind a tree. The woman panted, her light brown cheeks flushed with exertion. She glanced around nervously. There could only be one reason a woman from Kalon would be wandering so near to the Wolves. Odessa.

He reached out and snatched her by the upper arm. She yelped; her eyes wide like a startled deer.

Alaric released her arm, raising his hands in front of him. "I don't wish to harm you."

The woman stepped back but didn't run like he feared she would.

"My wife is from Kalon, as are you. Do you know anything about her?"

She breathed a sigh of relief. "You are Alaric of the Wolves?"

He nodded.

"Your wife sends a message."

"Where is she?" He cut her off before she could speak further, his desperation making him impatient.

"She's in an abandoned hunting cabin on the edge of Kalon, but there's more," the messenger rushed to get the words out before he could interrupt again. "She says Narah calls the four clans to Kalon."

"Narah calls the four clans?" The hair on his arms stood on end and his skin prickled beneath his tunic. What sort of message was this? "Is she alright?" He struggled for control, his whole body trembled. The woman's face softened in sympathy.

"She was well when I saw her."

He noticed her hedging. Odessa was alive this morning, but the sun was high in the sky now. It was anyone's guess how she fared.

"Was anyone with her?"

The woman glanced behind her and then back to Alaric. "The man, Nolan, had left for supplies. I waited for him to be gone before I approached. But it was the king's orders that she never return to the Wolves. That is all I know."

Alaric grasped the tree next to him. The king? Her father wanted her gone, but why? Why break the alliance now? He shook his head of all the thoughts buzzing in his skull. Only one thing mattered now.

"Why are you telling me this? Who sent you?" Could this be a trap?

The woman held her cloak open to reveal the seal of the Northern queen stitched to the inside. A white crescent moon on a scarlet background. "The queen herself."

"Why?"

"Odessa saved her daughter. A debt she can never

repay, but this is a start."

The queen had gone against her king? Odessa had evoked Narah's name? The pieces began to fall into place. His path forward became clear.

Chapter 38: A Forgiving Man

Warm fingertips brushed the hair from her face. Odessa smiled in her sleep, happy to be home. She breathed deeply, but the air was musty, the comforting smells of woodsmoke and pine were gone.

"Wake up, princess. I brought you something to eat." The voice was familiar and once beloved, but it was not the voice she was longing to hear.

She opened her eyes, squinting in the bright light of day. Nolan sat beside her on the bed. Nolan, not her husband. Not Alaric. She struggled upright, pain shooting through her side. She propped herself against the headboard as far away from Nolan as she could get.

"You're injured." He said it as though he wasn't the one who had caused it. His voice was almost sympathetic, almost kind as his gaze raked over her. Odessa shuddered.

"Why did you bring me here?"

Nolan laid a bundle in her lap ignoring her question. "Eat. You must be hungry." His voice was laced with all the kindness he had once shown her. Memories of his visits during her lonely hours in the castle raced through her mind. But the memories were tainted, spoiled by the rottenness that had only recently revealed itself.

Her resolve to refuse the food broke as soon as the smell of the warm bread wafted up to her. The grumbling of her stomach was impossible to ignore. She unwrapped the bread and tore off a small chunk. It was crusty and warm, and she held back a moan of pleasure when she bit into it.

"I'm sorry I had to leave you for so long. I went to get us supplies." He reached out to run a hand along her pale cheek. She flinched.

He narrowed his eyes at her and an image of his face as he dragged her to his horse flashed through her mind. "You never used to flinch from my touch. You loved me once." His voice was soft, the anger from last night had been pushed away. But she wasn't foolish enough to think it was gone for good.

Odessa had expected him to storm in here to carry out her father's wishes. She had not expected tenderness, however false it may be.

"Supplies for what, Nolan? Why did you bring me here?" she asked again.

He sighed as though she were trying his patience. "We are going away from here. Far away."

Odessa's mind spun. "You can't!"

Nolan's fingers caught her hard by the chin and lifted her gaze to his. "You are out of options, princess. You come with me, or I kill you like your father ordered me to."

She would rather die than go with him, and she nearly opened her mouth to tell him so. But she had a life now, one she wished to return to. And a husband. A family. Tears welled in her eyes. Alaric's family had become her own.

Nolan's fingers dug into her flesh as she blinked away her tears. "Please, Nolan. Don't kill me."

He dropped his hand, satisfied for the moment with

her answer. He stood from the bed and paced the small room. A nervous habit she had never seen him display before. He had always been so composed, so confident.

"I'm glad a life with me is more appealing than death." His words were no longer gilded with kindness. The bitterness had burned through the caring facade. The old floor creaked under his feet as he paced.

Odessa glanced out the window. The sun had already begun its descent in the sky. The queen's maid should have made it to Alaric by now. Perhaps if she could stall Nolan long enough…

"We will go far from here. Away from Kalon and Asherah's damn forest and the beast you call a husband." He spat the words, cursing everything she held dear. "The king wants you out of his sight, away from the clans. And I am nothing if not loyal."

He stopped his pacing to flash her a sickening smile. She didn't return it.

"Smile, Essa. It's everything you ever wanted."

Her stomach rolled and turned at his words, threatening to expel the small amount of bread she had eaten. He was right. It was what she had wanted. For a year she dreamt of Nolan taking her far from Kalon, but not like this. Never like this. Her hands shook in her lap, and she hid them in the folds of her skirt.

"You're right." The words burned her throat. "It is what I wanted. I will go with you, of course."

Nolan's smile grew, but his eyes remained hard. He came back to sit beside her on the bed and pulled her hand into his. Her flesh crawled at his touch, but she forced herself not to yank her hand away. It seemed safest to play along for now. This man she once knew was dangerous and unpredictable.

"But I can't go today. I can't ride with my injuries." She gently patted her ribs with her other hand and regret flashed briefly in his eyes.

He quickly schooled his features into the hardened mask he had taken to wearing. "We leave tomorrow at dawn. Injured or not."

"But Nolan—"

He grabbed her face again, hard, drawing a gasp from her mouth. He turned her slightly, so he only had to look at the pale cheek. "Do not try my patience, Essa. You have put me through enough already."

A laugh rose in her throat at the absurdity of his statement, but he gripped her so tightly she could do nothing but whimper.

He pulled her face closer until his breath was loud in her ear. "You are lucky I am a forgiving man."

Her mind raced even as her body recoiled from this man and his threats. Would Alaric find her by morning? Could he possibly convince the clans to face Kalon together?

Nolan stroked the pale side of her face. The bile rose in her throat as he traced the neckline of her bodice, his fingers dipping into her dress to follow the swell of her breasts.

"Do you remember the things I used to do to you? The things you let me do? The things you begged me to do?"

Her breath caught as he pressed his lips to the sensitive skin behind her ear, kissing a poisonous trail down her neck.

No, no, no. Please, not this. Her fervent prayer played on a loop in her mind as Nolan sucked on the skin where her neck met her shoulder. She remembered with shame how she used to melt into his touch when he kissed her right there.

But not anymore, not now, not like this.

She pressed her hands against his chest and pushed him away. "Nolan, stop. I can't."

His face went red with anger. His rapid breathing was no longer from passion but rage. She braced herself for the impact of his strike, but he held back.

"I will erase that bastard from your heart and your body if it is the last thing I do."

Impossible! The word screamed through her head, but she bit her tongue. No matter what Nolan did to her, Alaric was imprinted forever on her heart. He was hers and she was his. Why had she ever fought with him about the circumstances that brought them to each other? They were together. It was the only thing that mattered. She wished she could tell him.

Nolan stood abruptly and Odessa sank down in relief.

"Tomorrow morning. We leave. It would be wise to remember the alternative." He strode from the room, slamming the door behind him. Odessa sat in stunned silence, listening to the key turn in the lock.

How had she managed to become the cursed princess again, locked away from the world? Had she not shaken that life?

A wolf howled in the distance and the key to Alaric's home, her home, hung between her breasts. She stood and went to the window. The white wolf was back.

Tomorrow the clans would come. Tomorrow she would embrace her new identity. Odessa, Narah's chosen one, Alaric's wife. No longer a daughter of

Kalon but instead a protector of Asherah's Wood. And whoever else she damn well chose to be. Tomorrow she would shed her curse once and for all.

Chapter 39: Unity

Alaric strode back to the field, the woman's message singing in his ears. Narah calls the clans to Kalon. Odessa would not have invoked the goddess's name lightly, regardless of her beliefs. If this was the message she sent, she needed the clans united. And he trusted her with his life and the lives of his people. His belief in the goddess was strong, but his belief in his wife was stronger.

He walked through the crowds, head down, ignoring calls to eat or drink or compete. He climbed onto the wooden platform in the middle of the field. A few heads turned in his direction. He spotted his Uncle Merrick staring at him, his brows raised in curiosity. Arowyn sat happily upon Weylyn's shoulders, wearing a crown of flowers, her prize for winning the foot race. Alaric's guts twisted at the sight of his siblings. Rieka noticed him and gave him a questioning smile. His eyes scanned the crowd and he found Faolan laughing beside his aunt's fire, Asena clearly teasing him for something.

More clansmen had taken notice of his stance on the platform and an uneasy hush had begun on one side of the field, slowly flowing to the other side. From the corner of his eye, he saw Connell pushing his way through the crowd. Merrick grabbed his shoulder and held him for a moment. It was now or never.

"Fellow clansmen," he bellowed, his voice

carrying across the field. More heads turned his way until all the people of Asherah's Wood raised their gaze to him. Alaric stood tall. He was broad and muscled, weapons hung from his belt and a thick beard covered his face, but inside he shook with the fear of what he was about to do. He was a child again, cowering at his father's side, awaiting whatever punishment the man would dish out.

"I have a message."

Connell tore free of his uncle's grasp and continued his rush to the platform.

"But first I have a confession."

Connell froze in his tracks. Alaric met his gaze for the second it took to see the truth. With this confession, he would finally rid himself of Connell's hold over him. The man would pose no further threat.

"My father was not killed in battle. I was the one to put the arrow through his back."

Even the birds in the trees were silent after his confession. He sought out his siblings with his gaze. Their reactions were the only ones that mattered to him. Faolan's face had drained of color. Rieka stood frozen, her brow creased in worry. Arowyn peered down at Weylyn to gauge his reaction. Weylyn's eyes had gone wide, and Alaric's breath caught in his throat, he may have lost the boy forever.

But then Weylyn's face softened, and he gave Alaric a small nod, patting Arowyn comfortingly on the knee.

Unfortunately, his siblings were not the only ones in the field before him. Hundreds of his people burst into confusion. Shouts rang out from the Foxes demanding retribution. The Wolves' reactions ranged from angry and betrayed to worried and frightened. The Bears and Ravens watched in morbid curiosity.

Alaric held up the horn Connell had left on the platform and blew into the end. It took several blows to call the people back to order. Sweat dripped down Alaric's back. Regardless of what happened to him afterward, he needed to get Odessa's message to the clans. Odessa would not have used Narah's name simply to save herself. The clans were in danger. He felt it in his bones.

Finally, the crowd was quiet enough to hear him. He glanced at the Wolf elders out of the corner of his eye. They had already formed a small group at the edge of the crowd, ready to take matters into their own hands. He needed to make this quick.

"I am not proud of my actions, but I acted to protect my family. I would do it again."

A roar rose from the Fox camp and Alaric feared they may pull him from the stage and seek justice then and there. Wolf warriors had already begun to circle the unarmed families to protect them. The field was on the cusp of chaos.

"Do what you will to me, but please listen first. My wife, Odessa, was kidnapped." Several gasps and murmurs came from the Wolf camp and Alaric's gut twisted with guilt for lying to them all morning.

"She has sent word. Narah calls the clans of Asherah's Wood to Kalon."

Whatever loose restraints had held the clans before he spoke, snapped at his words. The people from all four camps erupted. The once organized field turned to bedlam. Alaric jumped from the platform in a panicked rush to his siblings. He gathered them close as the clan leaders attempted to regain control of their people.

"I'm sorry." He scooped Arowyn from Weylyn's shoulders and she snuggled into him. Rieka held tight to his side. "I should have told you sooner."

Weylyn nodded. "You should have." His voice was tight with emotion. "But the bastard deserved it."

Alaric swallowed hard. Faolan rushed to their sides, aunts and uncles close behind him. Alaric could see the forgiveness on the boy's face. Words were not necessary between them. If nothing else, his siblings now knew the truth.

"Is it true?" Merrick asked over the noise of the crowd. "The message from your wife."

"Yes. I received word from the queen's maid. Odessa was taken to a hunter's cottage outside Kalon." He glanced to where Connell glowered at him, the other elders by his side. "And Connell played no small part in her kidnapping."

He grabbed his uncle's arm. "She wouldn't have invoked Narah's name without cause. The goddess calls us to Kalon. We must go."

Arowyn's arms tightened around his neck, and he held her close.

"I will take your words to the other elders, but I don't know how this will turn out Alaric." His uncle ran a hand down his beard. The crowd around them quieted, but arguing still could be heard from every corner of the field.

"I plan to be in Kalon by dawn. I will stand before the Northern king myself if I must, but I will get my wife back. Narah calls the clans, Merrick. We must go."

Merrick hesitated and Alaric went on, "Since the kingdoms rose around us, we have been at their mercy.

293

We allowed them to desecrate our forest and march through our lands. Why? Because we couldn't put aside our petty grievances with each other to stand against them? We are strongest together. Now is the time."

A small group of Wolves had gathered around him as he spoke. He saw heads nodding in agreement. The tide of opinion was beginning to turn.

"You make a good point, nephew." A slow smile graced Merrick's face. "You may not walk to Kalon alone after all."

He strode off to join the other elders, and Alaric's body sagged under the weight of all that he had said and done. It was up to the clan chiefs to decide now. Connell's glare was like a hot brand on his back. He refused to turn around.

****

Alaric spent the rest of the afternoon sitting beside his aunt Layla's fire, waiting. His body ached. Every muscle remained tense and rigid as he watched the elders argue. By nightfall, he was fairly certain he was not going to be dragged away from his family and exiled for his crimes. At least not today. But still, he waited to hear the leaders' decision.

Arowyn was curled up in his lap, asleep with her head resting on his chest. Rieka sat beside him. She hadn't said much since his speech, but she also had not left his side. He didn't have the heart to send the children home to bed. They deserved to know what would happen next as much as he did.

Faolan sat across the fire, his cousins Asena and Sairsha doting on him. His plate had not been empty since noon. The sight brought a bittersweet comfort. His siblings would be fine without him, whenever that day came. He met Faolan's gaze, and his brother gave him a small smile. Alaric thanked the gods again for his family's understanding. His brothers knew why he did what he did.

Weylyn had wandered off sometime after sunset, and Alaric couldn't help but repeatedly scan the field for him. Now was not the time to chase Connell's daughter.

Layla sat beside Rieka with a soft groan. She handed a fresh cup of ale to Alaric. "My sisters and I, we…" she began but then stopped, sighed, and tried again. "Oh, Alaric. We are sorry."

When he turned to face her, slowly so as to not wake the child in his lap, there were tears shimmering in his aunt's eyes. Her face in the moonlight was so similar to his own mother's, he nearly gasped.

"What do you have to be sorry about, auntie? I'm the one who should apologize for bringing such shame to our family."

Layla shook her head, stroking a hand through Rieka's dark hair. The girl had dozed off against Alaric's side, the solid warmth of her comforted him.

"No. We failed you and these precious children. We failed your mother, my sister. We didn't see what was happening right in front of us. We didn't want to see." The tears fell freely now.

"I think my mother was ashamed. She didn't want you to know." It had never occurred to him to go to his aunts or uncles for help. He was only a child. His father's abuse was all he knew. By the time he was old enough to understand that hitting your children and wife was not something every man did, he too was ashamed. His father's actions had been his family's secret and now the secret was finally out.

He hated to see the pain on his aunt's face. "It's over now."

Layla nodded, hastily wiping the tears from her face. "Whatever happens," she paused and all the possibilities of what could happen ran through his mind. "Whatever happens, these children will be cared for. I swear it."

Alaric swallowed hard, glancing at the sleeping forms of his sisters. Faolan's soft laugh drifted to him from across the circle.

"I know. Thank you."

Layla sighed, her burden eased, and continued to stroke Rieka's hair. The firelight flickered over her familiar face, and Alaric's muscles relaxed for the first time since Odessa went missing. He would find her. All he needed to know was whether or not he would go alone.

Weylyn burst into the circle of light surrounding the fire, followed closely by Daciana. The girl's cheeks were flushed pink, and wisps of hair escaped her braids and stuck to the side of her face. Weylyn wore a huge grin and Alaric was about to drag him off into the trees to tell him exactly how inappropriate a time it was to be manhandling the chief's daughter when the boy spoke.

"The Wolves are with you." He was panting as though they had run across the field to tell Alaric the news and his eyes were bright in the firelight. "The Wolves will march to Kalon. They've gone off to speak with the other chiefs. To convince them to unite behind you."

"Behind me?" Panic spiked Alaric's heartbeat. "That was never my intention."

Weylyn's grin grew. "The elders say if we are successful in facing the Northern king, you will be named chief."

All the air left Alaric's lungs. He must have squeezed Arowyn too tightly. The girl squeaked and woke with a start.

"Sorry, little wolf," he mumbled, ruffling her hair.

"Alaric is to be the new chief," Weylyn repeated for his sisters' benefit as Rieka also awoke from her nap. Alaric's stomach tumbled and quaked. He had never intended to lead his people, only to answer the call of his goddess. Is this what she had been waiting for?

Alaric cleared his throat. "You are getting ahead of yourself, brother. Let's see if the other clans even agree."

"Oh, they will," Daciana chimed in. "We've been listening."

Alaric raised an eyebrow. "Something you seem to do often."

The girl's face reddened, and she gave him an apologetic smile.

"And what about your father?"

Her expression darkened but she gave a small shrug as though it didn't bother her. "He's been removed from the elders for his role in your wife's kidnapping." She squared her shoulders as if ready for a fight, but Alaric would never blame the girl for her father's missteps.

"I don't know what will become of him." Her chin quivered slightly. "But I will stay with the Wolves."

Alaric pitied the poor girl, but he was sure her relations would take her in. And perhaps Connell would stay, even after his fall from grace.

"She will stay with me, as my wife," Weylyn declared, proudly pulling Daciana closer.

Ale sputtered from Alaric's mouth as he nearly choked to death. Layla cackled happily beside him, and his sisters clapped with glee.

"Your wife?" Alaric managed between coughs. "There is no way—"

"We can discuss it later, brother. You have a clan to lead!" Weylyn called over his shoulder as he slipped away from the fire, Daciana's giggles lingering in their wake.

Alaric ran a hand down his face and Layla patted him on the shoulder. "Come now, nephew. Your people need you. Your brother's thrashing can wait until you return as chief." Layla beamed. Rieka reached up and planted a kiss on Alaric's cheek. He sighed. His aunt was right.

Chapter 40: Tomorrow

Odessa woke from her few hours of sleep cold and stiff. She had dozed off sitting against the headboard and her neck was sore from slumping over. The ache in her side had dulled to a persistent throbbing. Nolan had never bothered to start a fire, and Odessa shivered beneath the thin quilt. She reached for the last of the bread and choked it down followed by a few sips of the water Nolan had finally thought to bring her.

She rose gingerly from the bed and crept toward the window, her muscles aching in protest. A weak gray light had begun to seep from the horizon to the surrounding fields, illuminating the fact that the fields were still empty.

Odessa sighed and leaned her forehead against the cold glass. Alaric had not found her. The clans had not made it in time. Perhaps they would never come. But soon Nolan would be at her door ready to take her far from here, far from everything she knew, both the good and the bad.

As the sun peeked over the distant hills, Odessa weighed her options. They were few. Nolan's behavior the night before was erratic and dangerous. His former kindness had nearly surfaced but had been crushed by the man's self-righteous anger. A shiver of dread ran through her as his threats echoed in her mind.

She stilled at the sound of the key turning in the

lock.

"Good. You're awake."

She didn't turn and Nolan came to stand behind her, his words hot in her ear. She squirmed away from him, but his body kept her pinned to the window.

"There's no point in pretending you are sad to go, princess. I, of all people, remember what your life was like in that castle."

"It's not the castle I will miss." Her breath fogged the glass in front of her. Nolan wrapped an arm around her waist and tugged her close.

"Don't dare speak his name, Essa. I will not stand for it."

She gasped as his grip tightened, his teeth sharp on her ear as he bit her. Any struggle on her part only made him squeeze her harder. His breath was ragged, his erection pressed into her back.

"In fact, I will make you mine before we leave this place. I won't have you taking his memory with you." He spun her around roughly, slamming his lips onto hers. She tasted blood. He held tight to her arms, his fingers digging into her flesh. How cruel of him to make this her last memory, to make this her last kiss. She pushed Alaric from her mind, refusing to think of him while Nolan pawed his way into her dress.

Nolan had been fully dressed for traveling, but now he shucked off this coat as he dragged Odessa toward the bed. She shrieked as he tossed her onto it; pain radiated through her already bruised body. He yanked his shirt over his head and climbed on top of her.

"Don't be so dramatic. I've fucked you plenty of times before."

She twisted beneath him, and he pinned her wrists

to the mattress.

"Why must you make things so difficult between us?" he ground out, struggling to keep hold of her hands. "It used to be so simple." Again, a flash of the man he used to be crossed his face.

Odessa calmed beneath him. He studied her, his gaze flicking quickly over her face and landing somewhere above her rapidly beating heart.

"You're right," she whispered. "It used to be simple."

His grip relaxed slightly on her wrists. She flexed her fingers open and closed.

"I'm sorry, Nolan." Her throat burned with the lie.

His gaze rose to hers again and she smiled at him, the way she used to. She smiled at him the way she did when he was her whole world, when she had nowhere else to direct her love. She smiled at him the way she did when she thought he was the one person who truly understood her.

She smiled, and he released his grip on her wrists. Odessa wrapped her arms around his back, pulling him closer and he sighed into her neck, kissing, and murmuring his love for her.

Odessa's hands roved over Nolan's back. His ribs stuck out like ridges in his side and the knobby bones of his spine were raised beneath her fingers. He had once been so strong and healthy. He had let his obsession ruin more than his mind.

He grabbed her skirts and began pushing them up over her legs just as Odessa grabbed the dagger from his belt.

"Mine," he growled as he freed himself from his pants. What a terrible last word, but there was no turning back now. Odessa drove the dagger up and under his ribs, hard and fast. It sank into the soft flesh between the bones, and Nolan's eyes went wide with pain and betrayal.

His blood seeped through her fingers, sticky and warm as he wriggled on top of her. She managed to push him off her body. She stood on trembling legs as the life drained out of him.

In the distance, a wolf howled.

Odessa stumbled to the window in time to see the clansmen filling the fields beyond the cottage. Hundreds of them. She looked at her hands, covered in Nolan's blood. Her mind was filled with the buzzing of a thousand bees, keeping her thoughts at bay.

She hurried past the bed, not daring to look at Nolan again, and opened the door to the bedroom. She found her boots and cloak waiting for her outside. She pulled them on, focusing only on the next task, the next step, not letting her mind wander back into the bedroom. Not letting herself think about the life she had taken.

Her injuries no longer hurt, although she was sure they would later, later when she could think, later when she would catalog her experience here. But for now, her blood raced through her veins with a new determination.

Odessa tore open the door of the cottage and found herself in a small, overgrown garden on the edge of the forest. To the north, the fields of Kalon stretched to the castle on the hill. To the south, Asherah's Wood. And from her sacred trees more and more clansmen poured out into the sunlight.

Before she could fully comprehend what this

meant, the one face she longed to see more than any other appeared before her. His eyes went wide when he noticed her standing among the tangled vines. She followed his horrified gaze down her body. Her dress was streaked with bright red stains. Nolan's blood coated her skin. She didn't have time to explain it wasn't hers before she was wrapped in Alaric's arms, his tears falling softly in her hair.

Chapter 41: Wolves and Ravens

"Odessa, Odessa…" Her name spilled from his lips like a prayer whispered fervently in the dark. "You're alive." It was then he remembered the blood. So much blood. He held her away from him and she smiled weakly at him.

"Are you hurt? Where is he?" All his fear and relief and guilt quickly transformed into rage when he thought of Nolan, the savage wrapped in shining armor.

"He's dead." Odessa's words were stilted, her eyes unblinking.

Realization settled heavily in Alaric's gut. She never should have had to do this alone.

"I should have gotten here sooner. I never should have let you out of my sight." He cursed himself for ever leaving her, for ever arguing with her. But one more look at her ashen face, and he paused his self-recriminations. Plenty of time to torture himself later.

He brushed a gentle hand down her cheek and bit down hard on his rage when he noticed the bruises on her chin. Fingerprints. He pulled her close again, smoothing her hair, and murmuring whatever gentle words came to mind. When he finally felt the dampness of her tears seeping through his tunic, he breathed a sigh of relief.

"I'm so sorry," he whispered into her hair.

Odessa sniffled against him. "It's over now."

He kissed the top of her head, the silk of her hair brushing against his lips.

"Your heart is racing." She placed a hand over the ache in his chest.

"I thought I lost you. And seeing you covered in blood…" His throat closed and the words died in his mouth. He swallowed hard. "Did he hurt you?" There were other ways Nolan could have hurt her, ways he wouldn't be able to see. He squeezed his eyes shut at the images that sprang to mind. He wished Nolan was alive if only so he could kill him again.

Odessa ran a hand down Alaric's face, bringing him back to her.

"He didn't hurt me. I…I…killed him before he could."

Alaric pulled her close again. He should be comforting her, not the other way around. What was he doing? He sucked in air and blew it out in a harsh sigh. It took several tries before he was calm enough to speak again, but the time helped Odessa as well. Her breathing had evened out and her sniffling had quieted. If only they could stay like this, pressed together in each other's arms, forgetting about the outside world entirely. But it was a foolish wish. His people were waiting for him, and he needed his wife safe.

"I will take you home."

Odessa pulled back and stared at him with wide eyes. "Home?"

"To our home." A sudden panic hit him. Did she not wish to return with him? "If that is what you want."

She stepped out of the circle of his arms and placed her hands on her hips. Her hair had come undone from her braids and now cascaded down her back in dark waves. Nolan's blood stained her skirts and her hands. And her face, her face was fierce, her eyes narrowed, and her mouth set in a determined line. She had never looked more beautiful.

"I called your people here in Narah's name and you think I will turn and go home?"

The wind rustled through the trees around them. The branches bent toward her as though they too were listening.

"But you've been through so much. I thought—"

"You thought!" She threw her hands in the air at his stupidity. He struggled to bite back a smile.

"We are going to the Northern king. We will show him the clans stand together, and we will demand he stay away from the sacred wood, or the clans will rise against him." With every word he watched his wife claim her role as Narah's chosen one. And with every word his heart beat faster in his chest.

Alaric bowed deeply, the smile spreading across his face. "Lead the way, princess."

Odessa nodded once in satisfaction and then threw herself back into the safety of his arms. He caught her tight to his chest and she grimaced. She quickly schooled her features, trying to hide her pain, but it was too late.

"He did hurt you." Alaric's voice was nothing but a growl.

She reached up and tugged his face closer to hers. "He is dead, and we are still alive. I will not allow him a hold over us anymore."

Her lips met his with a ferocity that matched her words. She kissed him like she had nearly lost him, like she wanted to wash away the touch of Nolan on her skin. So, he kissed her back, sweeping his tongue into her mouth as she clung to him. She moaned and whimpered as he worshipped her with his mouth. He ran his fingers through the waves of her hair, afraid to hold her too tight. He could do this forever, but soon the voices of his people filtered into his thoughts.

Odessa planted one more gentle kiss on his lips before pulling away. Alaric glanced through the trees and nearly gasped at the sight of his people filling the fields of Kalon. Last night, he had been filled with an urgent dread, wanting nothing more than to reach Odessa. But now in the early morning light, to see his people finally united with the other clans of the wood, Alaric's heart filled with a new hope.

Odessa tugged his hand and led him to Nolan's horse. She spoke softly to the beast, calming her, and gestured for Alaric to help her into the saddle. He mounted behind her, and they rode slowly into the field to join the clans.

"It does not bother you to speak on Narah's behalf anymore?" he whispered the question in her ear as they rode. Even if it was simply the need to escape Nolan, he would have understood, but here she was planning to speak to the king on behalf of his people. Something had changed.

"My father made threats against the clans. Nolan told him the clans had taken to worshipping me, and he vowed to make them pay for it."

Alaric stilled as she spoke. She had done it to save them all, not to save herself. He left a trail of kisses along the curl of her ear, unable to keep his lips from her.

"I realized I could do the one thing my father

feared the most, unite the clans in Narah's name. It was like the night I realized I could be the one to save Faye." She shrugged a little against him, and he wrapped himself around her. "I felt strong. Maybe it was Narah. Who am I to say?"

He held her tighter against him.

"You are strong. And clever. And braver than any warrior," he whispered the words against the pale skin of her neck.

She tensed beneath him as they neared the castle. They had skirted around his clansmen, wanting to go directly to the king and avoid bloodshed.

He placed a kiss behind Odessa's ear, then straightened and took a deep breath. It was time to face the man who had tormented his wife and threatened his people. He reminded himself it would help nothing if he smashed his fist through the king's face.

"Where's Connell?" she asked before they reached the gate.

"He was removed from his position for his role in your kidnapping."

"Oh." Odessa didn't sound surprised that the chief had conspired to have her taken from him. Perhaps he shouldn't have been either.

"Then who is the new Wolf chief?"

"Uh…I suppose it's me." His confession was quiet and nearly lost in the shadow of the looming castle, the noise from inside the walls nearly drowned him out. But Odessa heard. She turned slightly in the saddle and looked at him in disbelief.

"If this goes well, that is," he added.

Odessa stared at him a moment longer before a slow smile crept across her face. Despite his racing heart and the dread settling in his gut, he returned her grin before she turned toward the gate.

She yelled to the man on the wall above them. The Kalonian guards were already in a frenzy of activity thanks to the hundreds of clansmen now occupying their fields, but one man paused to listen.

"It's Princess Odessa. Let us through. I've come to speak to my father on behalf of the clans."

****

The king had kept them waiting for three days, and he still refused an audience. He had rejected their call for a meeting, and every messenger since had returned with the same answer. King Orion refused to meet with his daughter or any member of the Clans of the Woods.

Alaric stood outside the tent he shared with Odessa and scanned the field in front of him. He was soaked to the bone from the rain that had begun yesterday and refused to let up. His people were cold and miserable. No one could remember why they had come or why they should stay. He cursed the Northern king, muttering to himself in the early morning light.

"Nephew." Merrick strode up to where he stood in the mud. "Another fight broke out in the night between the Foxes and Ravens." His uncle shook his head, the rainwater dripping from the ends of his hair.

"Damn it." Could his people not remain united for more than a few days? Had he led them all here for nothing? A growl formed low in his throat. He would not come this close to peace for nothing.

"Several men are injured, and Brenna is threatening to leave with the Ravens," Merrick went on. "They have the largest numbers. Without them…"

"I don't need you to explain how damned we are,

uncle," Alaric snapped, wiping the water from his eyes. "I will speak to her."

"Speak with who?" Odessa emerged from the tent, her hood pulled tight around her, keeping out the rain.

"Go back to bed, princess."

"Speak with who?" she repeated, not budging from her place beside him. He could not even command his own wife. How could he ever lead his people?

He glanced at Odessa. Her mouth was set in a firm line and her arms crossed over her chest. Her feet were firmly planted in the mud next to his. A grin tugged at his lips. Who was he trying to fool? A pliable wife would have never suited him.

"I'm going to speak with Brenna, the Raven Chief. She's threatening to leave."

Odessa's eyes widened. "I'm coming with you."

Alaric sighed. "I expected you would."

They trudged through the mud toward the Raven's camp. The people had set up in the same way they had for the gathering, clustered together by clan. United, but still separate. Old tensions were not easily forgotten. How would they stand together in battle, should it ever come? Alaric prayed it wouldn't. This was meant to be a show of force, a message to the North that the clans were united and would no longer tolerate the desecration of their forest. But the king ignored them day after day. And the clans were growing restless.

Men peered at them as they passed, many still wanting to get a better look at Narah's chosen one. Odessa stayed close to his side, offering the warriors a nod or lift of her hand in greeting but nothing more. Her conviction from days before had waned with the waiting. His fierce warrior had turned anxious again. It was a mistake to continue to shield her from the clans. They deserved answers, but he would not parade Odessa in front of them. The words from their last fight still lingered in his mind, Odessa's worries and fears echoed even though she didn't repeat them. His clansmen would have to follow his word or leave. He wouldn't force Odessa to lead his people.

Alaric shook his head in frustration and Odessa squeezed his hand, bringing him back to the present moment. The Raven's camp was a flurry of activity despite the early hour and the driving rain. It wasn't hard to find their chief, Brenna, standing in the center of it all.

Her black hair was plastered to her head from the rain, and her dark eyes scanned her people. She was tall and slim, dressed in her black fighting leathers. Even without her face painted black for battle, she was ominous as death itself as they approached her.

The Ravens handed the chiefdom down through the women of the clan. A picture of young, rosy Daciana as the next leader of the Wolves nearly brought a laugh to his lips. Although, she might have done better than he was.

Alaric swallowed the dread rising in his throat. He was not ready to lead his own clan, and convincing others to remain with him seemed more impossible by the minute.

"If you've brought your little wife here to convince us to stay, it's not going to work."

"I only came to see what the trouble is."

Brenna stepped closer, crowding him, but he didn't budge. She had fine lines around her eyes and a few streaks of silver through her hair. Older and wiser than him in every way and here he was about to argue with her to stay.

"The trouble is those sneaky Fox bastards snuck into our camp last night and stole from my warriors."

Alaric opened his mouth to speak, but Brenna continued, "We are sleeping in the mud like pigs, and for what? Where is the Northern army? If we are not here to fight, then why are we here?"

The Raven chief's voice had carried across the field. They didn't have a council of elders like the Wolves. Brenna ruled their every move, and now her people stopped to listen to Alaric's answer.

Cold rain dripped down his back, and the wind lashed his hair across his face. Odessa clutched his hand in hers, her steady warmth beside him never wavering. If this was the only way to gain peace for his family, for his wife, then he would forge ahead regardless of how his stomach clenched into knots and his body begged for rest.

"Narah called us here to finally stand against the Northern king."

"The same king who sent healers to save your people?" Brenna scoffed and the warriors closest to them shifted warily, ready to do their chief's bidding. "Do you not have an alliance with him? How can we trust you?"

Whatever fervor had caused the other clans to follow him here was fading by the day. And in its place were questions and doubts.

More and more warriors stopped to listen to them. Alaric watched as Brenna's words were passed from person to person like a wave through the water. It was no longer just the Raven chief he was speaking to.

"We did have an alliance with the North."

Odessa's body went rigid next to him. He squeezed her hand tighter and went on.

"Until my wife was kidnapped and our people, the people of all the clans, were threatened with the king's vengeance."

Brenna raised a single black eyebrow, but she held her tongue.

"I have a family to protect, a clan, and so do all of you. But we cannot keep living like this--fighting for whichever kingdom benefits us most in the moment, refusing to defend each other, or fighting amongst ourselves.

Kalon and Melantha will continue to wage war against each other, and the clans will pay the price. It is time to fight back. It is time to protect what is ours. We are the clans of Asherah's Wood. If we stand together, she will protect us."

A roar rose up around them, spreading through the clans until all the clans' people shouted their agreement. Alaric's heart thundered in his chest, threatening to gallop off without him. The white castle on the hill towered above them, mocking him. But when he glanced down at Odessa she was beaming, tears glistening in her eyes.

For her. It was all for her.

Brenna stood silently, waiting for the war cries of each clan to die down. She appraised Alaric with narrowed eyes and apparently found something new.

She nodded once. "We will stay."

Alaric's shoulders slid down his back in relief.

The corner of Brenna's mouth lifted in a smirk. "It is good luck when a wolf and a raven go into battle together. So, lead the way, little wolf."

Chapter 42: Enemy at the Gate

Odessa had insisted on staying at the Raven's camp to speak further with Brenna. His wife was fascinated with the woman warrior. He never should have told her so many tales of Brenna's feats. But the winter had been long.

As much as he didn't like the idea of leaving his wife with the war chief, one fierce look from both women told him he had no say in the matter.

He walked away from the Ravens still trying to shake the feeling that he was nothing more than an imposter. But hadn't the clans followed him here? Hadn't they cheered his words? It was time he got used to the fact that he was to be the next Wolf Chief.

The rain slowed to a cold mist, and Alaric shook the water from his hair. He pushed thoughts of his warm bed from his mind as he returned to the Wolf's camp. His people had begun to make small, smoky fires in the damp morning, eating whatever rations they had left. They hadn't planned on being here for so long.

Alaric sighed and looked back toward the tree line of the forest. A figure there caught his eye and even from a distance he recognized the man. He strode toward him, dread pooling in his gut.

"That was a very rousing speech," Connell growled as soon as Alaric was in the protection of the trees. Connell leaned against the thick trunk of an oak, his casual posture hiding the fury simmering behind his eyes.

"What are you doing here?" Alaric glanced behind him, wondering if he should call the other elders.

"Are you the chief now, boy, or do you need to go running to your uncle?" he hissed from the shadows.

Alaric's gaze snapped back to his former chief's. The man sneered and pushed away from the tree.

"Did you think I would just lay down and allow you to take everything from me?" Connell crept closer, stalking his prey.

"It was not my decision." Alaric rolled his shoulders back. From his full height, he towered over the older man.

"Perhaps not. But ever since you brought that Kalonian bitch home with you, everything has gone to shit."

In one swift movement, Alaric stepped toward him and grabbed him by the front of his vest, nearly lifting Connell from the ground.

"Never speak of my wife like that again."

Connell huffed a laugh. "You think you are invincible now? Narah's chosen one?" Alaric flinched as Connell spat the words in his face. "Kill me and be done with it. If you are going to take what is mine, do it like a man."

Alaric dropped him, and Connell stumbled back a step before laughing again. The man's eyes were wild, his huge pupils turning his gray eyes black. Alaric curled his hands into fists at his sides. This was the man who nearly murdered his wife. He should kill him. He had every right to.

He placed a hand on the hilt of his sword, and

Connell grinned maniacally. "That's right. Fight me like you didn't have the guts to fight your father." Connell pulled his own sword from its sheath.

Alaric's hand stilled on his sword. What good would it do to fight this man now? Connell held nothing over him any longer. No power to harm his family or his people. He was nothing more than a hysterical old man. Alaric had already won. And he had no desire to take any more lives from this earth.

"Put down your sword, Connell."

The former chief sputtered. "You won't fight me?"

Alaric shook his head, removing his hand from his weapon. "Go home. I'll speak with the elders. They will let you stay, but no more of this."

Connell narrowed his eyes. "You are soft. Always have been. You don't deserve to rule my people." He lunged forward, his sword barely missing Alaric's stomach as he dodged to the side.

"Fight me like man," he bellowed, lunging again.

A vision of Odessa crying over his bloody corpse nearly had him pulling his sword from his belt, but he refused to begin his life as chief this way, with more blood and violence.

"Leave, Connell," he growled low in his throat.

The man paused, panting loud, uneven breaths. Perhaps he would go.

Alaric took a step back, and Connell dove forward, his sword slashing across Alaric's torso. The pain sliced through him, hot and quick. He clamped a hand over his middle, his own blood quickly soaking through his fingers.

He had no choice. He pulled his sword, but Connell's wolfish grin twisted into a grimace as he collapsed to the ground, the arrow still quivering in his back.

Holy gods, what now? Alaric's head spun, looking frantically for the killer.

"Show yourself."

The trees dripped rainwater from their leaves, the sound pattering on the forest floor. Noise from the camps behind him filtered through the trees, but the woods were still. He pulled his hand away from his wound, wincing at the sting of air on the cut. It wasn't deep and the blood had already slowed. At least there was that.

"Who's there?" His voice was nothing more than a rasp, his throat burned with the effort to speak. He wanted his wife and his bed, not this waterlogged forest and hidden threats.

"Show yourself," he bellowed, summoning a strength he didn't feel. The birds fluttered up into the treetops.

Weylyn stumbled out from behind the wide trunk of a tree, his bow hanging at his side and tears sliding down his cheeks.

"Weylyn? What...?" Alaric closed the distance between himself and his brother, taking the boy by his shoulders. He shook him. Hard. "What have you done?"

What was he doing here? He should be home, safe with his sisters and Faolan. Why was Alaric doing any of this if not to spare his brothers from battle?

Weylyn swallowed hard, lifting his gaze to meet Alaric's. "It's Daciana—"

"Do not tell me you killed a man because some girl asked you to." A sharp pounding had taken up residence inside Alaric's skull and the wound on his stomach ached. He pressed his hand harder into it to stop the bleeding, sucking in air between his teeth.

This was how he would start and end his time as chief, with his own brother murdering their former leader. Everything was slipping through his blood-covered grasp. He suddenly wished Odessa was by his side, keeping the ground solid beneath his feet.

His brother took a steady breath in, keeping the tears from his voice. The weak daylight seeped through the branches and lit his face. His skin was still smooth, but his eyes already held so much sorrow.

"He beat her, Alaric. She showed up at our door bloody and bruised." His voice cracked and his shoulders trembled under Alaric's hand. The words sunk slowly into Alaric's consciousness, even as he fought to keep them out.

"He found out she told you about the kidnapping, that she told you he was involved." He sucked in more air, his voice wavering and Alaric prayed for him to stop but the words kept coming. "She was crying, and it was just like mother all over again. I couldn't let him live, Alaric. I couldn't."

Whatever small amount of pity Alaric had felt for the man the moment before was replaced with disgust. He glanced back to where Connell lay face down in the dirt, unmoving. His brother had excellent aim.

He turned back to Weylyn, squeezing his shoulder. The boy lifted his chin, waiting for Alaric's response.

"You did what you had to do. I will explain everything to the elders."

Weylyn hastily wiped a tear from his mottled face. He sniffed hard and nodded.

"Go home and take care of Daciana. We will be done here soon enough."

"I can stay—"

"Go. If nothing else, I will spare you this one fight. By summer you will be a man, and I will no longer be able to keep you safe. Now go."

For perhaps the first time in their lives, his brother didn't argue. With another glance at Connell's body, Weylyn took off through the woods back to the Wolf village.

Alaric stood over the body, his muscles trembling, the memories flooding his thoughts. His father with an arrow in his back, Alaric's own fear and anger bubbling over the surface. And now Weylyn had done the same. But this time there would be no lies. He would face the elders and tell the truth. Connell got what he deserved and so had his father. There was only one man left that still stood in his way.

He couldn't ask his people to wait in this field any longer. The king either met with them today, or they would attack at dawn. He filled his lungs with the piney scent of the forest and winced in pain. But first, he needed stitches. Luckily, his wife was a better seamstress than she was a cook. He left Connell's body for the wolves and set off to find Odessa.

****

Odessa laid her hand on Alaric's chest as he slept, the steady thrumming of his heart comforting her. The early morning light filtered through the walls of their tent. Soon he would wake. Soon the clans would prepare for battle against her people. Her father ignored their last plea for an audience. Odessa sighed, allowing Alaric's smoky scent to fill her one more time before she quietly crept from the tent. This was not what she intended when she called the clans here. She only meant to show her father the strength of the clans, and if she was honest, her own strength as well.

She stepped out of the tent into the chill of the morning. Everything was wet and filthy, but mercifully the rain had stopped. A weak sun was just appearing over the horizon, lighting the castle in a soft white glow. It was beautiful and yet it hid such ugliness.

The men around the camp began to stir and wake for the day, paying her little attention anymore. She had lost her fantasized version of the clans after her time spent among them, but she still believed they deserved to live a life undisturbed by power-hungry men. And so did she.

With another glance at the tent, she stalked off to find Brenna.

It wasn't hard to find the woman. She always seemed to be in the center of her people. Like a long dark shadow, she looked over them. But there was safety in her darkness.

"Morning, princess." Her mouth quirked into her half-smile.

"Good morning." Odessa ran a hand down her stain-covered dress, flustered by the other woman's composure.

"Still think this is a good idea?"

Odessa straightened and met her eye. "As good an idea as any."

"Did you tell that fresh-faced husband of yours?"

The heat rose to Odessa's cheeks, and she shook her head. "No." She ignored the pang of guilt Brenna's question raised.

Brenna's smile grew, and it was foolish, but Odessa's chest filled with pride.

"You are braver than you look."

"Uh…thank you."

Brenna turned and wove her way through the groups of men and a few women warriors preparing for the battle ahead. "This way. You can take my horse."

Odessa followed her dark shape, ogling at the Raven women as they painted each other's faces with black paint. She touched the dark side of her own face and a smile tugged at her lips. Perhaps this was where she belonged after all.

"Here she is." Brenna stood beside an enormous black horse, gently patting its side. Odessa suddenly wished she had spent more time riding.

"We don't have much time." The Raven chief pulled her close and began tying raven feathers into Odessa's hair. The bear claw necklace already hung around her neck. Odessa clutched it with nervous fingers. She carried the Fox's torch with her, the one she had borrowed from Alaric's cousins the day before. She only needed to light it. And of course, she had her face, light and dark like Narah's. Something from each of the clans to adorn her.

Brenna stepped back, a frown creasing her face. "That will have to do." She took the torch from Odessa and lit it in a nearby fire pit as Odessa mounted the horse. She swallowed hard and looked down from her new vantage point. The clanspeople were lining up, ready to finally act after so many days of waiting. Men had been injured already by their fellow clansmen, centuries-old fights rekindled again and again. The alliance might not last much longer.

The air was filled with their impatience and their fear as well. It clung to her, suffocating her. She prayed this would be her first and last time on a battlefield.

Across the expanse, the Kalonian soldiers were also preparing. Their horses' hoofbeats vibrated the earth. Odessa's stomach quivered with nerves, and she prayed, not for the first time, that her plan would work.

Brenna handed her the lit torch and smiled, her teeth white in her blackened face.

"Good luck, princess."

Odessa nodded her thanks, her throat too tight for words. She rode to the front of the warriors, one hand trembling on the reins and the other gripped tight to the torch. She crossed in front of them, first the Ravens, then Foxes, Bears, and finally Wolves. It didn't take long to catch the men's attention and the din of the crowd began to quiet.

This was it. One last chance to end this fight before it began. She glanced toward the castle and the men gathering beneath it. They were too far away to know for sure, but it seemed they had stilled in their preparations as well.

She turned back to the clans and cleared the emotions from her throat. It was now or never. It was time to claim everything they thought of her, every name they called her; cursed, blessed, goddess, devil. She would use it all to get what she wanted. Peace for her family and freedom for herself.

"People of Asherah's Wood." Her voice rang out across the field carried on the wind. "You are my father's biggest fear. This, the clans united, is his greatest nightmare."

The clans roared as one, weapons clanging against

shields. Odessa shook with fear but forced more words from her lips. "I called you here to prove to King Orion that the clans stand together, that Asherah's wood is no longer open to him. To show him that he has no power over the clans of the wood."

Or me. The words rang through her as the crowd cheered again. She scanned the faces she knew and so many that she didn't but couldn't find the one she was looking for.

"But perhaps, the king doesn't believe us. Perhaps he has seen the fighting amongst you and does not believe the clans can defeat him." She continued trotting the horse back and forth in front of the crowd as she spoke. "Perhaps we need to show him."

The sound of metal against metal as the men banged their weapons against shields and breastplates was deafening. Odessa looked again toward the castle. Her father's men were shrinking back toward the castle walls, their carefully practiced formations falling apart. Her heart thundered in her chest; her blood rushed through her veins. Let her father see this. Let him be filled with terror and regret.

"Wife!"

Odessa's head swiveled back to the clans. Alaric stood at her side, his eyes blazing. Was it anger? Fear?

"Alaric, I—"

The words died in her throat as her husband fell to his knee in front of her. The world went still. The wind whispered in her ears. Every warrior held their breath and then dropped to the ground. Alaric gazed up at her. He was beautiful in his leather armor, every muscle tense and ready for the fight. And the look in his eyes, it wasn't anger or fear. No, it was pride.

She reached down to him, and he stood, taking her hand. He pressed his lips roughly to her fingers and then swung himself up into the saddle behind her. She leaned into his unwavering support.

The clansmen rose, roaring and stamping, but the Kalonian army was fracturing, fleeing, and deserting faster than their commanders could contain them.

"We bring our message to the king!" Odessa shouted above the noise. She rode toward the castle, the Clans of the Wood behind her, to finally free herself from her father's grasp.

****

Her father sat, red-faced and surly, on his throne in the great hall. The sounds of metal against metal and the screams of the wounded carried to them through the echoing halls of the castle. The clans hadn't met much resistance on their short march to the castle, but some of the king's army remained.

Odessa's horse had been escorted through the fray, surrounded by clansmen, Alaric's sword drawn to take down any that dared to come near. But even the Kalonians that stayed to fight gave her a wide berth. And for once, the curse that kept her isolated from her people worked in her favor. She arrived unscathed, but her hands still shook, and her ears rang with the sounds of war. Her father had no choice but to finally let her in.

Queen Louise sat next to the king, her placid demeanor giving away none of her inner turmoil. Odessa didn't miss the lift of her smile as she bowed before her.

"Father." She dipped into a shallow curtsy in front of the man. His face turned a deeper shade of red at the title. Alaric didn't bow. He stood beside her, a steady hand on her back, the barely contained anger radiating off of him.

There were dark circles under the king's eyes and his hair stuck to the sides of his head with the sweat that dripped from his brow. He looked as though he'd aged ten years since Odessa had last seen him.

He raised his gaze to her face, and she braced herself for his harsh words, for his anger, and his bluster. But instead, the king blew out a long sigh, ruffling the hairs of his beard.

"For twenty-four years I have not slept a full night." He pinched the bridge of his nose and closed his eyes.

Odessa waited. Alaric shifted beside her. She glanced at the blood dried onto the hem of her dress. She quickly raised her gaze back to her father.

"For twenty-four years your mother has haunted my dreams. She became a thing of nightmares."

Odessa held her breath. Never had her father spoken to her about her mother. Queen Louise shifted in her seat. A slight crease between her brows gave away her own confusion.

"Last night was the first night since your birth I slept undisturbed. Your mother finally rests." The king's eyes were still closed, and he ran a weary hand over his belly.

Had the old king lost his mind? What was he talking about? And why now, when hundreds of clansmen fought outside his gates? Odessa glanced at Alaric. He raised his eyebrows and gave a slight shrug but kept a reassuring hand on the small of her back.

"Father, the clans of Asherah's Wood have united. Your men fled."

He slammed a hand on the arm of his chair and his eyes sprang open. "I can see that, daughter. The enemy is at the gate. And your mother no longer haunts these halls." For once he looked her in the eye and didn't flinch, didn't turn away. She met his stare and refused to cower.

"It seems you have fulfilled your destiny after all. I expect no mercy from you, but I ask before you send your barbarians over the walls to remember who your people truly are."

Alaric stiffened beside her. But Odessa's breathing remained calm and even. She rolled her shoulders back. Here was the father she was expecting. Full of hatred and manipulation. She stepped closer until she was at the man's feet. He recoiled further into his throne as if he wished to be as far from her as possible.

"The clans at your gate have no intention of causing your people any harm."

The king's lips curled into a sneer.

"Yet…" Odessa dropped the word, and it echoed in the cavernous space. Everything here was cold stone, and she longed to be back in her cozy wooden house. But not until she was finished here for good.

"The clans will no longer grant you access to the Warrior's Pass. If you wish to continue your feud with the Melanthians, you will have to find a new route."

The king opened his mouth to speak, but Odessa continued before he got the chance.

"Mistreatment of any of the clans will be rectified by all of the clans. So, I suggest you consider the consequences before you send your men into the woods."

The king chuckled a joyless laugh. "And you

expect me to simply accept your terms? To roll over like a whipped dog and obey you?"

Alaric stepped forward. "You would rather fight the four clans?" The menacing growl of his words was at odds with the king's affected speech. "With what army?" He stepped closer to the king, and her father's eyes darted to his closest guard. The man placed a hand on his sword and Odessa placed a hand on Alaric's arm.

He stilled in his approach but brought his gaze to the king's. Odessa knew how it felt to have Alaric's two-toned eyes pinned on you. A small shiver ran through her. The king's fingers clenched tighter onto the arms of his throne.

"Your fields are full of savages," Alaric went on, using the term so often used for his people. "Do you truly wish to sacrifice more men to cling to some forest path? It is one thing to pick us off one by one, your majesty, but to face us all at once is foolish. Bloody and foolish." Alaric grinned a wolfish grin.

Her father sputtered, his mouth opening and closing like a drowning fish. A slow smile spread across Odessa's face. The king swallowed and ran a hand down his beard. Odessa watched as he calculated the risks in his mind. The old man had nothing. What was left of his army could be heard shouting in pain from beyond his walls. Unless he intended on fighting the clans himself, he had no choice but to agree.

At last, he gave a stiff nod. "Kalon will stay out of the damned woods."

Odessa heard the unspoken words between them. For now. Her father would agree to the terms for now, while the clans stood outside his doors. She did not trust for a moment that he would keep his word for long. But this was the best she could do for her husband's people. For her people.

She turned to address her stepmother.

"Any Kalonians who wish to visit or trade with the clans will be welcome as long as they come peacefully. I do hope you and my sister will visit us soon."

The queen's eyes widened a fraction of an inch, the most surprise Odessa had ever seen on her face.

She nodded. "I am sure Faye would like to see you. Please come back to the castle any time."

At this, Alaric coughed and cleared his throat, but Odessa ignored it. "That is very kind, your majesty."

Odessa turned back to her father one last time. "I do hope you can find another way to spend your time, father. Perhaps you can take up gardening." With that she spun on her heel, leaving the queen cackling in surprised delight.

She took Alaric's hand, and they left the king's great hall, the tapestries blowing in the windowless room as though they were waving goodbye.

Epilogue

Alaric traced a finger idly across her stomach, and she squirmed under his touch. Odessa's skin was sticky with sweat, and she was attempting to stay as still as possible in the relative coolness of the little house. Summer had descended on the forest, and the heat outside their door had been oppressive for days.

"What are you thinking about?" Odessa asked, rolling to face Alaric. Neither of them had bothered to dress, and she took a moment to enjoy the sight of him beside her. His skin had bronzed in the summer sun, and his face was clean-shaven. His hair was pulled back from his face in an attempt to stay cool. He looked young, but the crease had returned to its place between his eyebrows.

"Only, it's been nearly seven cycles of the moon since we married, and yet…" He glanced at her still flat stomach.

Odessa sighed. She thought that might be troubling him. It troubled her enough for the both of them. She ran a finger over the ridges of his arm, brushing lightly over the scar running from shoulder to elbow.

"Does it upset you? That we've yet to conceive a child?"

The crease deepened, but he shook his head. "No. There's time." He leaned forward and dusted a line of kisses along her cheekbone. She tipped her face up to his and caught his lips with hers.

Alaric pulled back. "I wouldn't mind if we never did." He said it quietly as though it were a confession. "I only mean, I'm happy with you either way."

Odessa pulled him closer until the hard lines of his body met the soft curves of hers. Alaric hummed his approval, sucking on the tender skin of her neck as she slid a hand up and down his back. Every part of him was hot, pressed against her, but this heat she welcomed.

"But it doesn't mean we should stop trying," he murmured into her neck.

She laughed as he rolled her onto her back. She grinned at him, and he returned it, his smile still causing her heart to race. He braced himself over her, and she wrapped her legs around his lower back, inviting him in.

Alaric growled as he returned to lavishing kisses and bites along her neck. The muscles of his back flexed under her fingers. She arched against him as he sucked on one nipple and then the other. Odessa gasped and tangled her fingers in his hair as it tumbled around his shoulders.

A pounding on the door stilled him above her.

"Alaric!" Arowyn's voice cut through the sound of their heavy breathing. "Alaric, we want to go to the swimming hole!"

Alaric groaned into Odessa's shoulder, and she bit back a laugh.

"Where are your brothers?" he yelled, not bothering to roll off Odessa.

"Weylyn's with Daciana and Faolan left hours

ago!"

"Always the same story," Alaric muttered. "I'll take you myself in a half-hour."

"Better make it an hour!" Odessa shouted. Alaric's eyes went wide and then he collapsed beside her in a fit of laughter. They waited in silence to see if that would satisfy the girl.

"One hour, and then I'm coming back!"

Odessa giggled into Alaric's shoulder.

"Perhaps it is best if we don't have children of our own too soon," she admitted.

Alaric nodded, a mischievous glint in his eye. "Perhaps we should keep trying and leave it to the goddess to decide."

He pulled her on top of him, a grin stretched across his face. It was a sight she would never tire of.

"Alright. We'll let the goddess decide when to send us a child." She leaned forward and kissed across his broad chest. "But for now, we have one hour before your sister is back at the door."

He ran his hands through the heavy mass of her hair, lifting it off her sweaty neck.

"We better get started then."

****

"Watch this!" Arowyn ran across the grassy bank and jumped into the clear water below. Odessa laughed beside Alaric, soaked from head to toe from the children splashing nearby. Rieka's dark head disappeared beneath the water and emerged closer to the bank. She grinned at him, her cheeks pink from the sun.

Daciana lounged on a rock near the pool as Weylyn strutted around her doing everything he could to impress her. Alaric rolled his eyes but found he couldn't suppress a smile. Faolan jumped in from the other bank, splashing both his sisters and sending them shrieking after him.

Odessa reached across the grass, placed her hand on her husband's, and made the day perfect. As he watched his family play and swim, he found himself thankful for all of it. For all the things the goddess had seen fit to give them, he no longer questioned the things she had taken away. Narah was light and dark. And so were they. And so was life.

He laid back in the grass, the sun on his bare skin, and his wife by his side, and he could think of nothing else he wanted. For this moment alone, he would do it all again.

A word about the author...

Melissa McTernan is an award-winning author of paranormal, fantasy, and contemporary romance. When she's not writing, she's most likely reading or wrangling her kids as a stay-at-home mom. She writes romance to keep her sanity.

For exclusive content, book recommendations, and plenty of pet pics, sign up for her newsletter at melissamct.com